Ain't nothing but a stray away...

Loran had only just heard the quaint expression while she was waiting in the checkout line at the little discount store in the North Carolina mountains. Two old women had been talking about someone's granddaughter, one who frequented places where she had no business being. And it wasn't that the girl "hadn't been raised" and didn't know better, they had assured each other. It was that she apparently was just like Loran's mother. Maddie knew better—but she did it anyway.

"Mother—"

"Loran, stop worrying. I'll feel much better after I shower and eat something."

"I wish I could believe you—you have no idea what it's like having such a liar for a mother," Loran said, and Maddie laughed.

"Ah, well. We all have our heavy burdens to bear."

Loran kept driving. They weren't far from the B and B now. Maddie did seem better. She was sitting up a little straighter, at any rate.

"You know what they say—if you don't sow your wild oats when you're young, you'll sow them when you're old."

"Couldn't you have picked someplace a little closer to home?"

"Home is a state of mind, my darling."

Cheryl Reavis

Cheryl Reavis is an award-winning short-story and romance author who also writes under the name of Cinda Richards. She describes herself as a late bloomer who played in her first piano recital at the tender age of thirty. "We had to line up by height— I was the third smallest kid," she says. "After that, there was no stopping me. I immediately gave myself permission to attempt my other heart's desire—to write." Her Silhouette Special Edition novel *A Crime of the Heart* reached millions of readers in *Good Housekeeping* magazine. Her books, *The Prisoner*, a Harlequin Historical title, and *A Crime of the Heart* and *Patrick Gallagher's Widow*, both Silhouette Special Edition titles, are all Romance Writers of America/RITA® Award winners. *One of Our Own* received the Career Achievement Award for Best Innovative Series Romance from *Romantic Times BOOKclub* magazine. A former public health nurse, Cheryl makes her home in North Carolina with her husband.

Blackberry WINTER

Cheryl REAVIS

BLACKBERRY WINTER

copyright © 2005 Cheryl Reavis

i s b n 0 3 7 3 2 3 0 5 2 4

This edition published by arrangement with Harlequin Books S.A.

® and TM are trademarks of the publisher. Trademarks indicated with
® are registered in the United States Patent and Trademark Office, the
Canadian Trade Marks Office and in other countries.

TheNextNovel.com

 HARLEQUIN®

PRINTED IN U.S.A.

For my editor, Tara Gavin, and my agent,
Maureen Moran. Thank you both
for bringing shovels.

With appreciation to Dawn Aldridge Poore,
fellow writer and my "mountain friend,"
who graciously answered all my questions
about the Appalachian experience.
Any mistakes are mine, not hers.

And special thanks to Linda Buechting and
Janet Wisst, and to Pat Kay, Lois Dyer,
Julia Mozingo, Myrna Temte, Lisette Belisle,
Laurie Campbell, Chris Flynn and
Allison Davidson—for their wisdom,
encouragement and boundless generosity.

PROLOGUE

She stood at the open window, feeling the cool breeze that always rippled off the mountain after the sun went down. She turned her head slightly to savor the feel of it on her face, never once taking her eyes off the line of trees that obscured the old logging road deep in the shadows on the mountainside.

She had no idea what time it was or how long she'd been waiting. There were no working clocks in the house except for the small windup alarm clock she used to catch the school bus on time. She didn't dare leave the window long enough to go and get it for fear of missing the small flicker of light among the trees that would mean he had finally come for her.

A question formed in her mind, but she immediately pushed it aside. It was the kind of question her mother would have asked, the unanswerable kind a woman who didn't matter couldn't keep from asking. She didn't want to think about her mother now—or her father. *He* lied when he didn't have to, and he did as he pleased—always. Tommy wasn't like him. Tommy wouldn't—

Where is he?

For a brief moment she was afraid she'd spoken out loud, because if she had, if she voiced the fear she didn't dare give a name, it would become real, inescapable.

She took a deep wavering breath and forced her hands to unclench.

No. He wasn't like her father. Never.

Always before, meeting Tommy had been so easy. She would stand exactly where she was now, and in no time at all she would see the blink of light among the trees that meant he was waiting for her, for *her*—Maddie Kimball—when he could have any girl in the valley, girls whose families had money and whose fathers weren't Foy Kimball.

It had never taken this long for him to get here before. If anything, he was apt to come too soon, before it was even dark enough for her to be absolutely certain she'd seen his signal. And when she did see it, she always waited just a little longer before she slipped away from the house, in case her father had seen it, too. Foy Kimball was a hard man to fool, primarily because he had done so many devious things himself and because hindering other people was a pleasure to him. Getting away tonight should have been easy. Foy wasn't here. Her mother wasn't here. The house was wonderfully and unexpectedly quiet, and all she had to do was watch for the light, then pick up the brown paper grocery bag that held a few of her carefully ironed clothes and go.

Easy.

And permanent.

She would never have to come back here again if she didn't want to, never have to live hand to mouth with two people who only knew how to cause each other pain.

She could hear the faint rumble of thunder in the distance. She forced herself to move away from the window and cross the cluttered room to the front door. She stepped outside onto the porch, careful of the warped and rotted boards under her feet.

She knew that she wouldn't be able to see the trees along the ridge any better from the porch, but she still looked in that direction, straining to find something, anything in the shadows.

She could smell the rain coming. The trees in the yard began to sway, and she could hear the wind moving along the mountainside treetop by treetop.

Tommy.

"Tommy," she said in a whisper.

"Tommy!"

His name echoed into the distance.

If he was out there, he would hear her, and he would know that she'd missed the signal somehow. He'd know, and *he* would come to *her*.

She waited.

Listening.

Listening.

She stood at the edge of the porch, her eyes focused on the trees along the ridge until the shapes became meaningless, until the raindrops began to fall, until she knew.

He was like Foy Kimball after all.

CHAPTER 1

For some reason, the drive from D.C. into Arlington was less hair-raising than usual this morning. Loran Kimball tried to put her worry aside enough to be happy about it. She wanted—needed—to see her mother today, and for once she might actually arrive only minimally stressed by the Beltway traffic.

She never knew what to say to Maddie these days, what to do. She didn't know if coming to visit so often was making things easier for her or not. She couldn't tell without specifically asking, and even if she did ask, she could never be certain of the accuracy of the answer. Maddie was so adept at seeming to indulge an inquiry, but, truly, she was the quintessential self-contained "private person." Not standoffish. Not rude or unfriendly. Just private. She didn't respond with precise answers to the things people asked her; she responded with whatever she wanted them to know. And, as far as Loran could tell, Maddie's illness hadn't made her any more forthcoming. She was quite willing to make some morbid joke about her imminent demise, but she was typically sketchy regarding what was actually happening to her body and how she felt about it. Loran had only lately come to recognize that she had never really known with any certainty how Maddie had felt about anything—except in the strictest parent-child context. She knew Maddie's Rules of Etiquette and Social Behavior inside out, but Maddie herself was, and always had been, an enigma. What little real information Loran had gleaned about her mother had come from the example she'd set, not from anything she'd said. Did her mother have hopes and dreams beyond getting herself and her daughter educated and well-employed? Loran had no idea, and, at this late date, she wasn't at all certain she wanted to find out, not when it was too late for Maddie to realize them.

She gave a quiet sigh and made the first of a series of turns that would take her deep into Maddie's peaceful residential neighborhood, driving slowly down the tree-lined streets toward the bungalow where Maddie lived, for once paying attention to the houses and the front yards as she passed. They all reminded her of 1950s television somehow, of a world where families thrived intact and where wives stayed at home, mindlessly happy and wearing high heels and pearls, women who never worried about anything beyond the boundaries of their neatly manicured yards. They kept their houses and raised their children themselves, while their husbands went out into the real world every day and earned a decent living. It was *not* the kind of place she would have thought would appeal to Maddie, but clearly it had. Maddie had been living there ever since Loran had graduated from college eighteen years ago.

"Oh," Loran said out loud as her mother's house came into view. Maddie was an early riser, but her driveway shouldn't be empty this time of morning. Her car was gone and the drapes at the windows were still drawn—a sure sign that her daylight-loving mother wasn't at home.

Loran pulled sharply to the curb and parked. She hadn't called first to let Maddie know she was coming today, and her immediate thought was that Maddie's condition had worsened, that she had unexpectedly taken herself to the hospital again, and she hadn't called yet to let Loran know.

Except that Maddie was Maddie, and it was just as likely that she wouldn't call at all, if she could help it. Loran didn't want to think that she might be physically unable to use the phone—but either way, it was a contingency she had planned for. She had the patient-information number at the hospital programmed into her cell phone.

When the woman at the hospital answered, Loran made no attempt to try to explain or to justify the reason for her call.

"I'd like the room number for Ms. Maddie Kimball, please," she said, spelling both names.

There was a pause, one filled with the staccato clicking of computer keys.

"We have no one listed by that name," the woman said.

"It's possible she could still be in Emergency," Loran said, trying to keep her voice steady and not grip the phone so tightly.

"I'm sorry. That name hasn't been entered into the system."

"If she just arrived—"

"All patient data should be entered right away. You could try again later, just in case there's been some unforeseen delay."

"Thank you," Loran said. She snapped the cell phone shut and stared out the windshield. "Okay, Maddie, where are you?"

Out hitting the yard sales? Gone to meet some other early bird for breakfast? Either would be unlikely, Loran thought. She had no choice but to wait. She had the key to Maddie's house and she rummaged through her purse until she found it.

She glanced at the bright blue sky as she got out of her vehicle—the new and far too expensive SUV Maddie called the domestic version of a Sherman tank—and walked toward the back door. It was going to be a beautiful fall day, crisp and clear. A group of children rode by on bicycles. Someone was burning leaves somewhere—probably illegally.

Loran stopped abruptly when she reached the carport. The back door was slightly ajar. She hesitated, then pushed it open wider and stood on the threshold, ready to run if she had to. She listened intently and she could hear a child babbling somewhere in the house and a man's voice. After a moment, a portly bald man wearing a bow tie came into view. He was carrying a little girl and holding Maddie's red watering can.

"What are you doing in here?" Loran asked bluntly.

He looked around in surprise. "Oh—we're just watering the plants," he said, clearly unperturbed by the question. He held up the red watering can for Loran to see.

"Water pants," the little girl echoed and the man smiled at her. She smiled at him in return, then gave him a hug. "Hi, Daddy," she said.

"Hi, little miss," he said to her. "Aspiring linguist," he said to Loran.

Loran stared at him. "You are…?"

"Andrew Kessler—this is Sara—we live next door."

"Nest-or," Sara said, making her father smile again.

"You have to be really careful at this stage," he said to Loran. "They're a walking instant replay, only the replay might not be instant. It might show up three days later in the middle of church." He proceeded to water the herb pots on the kitchen windowsill.

"Do you…know where Maddie is?"

"Yeah—she gave me the address. Or the vicinity, anyway."

"Where is she?"

"You are…?" he asked pointedly, in the same way she had done.

"Her daughter."

"Oh, yes. Loran. We nearly stole your name and gave it to Sara, didn't we?" he asked the child.

Sara nodded solemnly.

"Could you give me the…vicinity?" Loran asked.

"Sure. I don't see why not."

"Did she say how long she'd be gone?"

"Nope. Not really," he said, watering another plant.

"Nope," Sara echoed.

He set the watering can on the counter and reached for his wallet. It took him a moment to shuffle Sara, who didn't want to be put down, and the contents of his billfold until he found a slip of blue paper.

"I'll need that back," he said as he handed it to Loran.

She looked at the paper. *Lilac Hill* had been written in her mother's careful hand, with a phone number below it.

What and where was Lilac Hill?

"It's a North Carolina phone number, I think," Andrew Kessler said helpfully. "She said something about the mountains. That's about all I know."

"Was she—did she—?" Loran stopped, not quite knowing how to frame the question. This man might be allowed into Maddie's house to look after her greenery, but that didn't mean he knew anything about her health.

"She seemed fine," he said, still being helpful. If he thought it odd that Loran didn't know about her mother's travel plans, it didn't show. "Better than I've seen her in a while, actually. Kind of excited about going."

Loran moved to the pad beside the telephone and scribbled down the number, then handed the blue paper back to him.

"Thank you," she said absently, trying to process the information he'd just given her.

"Will you be staying for a while?"

Loran looked at him blankly.

"Do we still need to come and water the plants, is what I'm asking."

"Yes. I won't be staying. Thanks for doing that, by the way."

"Oh, it's our pleasure."

"Pay sure," Sara said, and this time Loran smiled.

"She's very…pretty," she said, but she'd been about to say "lucky." Little Sara Kessler had a father who clearly wanted to be in her life, to talk to her, to carry her around with him—something far beyond Loran's experience.

"We think so," he said. "Well, that's it for today. Come on, little miss. We're off to wake up Mommy and take her to McDonald's."

"Mommy!" Sara cried, clasping her hands together.

"That's right! Mommy! It was nice to finally meet you," he said to Loran, making her feel slightly...absentee, in spite of the fact that she had never neglected Maddie. She had come to Arlington as often as she could.

She stood and watched him walk back across the yard. At one point, he set his daughter on the ground and they continued the rest of the way hand in hand, underscoring something Loran had realized a long time ago. Some men were meant to be fathers—and most men weren't. Clearly, her own hadn't been so inclined.

She thought suddenly about leaving the house this morning and about Kent, cranky and half-asleep when she'd tried to tell him about her restless night and her impulsive decision to go to Arlington again. He'd made a token offer to come with her, but he hadn't meant it. She hadn't really wanted him to come along. What she had wanted—needed—was some small indication that he understood a little of what she was going through. They had lived together for months. Her mother was dying, and her heart was breaking, and he had given her...nothing.

She was still watching as Andrew Kessler and his daughter carefully climbed the steps to their front porch and went inside the house. Step-climbing was clearly another much appreciated milestone. She tried to imagine Kent taking that kind of delight in a child's simple accomplishments and couldn't. He wasn't interested in being a father, or a husband. He was interested in living unencumbered and in having a large corner office with his name on the door—not unlike herself. She and Kent made a beautiful, career-minded couple. Everybody said so. Loran and Kent. Kent and Loran. Wunderkinds of the investment world. She knew that Maddie didn't like him much, regardless of the fact that she'd never said so. Loran had never quite gotten up the courage to ask why not. As inaccessible as Maddie's thoughts might be, one did *not* want to ask her for an honest opinion unless one was ready to hear it.

"Maddie, Maddie," Loran said wearily.

She didn't understand any of this. Her mother was a homebody. She didn't take unplanned trips, even when she'd been in the bloom of health. Apparently, Maddie expected to be gone for a time, or she wouldn't have made plans to keep her philodendrons and her window-sill herb garden alive.

She just didn't expect to be gone long enough to have to inform her only child.

The house was so quiet, in spite of the whirring of the refrigerator motor and the wall clock clicking off the seconds. The place looked homey, but it wasn't, not without Maddie in it. There should be music playing, the oldie-goldie doo-wop station, and Maddie singing along even though she claimed to hate the songs of that era. There should be a pot of soup bubbling on the stove or bread baking in the oven.

The phone rang sharply, making Loran jump. She hesitated, then answered it.

"There you are!" her mother said cheerfully—as if Loran were the one missing.

"Mother, where—"

"I just talked to Kent. He told me you took a couple of days off and you were coming to see me today."

"Well, that didn't work out," Loran said pointedly, and her mother laughed.

"Yes. Well. I...need you to do something for me," Maddie said.

"Who *is* this?" Loran countered in honor of the many, *many* times she'd offered her services and been summarily turned down.

"I'm serious," Maddie said. There was something different in her voice.

"What is it?" Loran asked, worried now. "Are you all right?"

"I'm doing great, considering."

"What do you want me to do?"

"I want you to come here."

"Where?"

"To North Carolina. To the mountains."

"When?"

"Right now. If you leave right away, you can be here before dark, if you don't take time to pack. The place isn't hard to find. You can buy what you need after—"

"Mother, I don't understand," Loran interrupted.

"I know you don't. I'm not sure I understand myself. I know I'm asking a lot, and it's short notice. I'll...explain when you get here. Or I'll try."

"Mother, you're scaring me. Can't you tell me something, at least?"

"I...not really. I don't want to go into it on the phone. It's important, Loran."

And that was the only thing Loran was reasonably certain about. It was important. Nothing else would explain Maddie's sudden disappearance or her unlikely request.

It was also inconvenient—for Kent. He had a big business dinner on Friday, one that required Loran's presence, not for her investment-banking expertise, but because she apparently had an uncanny and probably fortuitous resemblance to the client's late wife.

"Loran?"

"Tell me how to get there," she said, making up her mind.

She could hear Maddie give what could only be a sigh of relief.

"Have you got a pen? You drive to Charlottesville, then to Waynesboro—"

"Hold on—okay. Go ahead."

"Get onto the Blue Ridge Parkway at the first opportunity and head into North Carolina. Stay on it as far as the Highway 16 exit near Glendale Springs. The mountain scenery is going to be spectacular, and there's a church in Glendale Springs with beautiful frescoes, but don't stop. Take that exit…"

Loran wrote everything down, even the phone number she already had. "What is Lilac Hill?" she asked.

"It's a B and B. I'll get you a room. There's one called the Rose Room. Very Victorian-girlie. You'll like it."

Loran stood looking at what she'd written, still bewildered, still worried.

"Loran?" Maddie said when the silence on Loran's end lengthened.

"I'm here."

"Drive carefully, okay?"

"I will," she said. "Are you sure you're all right?"

"Don't I sound all right?"

"You *sound* all right. It's that answering a question

with a question thing that's bothering me. Does your doctor know about this?" It suddenly occurred to her to ask.

Maddie laughed softly. "Actually, it was his idea."

"He told you to go to the mountains?"

"He told me it was time to make sure the burners were turned off and the iron was unplugged—but this is what he meant. I'll see you later."

"Okay," Loran said. "Later."

She hung up the phone, stood for a moment, then dialed Kent's number.

"Kent," she said when he finally answered. "I have to— Are you awake?"

He said something unintelligible.

"Kent, listen. I have to go somewhere to meet Maddie."

"Okay," he mumbled.

"No, listen. I might not be back in time for the dinner Friday."

"What? Why?"

"I told you. I have to go meet Maddie. I'm not sure when I'll be back."

"Loran, this dinner is important. The old man specifically asked if you were going to be there."

"I know, but you can handle it."

"I'm not the one who reminds him of his first wife."

"I know. It can't be helped. I have to see what Maddie wants."

"Well, where the hell is she?"

"She's…staying somewhere in the North Carolina mountains—a B and B called Lilac Hill. She wants me to come, and I have to go. I'll call you when I get there. I'm sorry."

"Damn it, Loran! Well, if you have to, you have to. I'll make do, I guess. I'll tell the old bastard...something."

"The truth would probably work," she said, and he laughed, hopefully an indication that she was forgiven for causing him such a major inconvenience.

"The call-waiting just beeped," he said. "Catch you later."

He abruptly hung up, and Loran stood holding the phone, still full of apologetic gratitude for what could only be described as a piddling display of empathy and understanding. She would have probably apologized a few more times if not for call-waiting. She tried to imagine what Maddie would have said and done in this situation. She might have *said* the same things Loran had—but she wouldn't be feeling so tentative. Of that, Loran was certain.

"You are *not* your mother's daughter," she said out loud.

CHAPTER 2

The new guest shivered suddenly and moved closer to the fireplace. Meyer Conley kept glancing at her as he stacked the heavy cedar logs carefully into a wood box hidden behind an oak paneled door next to it. She stood looking at the flames.

"It's turning colder tonight," he said after a moment.

"I'm sorry— What?" she said.

"It's turning colder tonight," he said again, as if that possibility permitted his intrusion into her thoughts.

She looked at him and smiled suddenly. "I like your haircut. Does it have a name?"

"Cheap," he said, and she laughed softly.

"It reminds me of the boys I grew up with, their summer haircuts."

"Get buzzed in May and it doesn't grow out until school starts," he said.

"That's right. I had one like it myself not too long ago."

"Yeah?"

"It looks better on you, though."

She was teasing him a little bit; he understood that. But she wasn't being suggestive or flirty like some of the Lilac Hill guests. It was done more in a kind of natural friendliness some people seemed to have.

She went back to staring at the fire.

"My grandfather used to make things out of cedar," she said after a moment. "It's a little hard to watch these cedar logs going up in smoke."

Something in her voice made him look up.

"I know this old man—he's Cherokee, I think. Anyway, he says cedar smoke will take your prayers straight up to heaven. It's not so bad if you think of it that way, I guess." He put another log into the wood box. "So what did your grandfather make then?" he asked. "Out of cedar."

"Oh…trinket boxes. Pencil holders and wall plaques."

"You mean the kind they sell to the tourists, the ones with the poems on them?"

"Hillbilly humor," she said, and he smiled.

"Some people might call it that. Was he from up around here?"

The woman abruptly looked over her shoulder toward the front windows without answering. Apparently, she was expecting someone.

Mrs. Jenkins, the owner of the B and B, came to the doorway. "The second room is for two nights, too?"

"Yes," the woman said.

"You might find you like our little valley enough to stay longer—isn't that right, Meyer?" Mrs. Jenkins called to him. He hated being dragged into this kind of token social banter with the guests, but it went with the job. All in all, he preferred to start and end his own conversations.

"Just might at that," he said anyway. "A lot of people decide to stay longer than they expected to. It's helped me out more than once."

"Meyer is the competition," Mrs. Jenkins said. "When he's not teaching at the community college." The condescension in her voice was heavy enough to pick up and drop-kick. He'd been brought up to behave and not embarrass his kin, however, so he let it go. He also needed the employment Mrs. Jenkins so kindly provided.

"My little place can't compete with a house like this," he said, still stacking wood. "I get the deer hunters and the fly fishermen."

"Your cabin is...charming. Meyer built it himself," Mrs. Jenkins said, neatly putting him back in his place as wood-carrying employee, whether he sometimes taught at a community college or not. She turned her attention to her new guest. "Did you say your daughter would be here this afternoon?"

"She should be here any time now," the woman said.

"Would you like some coffee while you're waiting? Or tea?"

"I would love some tea," the woman said. "Earl Grey, if you have it."

"Just make yourself comfortable," Mrs. Jenkins said. "I'll bring it to you in here. You can enjoy Meyer's nice fire. Meyer, are you about done there?" Mrs. Jenkins asked, more to show her diligence as an innkeeper than because she wanted to know.

"Almost," he said.

"Well, leave some extra logs on the back porch."

The woman sat down in a Queen Anne chair near the window. "I hope she gets here before dark," she said, more to herself than to him.

Mrs. Jenkins brought the tea almost immediately, setting the tray on a low table, and then taking her leave.

The new guest sat for a moment looking at it, then leaned forward and poured herself a cup. She looked so…sad, suddenly.

Meyer checked for any wood debris he might have dropped on the carpet, then stood to go.

"I hear a car turning in," he said, and the woman immediately went to the window to look out. "Nice vehicle," he said of the big luxury SUV that was coming tentatively up the drive.

"That's her," she said, smiling and crossing the room quickly to get to the door that opened onto the back porch and the parking lot.

"You made really good time," he heard her say after a moment, and he stood back as she returned with an attractive younger woman he supposed was the daughter she'd been waiting for. The daughter glanced at him as she passed and he gave her a nod of acknowledgment. She looked flushed and unsettled.

"Welcome to Lilac Hill," Mrs. Jenkins said from the doorway. "Are you hungry? Would you like some coffee or tea? Your mother was just having hers in here by the fire."

"No, I'm fine," the younger woman said, getting her cell phone out of her purse. "I need to make a phone call," she said to her mother. "And then we'll…catch up."

"The reception is better if you're outside," Mrs. Jenkins said. She pointed out the nearest window. "There along the path that leads up to the gazebo is the best place."

"I'll be right back, Mother," the younger woman said. She went outside, and her mother walked back to the

Queen Anne chair and sat down again. Meyer could hear a sudden burst of laughter from somewhere upstairs—the other guests or the help. The woman did, too. He could tell by the way she stopped midway in the reach for her teacup to listen, as if she found it upsetting somehow. She let the tea go and leaned back in the chair, passing her hand briefly over her eyes.

He toyed with the idea of saying something to her— just to see if she was all right—but he didn't. If anything was the matter, it was none of his business. His business at the moment was the Lilac Hill fireplace. He went to get another armful of cedar logs.

The reception wasn't any better outside. Loran walked farther up the steep hill, finally standing at the bottom of the gazebo steps before she tried again. This time, when she punched in the number, it went through.

She stood waiting in the cold wind for Kent to answer.

"Hello?" someone said finally. The voice wasn't Kent's. The voice wasn't male.

"Don't answer the phone!" Kent yelled in the background. "Damn it—!"

"It was *ringing*, silly," the first voice said. "It might be impor—"

There was a sudden click and the line went dead. Loran stood staring at the phone in her hand. Her first impulse was to redial the number, but she stopped halfway through.

Her heart was pounding and her fingers trembled.

So.

She abruptly sat down on the steps of the gazebo, understanding now. She had been attributing Kent's recent distraction to his trying to close a lucrative deal with the man whose first wife looked like her. Now, however, she could give it a more precise name.

Celia.

Celia was the newly divorced investments counselor at the banking firm where Kent worked, the smart, pretty, ambitious and self-assured one, who had come into Kent's office without knocking one afternoon when Loran was there. The kind of woman Kent admired. A woman a lot like Loran herself, actually—except that she was annoyingly younger.

Damn it, Kent!

She didn't feel like apologizing now. Already she knew how this would go. He would be oh, so offended that she would jump to such an unflattering conclusion about him and a woman he worked with, whether she'd answered the phone or not. He'd try to convince Loran that *he* was the wronged party, and, when that didn't work, he'd tell her that Celia didn't mean a thing, that it had just "happened."

And Loran would show him that she was Maddie Kimball's daughter after all. She would tell him to get the hell out of her house.

Her house.

She wondered suddenly if having had a father would have made a difference, whether she would have been better at maintaining meaningful relationships with men if someone like Andrew Kessler had been in her life, someone who would have carried her when she wanted to be carried and let her walk on her own when she didn't.

Of course it would have, she thought immediately.

How could it not? Even if she'd had a bad father, she would have been better able to tell the gold from the dross—and before the wrong person answered the phone.

She gave a wavering sigh and put the cell phone into her coat pocket, wiping furtively at the tears she suddenly realized were sliding down her cheek.

"Do you smoke?"

"What?" she said, startled. The man she'd seen in the house stood a short distance away from her.

"I asked you if you smoke."

"No," she said shortly.

"I was going to offer you a cigarette. I carry a pack around in case one of the guests needs one. You'd be surprised how often that comes up. Quitting tobacco just doesn't take sometimes, especially if there's a bump in the road. I've got this great aunt—Nelda, her name is. She *thinks* she's quit dipping snuff. And she's just fine as long as the sun shines on her back door. But you let the least little thing go wrong and she's right back at it." He paused long enough to make her glance at him. "So how about this instead?" he asked.

He stepped forward and held out a peppermint candy wrapped in cellophane, the kind that pizza restaurants gave out to customers, ostensibly to keep them happy and coming back to buy pizza again.

She stared at it as if she'd never seen one before.

"Go on," he said. "You need it."

"I don't need it," she said, getting to her feet. It put them at eye level, but she still felt at a disadvantage.

"You might feel better."

"No, I won't—and who *are* you?"

"The name is Meyer," he said.

"As in *Oscar?*"

He smiled. He was older than she'd first thought, and he had dimples.

"Now, you know what? I may not look it, but I've been out of the hills enough times to actually get what you just said. That was pretty good, too—only I'm *Meyer* with an *e*, not an *a*. So…you don't want the peppermint."

"I don't want the peppermint," she said, feeling close to tears again.

"Okay," he said. "I'm going to put it in my coat pocket. If you change your mind, I'll give it to you. I'm just about always around here someplace—except when I'm to home."

"And where is that?" she asked in spite of herself, even knowing that the quaint colloquialism was likely affected just for her benefit. "'To home'?"

"It's up there. See?" He pointed off into the distance— toward a hillside with a winding road going up it. "See where the sun is shining on that silver roof? That's my place—except when I'm letting people rent it. I'll show it to you sometime, if you want. Don't worry. I don't have any etchings," he added in a whisper.

She smiled slightly without wanting to. "Well, that's…good to know."

"Got a couple of deer heads, though. They're kind of scary if you're not used to them. You do understand that nothing helps when you're feeling down and misplaced like a good piece of peppermint."

"You've felt down and misplaced enough to know, I take it."

"Damn straight," he said. "I've pretty much made a career of it."

"And what career was that?"

"The United States Army. I'm telling you, if you don't let the little things make you feel better, you'll have a hell of a time getting through the big things."

"If you think—"

"It doesn't matter what I think. What I *know* is you look like you're running on empty—and when that happens, a little hit of sugar can help. I used to carry these all the time when I was deployed—my aunt Nelda would send them to me, whether she could afford to or not. They'd help when you were so tired you thought you weren't going to make it, and if your mouth was full of sand. I used to give them to the kids sometimes—they were scared of us, and maybe it helped. I don't know. I liked to think even if they hated the taste of them, they could still appreciate the effort."

She glanced at him, not certain if he meant some foreign child or if he meant her.

"All right," she said impulsively. He was trying to be kind when he didn't have to.

"All right what?"

"All right, give me the peppermint. Please," she added, letting him make her work for it.

He smiled slightly and handed it over. She unwrapped it carefully and popped it into her mouth. It was rather good, actually. She couldn't remember the last time she'd eaten this kind of candy.

He stood quietly, with his hands in his pockets. She glanced at him, but she was afraid she was going to cry again.

"Okay, then. I'm just going to go do what I'm supposed to be doing," he said. "You ought to sit out here for a while. Give that peppermint a chance to work. Admire the view. You ought to enjoy nature every chance you get—that's what it's there for—especially when you're going through a rough patch. Everything's going to be all right," he added in a quieter voice, as if his impertinence might offend her if he said it too loudly. "You'll see."

She tried to take offense at his unwelcome reassurances, but he didn't give her the chance. He turned and walked away toward the woods beyond the gazebo.

"Hey!" she called after him. "Oscar!"

He looked around.

"Thanks."

He gave her a thumbs-up and walked on.

She sat down on the steps again. She was a grown-up, independent woman. She had a high-paying job with a lot of responsibility. She had a house *and* an expensive vehicle she'd bought for no reason other than the fact that she could. And—incredibly—a piece of peppermint candy was making her feel better.

She cried a little anyway. She didn't want her mother to die. She didn't want to be here. She didn't want strange women to answer *her* telephone at *her* house.

Damn it!

It was some comfort knowing that she wasn't really in love with Kent. But in love or not, she still wanted his head on a stick.

In love.

She would be forty years old on her next birthday, and she still wasn't sure what the term meant. She had tried more than once to identify the elusive emotion she as-

sociated with Kent. A certain pride, she supposed. She
was proud to be seen with him, to have people know that
they were a couple. He mirrored her own accomplishments. Like her, he had an intense drive to get ahead and
stay there, so intense that she couldn't let herself trust
the regard he *said* he had for her. She had never told him
about her illegitimacy, for one thing. She didn't talk
about it as a matter of course, but she wasn't ashamed of
it, either. She didn't mind people knowing that she had
been brought up by an unwed mother, not when that
mother had been Maddie Kimball, who was dedicated
enough and strong enough for the both of them. Even
so, she'd let Kent assume that her parents had divorced
when she was very young—because she wasn't sure that
it wouldn't matter to him. All she knew for certain was
that he would never have tried to give her solace with a
piece of peppermint candy. He would never have noticed
that she was feeling "down and misplaced," much less
have any inclination whatsoever to *do* something about
it.

No, that wasn't quite true. To be fair, if she'd been obvious enough, she might have gotten some all-purpose
flowers from him, the ordering of which he would have
delegated to an underling. Loran would repay him for his
thoughtfulness by willingly and enthusiastically offering
him access to her body, and afterward she would lie in
the dark not feeling nearly as "cheered up" as she did
right at this moment.

Incredible, she thought. She was by no means happy,
but she did feel a little less...forlorn. Maybe there was
something to the peppermint, after all.

Or maybe it was having someone offer his own unique

brand of commiseration—a simple act of kindness—
even if he was paid to do it.

She gave a sharp sigh. She would have to admit he
was rather good at it.

The wind grew colder suddenly. She needed to go back
to the house and find out where the nearest town was so
she could buy the things she needed. And she needed to
see what in this world was going on with Maddie.

Maddie's doctor had warned Loran what to expect as
the illness progressed. Frailness, fatigue, a gradual fading
away. Maddie would begin to lose her interests and her
appetite. And there would be pain, the kind of pain the
two of them couldn't begin to imagine. Indeed, he'd
said, she should be suffering already, and why she wasn't,
he really couldn't explain. Maddie's X-rays showed significant metastasis to the bones. She *should* be in pain
all the time, but obviously she wasn't—not yet.

Not yet.

Loran had never seen anyone in the process of dying
before, and having to watch Maddie do it was more than
she could bear to even think about. She couldn't imagine a world without Maddie in it.

What will I do without her?

But Maddie was definitely getting around at the moment, and whatever interests she might have lost, she'd
clearly replaced with new ones—like surprise jaunts
down the Blue Ridge Parkway.

In spite of her worry, Loran made a mild attempt at
taking Meyer's advice. She stayed put for a few moments
longer and looked at the surrounding mountains. Coming here was a crazy notion for her mother to have, but
Meyer was right. The place *was* beautiful.

She heard a burst of laughter and a slamming door. A teenaged boy and girl came out of the house carrying a large, green plastic garbage can. They were having to fight the wind to keep it upright, but eventually, they reached the Dumpster and emptied the bagged contents into it. The girl squealed suddenly as the wind shifted and snatched the can out of their grasp. It bounced and rolled down the hill. Still laughing, they chased after it, scuffling to see who would claim it—but only for a short distance. The garbage can banged into the side of a pickup truck, and the boy and girl suddenly stopped chasing it and went into each other's arms, the embrace they shared so joyful and so unlike anything Loran had ever experienced that it made her catch her breath. The sheer spontaneity of it spoke volumes about the love and the delight they inspired in each other—maybe because they were so young.

Loran wondered suddenly if Maddie and the unnamed male who had been Loran's father had been like these two, if she, Loran, had been a "love" child.

Love child.

Love.

She had never felt anything even remotely like what she'd just witnessed, and it was somehow more than disconcerting to think that her mother might have enjoyed that kind of bond with another person—a man—when she herself had not.

Someone in the house suddenly began playing a piano with great flair. After a few false starts, Loran could recognize something classical—and melancholy—Mendelssohn, she thought.

The boy and girl stepped apart, but not before he

kissed her lovingly on the forehead. Watching, Loran could almost feel the pressure of the lips that must be firm and warm on her own forehead.

She abruptly looked in the direction Meyer had gone, wondering if that was his first name or his last. Not that it mattered. She wouldn't be here long enough to call him anything.

The unwelcome memory of Kent's irate voice slid into her mind.

Don't answer the phone!

How was she supposed to get through this? Maddie was the only person she had in the world. She couldn't rely on Kent now, couldn't have relied on him even if Celia hadn't answered the telephone.

She closed her eyes for a moment and took a deep breath. Maddie and Loran. Two orphans in the storm as much as mother and child. Loran had always felt that they were survivors somehow, but she didn't quite know of what. Life, she supposed. And single-parent family-hood—except that that had been much less of a disadvantage than most people wanted to believe. From the time Loran was very young, she had understood that she and her mother were a formidable unit. Not much taken individually, perhaps, but together there was nothing they couldn't accomplish.

It occurred to her suddenly that Maddie may have simply settled for their life together. She sat there, as surprised by the sudden, unbidden thought as if it had come from someone else. It was something she didn't want to consider—that, for her sake, her mother might have let go of her own dreams. Loran had never asked her about it, and she wasn't astute enough to guess. Or perhaps she had been too self-involved to make the attempt.

She frowned slightly. She had *no* idea why Maddie wanted her to come here, and the last thing she needed was to discover that Maddie considered her life wasted.

She looked toward the woods. Meyer was back. She saw him walking through the trees, but he didn't come in her direction. Instead, he left the graveled path and went down the landscaped hill to get to the parking area without having to pass by the gazebo. She sat openly watching his progress and the strong and assured way he carried himself. She had no trouble believing that he'd been deployed somewhere. He had the military bearing and attitude. There was nothing tentative about him.

He went directly to a truck, the same one the green garbage can had tumbled into, got inside and drove away, never once looking toward her.

Her mouth still tasted of peppermint.

CHAPTER 3

Meyer waited on the church steps. It was warmer in the sun, but the wind was too cutting for him to stand out in the open for long. He stepped back into the alcove and glanced toward the sound of a backhoe digging a new grave in the cemetery across the road, all too aware that he could easily have ended up over there—and a lot sooner than later.

There had to be at least five generations of valley people buried in that patch of ground, friends and enemies, relatives claimed and unclaimed, but he had no idea who they were digging this grave for. There had been a time when everyone in the valley would have known, and friends and neighbors would have dug the grave themselves with a pick and shovel. He could remember when it had still been done, and when people had brought the best food they'd had to offer and sat up all night with the homemade wooden coffin placed on sawhorses in the living room. There was a lot to be said for the kinship of it, for neighbors coming together in times of trouble and sadness. It was the main reason he'd returned to the valley—that and the fact that he belonged here and whatever he needed to be—friendly or standoffish or something in between—he could be, and no one would hold it against him. Unfortunately, he had returned just in time to see that sense of community die away. He didn't know half the people who lived around here anymore.

It occurred to him that the two new guests at Lilac Hill might be friends or relatives of whoever had died—which would explain the younger woman crying after her phone call. It hadn't looked like grief to him, though. It had looked more like "significant other" or husband trouble.

Significant other, he decided, because she wasn't wearing a wedding ring.

It surprised him a little that he found her…interesting. He hadn't been interested in much for a long time. And it wasn't just that she was self-assured and attractive and drove an expensive vehicle. Caught crying, she'd still had the presence of mind to conclude that he was an idiot for bothering her and react accordingly—but she wasn't rigid about it. She'd revised her initial opinion of him once she'd understood that he only meant to help. He liked women like that—feisty, but still reasonable. He also liked the fact that she didn't seem to be all that aware that everything she had was working for her. Or maybe she just didn't waste such an obvious advantage on the help unless she wanted something.

In any event, she was obviously rich and she was definitely good-looking. She was also about as unhappy as he'd first thought, even before he'd seen her crying on the gazebo steps. He didn't like having to witness a woman's sadness. It reminded him too much of the things he was trying so hard to forget. He had seen enough sadness when he'd been in the army. All over the world. That relentless kind of sorrow that beat a woman down until she couldn't hide it no matter how hard she tried. Hundreds of them. It lived inside them and looked out of their eyes.

The image of an altogether different woman's face suddenly rose in his mind, and he had to work hard to push it away and force his thoughts back to the present. Whatever was going on with the Lilac Hill guests had nothing to do with him, and he had too many things on the concerns list already. Things like not sleeping night after night and not being able to find enough work to make ends meet. He had told the younger woman that everything was going to be all right. He shouldn't have done that. He certainly didn't believe it. Whatever optimism he'd once had had desiccated in a foreign desert. Nobody knew any better than he did that good deeds never go unpunished.

Which should have kept him from hanging around the church steps now.

He walked to the double doors of the church, expecting them to be locked. They were, but he thought not for long. If there was a funeral on the church schedule, then Estelle Garth would be arriving soon for one of her white-glove inspections. If it was possible for any one human being to own a house of worship, then Estelle Garth owned this one. She lived halfway up the hill just beyond the church, where she could see *everything*. Nothing happened on the premises night or day that she didn't know about, and he expected that sooner or later she'd see him down here.

Estelle didn't like him. As a boy, he'd spent an extraordinary amount of time trying to stay out of her crosshairs. At first, he'd thought it was because he'd lived in Chicago with his parents before they'd died, and those years had somehow canceled out the fact that he was a Conley and he'd been born here. Somehow, his brief absence had turned him into an outsider, and everybody knew how Estelle felt about them.

By the time he was ten or eleven it had gotten so bad that he'd had no alternative but to ask his great-aunt Nelda about it—and she hadn't been nearly as helpful as he'd hoped.

"I reckon everybody's got their cross to bear, Meyer, and she's yourn," she'd said.

He owed Nelda a lot, and he wanted to accept her simple philosophy of life, but he couldn't do it, regardless of the fact that he was the pitiful homeless orphan none of his other relatives wanted. He must have lived in a dozen foster homes before Nelda stepped up to claim him and bring him home to the mountains again. By the time he came to live with her, he'd already had plenty of crosses to bear and the last thing he needed was Estelle Garth throwing another one on the pile. So he kept after Nelda. He needed a *real* reason, so he could deal with it.

"Maybe she thinks you done something," Nelda said finally.

"If she thought that, she'd come to you about it—or she'd make the preacher do it. I've not done anything, Nelda. I swear it!"

"It...might not be you, Meyer."

"Well, who then? She's after me all the time—accusing me of things when there's not a word of it true. I ought to know what it's about, Nelda. How else am I going to stand it?"

"It might could be it's got something to do with me, honey, something Estelle thinks *I* done, and the Lord knows I'd be sorry if you was having to suffer for it. Estelle, she thinks what she thinks, and whatever it is, can't nobody on this earth change her mind about it. She's been that way ever since I knowed her—when we was little girls even. If I was to go to her about you, it would just make it worse."

The possibility that Nelda was the real target led to a certain moral indignation on his part. He didn't like being chastised for his sins when he was guilty. He *really* didn't like it when he was innocent, especially when it was done to persecute his beloved Nelda.

Estelle Garth.

There was something about being innocent that made him bold, made him just *have* to annoy the woman, if the opportunity presented itself. He was always respectful when he did it—he had Nelda's standing in the community to consider—but he didn't just toe the ground and let Estelle blame him for everything but the Great Flood after that. He spoke up for himself, no matter how many people were around to hear it, stating his innocence and politely reminding her of all the *other* times she'd thought he was guilty of something when he wasn't. He especially enjoyed pointing out the time she'd accused him of throwing rocks at the church windows when he'd gone on a school trip and wasn't even in the county.

Estelle had understood immediately that there had been a big change in their relationship, and that, for all intents and purposes, they were at war. And still were, as far as he knew. Nelda had been right about one thing. Estelle Garth didn't change. Not too long ago, he'd overheard some of the women in Poppy's store talking about how she still marked on her kitchen calendar exactly when every wedding took place. Evidently, she didn't do it to avoid scheduling conflicts. She did it so she'd know in nine months if the marriage was a case of "have to." Mostly legitimate wasn't good enough for her. She was the self-appointed gatekeeper to eternal salvation, and she took the job seriously. Nothing deterred her, not even finding out that her late husband, Emlin, hadn't walked the chalk line she had so carefully laid down for him. It had to have been a terrible shock to find out that the meek and mild Emlin had been on a first-name basis with every waitress in the county. Meyer smiled slightly at the memory of all of them coming to his wake and telling Estelle what a generous tipper her Emlin had been. Big bad Emlin had also taken money Estelle didn't know he had and slipped off to Cherokee gambling with his fellow veterans from the American Legion Post.

But, worst of all, he hadn't disowned his and Estelle's only son the way Estelle told him to. She'd had to take to her bed after the will was read—a will she'd forced Emlin to hire a lawyer to write because she wanted to make absolutely sure it couldn't be contested. Emlin and his lawyer had certainly gotten that part of it right.

Even so, it seemed to Meyer that the more Emlin's sins came to light, the more high-and-mighty Estelle got, and, as much as he enjoyed it, he just wasn't in the mood to aggravate her today. He owed her a little something, he supposed. She was the reason he'd thought army drill sergeants were rational.

"Come on, Bobby Ray," he said aloud, stomping his feet to get the circulation going. All he knew about his being here was that Bobby Ray Isley wanted to talk to him.

Now.

And, because he'd known poor old Bobby Ray for as long as he could remember and because Bobby Ray was like a big overgrown and easily disappointed child, *here* he was.

He couldn't even begin to guess what was happening with the man. Bobby Ray was scared to death of Estelle, and that alone made this location *not* the best choice for a meeting place. Besides that, he was scared of being struck by lightning whenever he used the telephone, storm or no storm, regardless of the season, and he had actually called Meyer at Lilac Hill—a huge indicator of how serious Bobby Ray thought the situation was. Needless to say, the conversation had been quick. Bobby Ray hadn't given him a chance to ask anything. About all Meyer had gotten out of it was how distressed the old boy was.

But, there was a definite limit to how accommodating Meyer intended to be, and Bobby Ray drove his truck into the circle drive in front of the church just about the time Meyer reached it. Meyer stepped out into the cold wind to meet him, waiting impatiently while Bobby Ray struggled to get the driver's side window down.

"Did she say her name, Meyer?" Bobby Ray asked when he finally got the glass to move an inch or so. "Did she?"

"Who, Bobby Ray?"

Bobby Ray's train of thought constantly derailed,

leaving big gaps in his conversations. He never could seem to tell the difference between what he thought to himself and what he'd actually said out loud.

"That woman. The one that went—to stay—up—at the house where you work," he said, still struggling to roll the wobbly window in his truck the rest of the way down. "Did you find out what her name is?"

"No, I didn't," Meyer said, hunched against the wind. "I didn't know you wanted me to."

Bobby Ray quit fiddling with the window. "How come she wouldn't tell you, Meyer?"

"Because I didn't ask her. I'm the hired help, Bobby Ray. If the guests don't come right out and say who they are, I don't go asking things like that for no reason."

"You got a reason."

"No, I don't."

"Yeah, you do. I'm wanting to know, Meyer."

"'Bobby Ray Isley wants to know' isn't what most people would call a reason. Why do you want to know her name anyway?"

"I just do," Bobby Ray said, his big hands opening and closing on the steering wheel. "She's driving that little gray car and she bought gas at Poppy's. And I want to know what her name is. Didn't you even see her up there?"

"Yeah, I saw her."

"Did you talk to her?"

"A little bit—"

"Didn't you find out nothing?"

"Not much, no. I think her granddaddy might be from the mountains, here or somewhere," Meyer said. "She said he used to make things—cedar boxes and pencil holders—stuff like that. Things to sell to tourists."

"Oh, no," Bobby Ray said. He gave a sharp sigh.

Meyer tried not to smile at Bobby Ray's growing alarm. Ordinarily, Bobby Ray was not the kind of man to let himself be troubled by anything. He might get his feelings hurt if Poppy forgot his birthday, but basically he lived in his own little world of simple and perpetual bliss. Nothing worried him, not the local happenings and not world events. He went to his more or less token job at Poppy Smith's convenience store every day, and then he went home to his trailer right next to the road that led to the Parkway, the monotony of it all broken up by coon hunting and trout fishing and an ice-cold bottle of beer now and again. That he would be so undone by a woman he'd seen buying gas at Poppy's store was more than a little unusual. That he'd wanted Meyer to meet him at the church to talk about it bordered on the absurd.

"So what's going on, Bobby Ray?" Meyer asked after a moment. "One of your chickens come home to roost?"

"Ain't *my* chicken," he said. "I ain't got no chickens. Not that kind anyways."

"Whose then?"

"I can't tell you, Meyer." Bobby Ray looked at him. "It might not be her, you know," he added hopefully. "Poppy didn't guess who she was."

"Did you ask him?"

"No! I ain't asking Poppy. His eyes ain't that good anymore anyway."

"Well, who do you think she is?"

"You reckon you can find out her name for me, Meyer?" he asked instead of answering. "Reckon you can?"

"Maybe. But names change, Bobby Ray. Especially women's."

"I know that, Meyer. I ain't that dumb. You find out both her names, okay? Her *first* name ain't going to change, is it?"

"No, probably not, unless she's a movie star or something." He was trying to make Bobby Ray laugh, but it wasn't working. For once, Bobby Ray was staying on topic.

"Will you do it? Will you ask?"

"If I get the chance, I'll ask. Why are you so worried about her? She seems nice enough."

"I just am."

"How did you find out where she was staying?"

"That car she was in went up where you work."

"What were you doing—following her?"

"No, I wasn't," Bobby Ray said, clearly insulted by the question. "Somebody told me it was there."

"Yeah? Who?"

"Poppy, that's who. He seen that car was up there when he took his wife to work. He was real glad about it, too, because it was still around and she'd be buying more gas."

"But you're not glad," Meyer said because he was beginning to get a little worried about him.

Bobby Ray ignored his observation.

"Addison got real mad," Bobby Ray said, looking out the windshield of his truck again.

It took Meyer a moment to adjust to the switch in topics. The only Addison he knew was a former sheriff who'd been dead for years.

"Did he?" Meyer said because that seemed the quickest way to get Bobby Ray to the point.

"He said, 'Shut the hell up, Bobby Ray! Quit that cryin'!' But I couldn't quit it. I didn't know what to do. He put Tommy in handcuffs and *he* was a-crying—"

"Addison was crying?"

"No, not Addison. Tommy. He was crying—and him a soldier—crying in front of people. And I knowed how he was wanting to ask Addison for a little bit of time. That was the bad part, Meyer. He was wanting to ask him so *bad*. But he never did. He just stood there with his hands locked in them things behind his back. And Addison—he was all mad. He never wanted to do it. He said, 'I got to, boy. The army's in it now.' I never seen nothing like that in my life, Meyer." Bobby Ray looked up at him. "It was raining real bad."

Meyer was about to ask who "Tommy" was, but he didn't.

"His fingernails was tore off," Bobby Ray said, his bottom lip beginning to tremble.

"Bobby Ray—"

"Don't tell nobody her name but me, okay?" Bobby Ray said, taking the conversation back to its starting point. "Don't you go telling Tommy Garth. Please, Meyer!"

"Now, Bobby Ray, how am I going to tell Tommy Garth? If he comes into Poppy's store even twice a year, he's doing good," Meyer said.

"And don't you go telling the preacher," Bobby Ray said, clearly unimpressed by Meyer's logic. In Bobby Ray's reality, happenstance was clearly a bona fide and terrible thing.

"Why don't you want me telling the preacher?"

"I just don't. He knows too many people."

"Like who?"

Again, Bobby Ray didn't answer him. He sat there instead, his face as sad as some old coon dog that got left tied to a front-porch post when its master went off hunting with the rest of the pack.

"Like Estelle?" Meyer asked, and Bobby looked at him with such alarm that he immediately regretted the question.

"Okay, okay," Meyer said. "I won't tell Tommy Garth. Or the preacher. Or anybody. But don't call me up at Lilac Hill anymore—unless it's something really important."

Bobby Ray gave another wavering sigh, his downhearted expression still in place. Clearly, *this* had been "really important."

"You're smart, ain't you, Meyer?" he asked after a moment, and Meyer laughed softly at this brand new topic.

"I wouldn't go that far," he said.

"You been places. You been in the army. You been to college. They let you teach school, Meyer."

"Yeah, but it takes more than that to make a man really smart, Bobby Ray."

"Tommy, he was in the army like you."

"Yeah?" Meyer said, trying to remember if he'd known that about the man and realizing that Bobby Ray hadn't changed the subject after all.

"He didn't stay in jail, though. He went back in the army anyway. Estelle, she—"

Bobby Ray abruptly stopped and stared through the windshield again—at nothing as far as Meyer could tell.

"Don't you let nobody hurt her," Bobby Ray said quietly, more to himself than to Meyer.

"Who are you talking about, Bobby Ray?"

"I hope she ain't come back," he said. He looked at Meyer. "And I hope she is, too. Now ain't that a crazy thing?"

There wasn't much Meyer could say about that, even if he'd actually understood it. "You better go on to the store before you get into trouble with Poppy—or Estelle sees us."

"Yeah. I better," he said. "You ain't going to forget to try to find out what her name is, are you?"

"I won't forget, but I'm not promising you anything."

"You got any candy, Meyer?" Bobby Ray asked.

"Yeah, I got candy," Meyer said. He reached into his coat pocket and tossed him a couple of pieces. "You're going to rot your teeth, you know that."

Bobby Ray already had a peppermint in his mouth. "I ain't worried," he said around it. "You ate these when you was in the army, didn't you, Meyer? Nelda used to send them to you, didn't she? She'd go to the post office and mail them."

"That's right, Bobby Ray."

Bobby Ray reached to start his truck, then looked at him. "His fingernails was tore off, Meyer."

Meyer didn't say anything. He stood back to let the truck labor forward, then stared after it, trying to recall what he knew about Tommy Garth—mainly that he was Estelle Garth's only public failure. Meyer vaguely remembered something about Garth's trouble with the army, that he'd gone AWOL one time when he knew he was going to be sent to Vietnam and his mama had been the one who'd turned him in.

That must have been when people knew once and for all that Sister Garth had a tight handle on what was right and what was wrong, and she didn't turn loose of it for anybody, not even her own son.

Today, the man was little more than a backwoods hermit, living on a piece of land up on one of the ridges most people here had once thought he didn't even own—until his daddy's will had been read. Nobody had known he had been letting his boy stay on it. And, now that they did, nobody knew exactly what went on up at the place, how Tommy Garth made his living or what sins he was guilty of. And Tommy clearly didn't care what went on down here in the valley. He hardly ever showed his face, and when he did, it was only to buy what little he could afford and then go. He never asked after anybody or commented on any of the ongoing topics—the government's latest doings, the apple crop, the flatlanders, the weather.

Every now and then somebody would see his truck pass through with a load of lumber on the back, and the rarity of that was enough to cause comment in the store and on the church steps on Sunday mornings, precipitating rampant speculation as to what he could be using it for. The more generous of the group thought he was doing carpentry work for the new people moving in— his daddy and his granddaddy both had been good with their hands. Others thought it had to be something illegal, growing marijuana or something like that, which led to a lively discussion about how there wasn't much money in running a still anymore, and Tommy Garth wasn't the kind who would do it anyway as a courtesy to his neighbors.

The few times Meyer had seen him, the man had certainly had no intention of staying in what passed for civilization any longer than he could help. He'd been in and out, and if he'd recognized any of the regulars sitting around the stove in Poppy's store or outside under the shade trees, it hadn't shown. Even Poppy, who knew every single person born and raised in the valley and everything about them past and present, didn't presume to be familiar with this man. He took Tommy's money in silence and skipped the usual "old home week" small talk.

His fingernails was tore off—

Meyer's thoughts suddenly went to the woman crying on the gazebo steps. Her mother might be mixed up in all this somehow, and if Tommy Garth was in it, then so was Estelle.

And Meyer wouldn't wish that on his worst enemy.

CHAPTER 4

"Mrs. Jenkins is looking for you," Poppy said when Meyer walked into the store. He could see Bobby Ray intent on dusting probably dust-free soup cans near the front window.

"I just left from up there," Meyer said.

"Which don't amount to a hill of beans. There's still a hour or so of daylight left. I reckon you ain't done till she says you are. And she *says* she needs you to take somebody somewhere. Right now."

"Did she say who?"

"No. She didn't say where, neither. That woman is way too high-strung for me to go asking her questions. I reckon you'll find out when you get there. You got some job, boy, you know that?"

"I've had worse, Poppy."

"Yeah, I reckon you have. Is there anything up there you don't do?"

"She hasn't got me cooking breakfast yet, so your wife's job is safe," he said and Poppy laughed.

"How are you doing these days, Meyer? You look like you dropped a pound or two to me. You sleeping all right?"

"I'm okay."

"You sound like me when I first got back home. I was as big a liar as you are."

"Yeah, well, don't tell Nelda you think I've lost weight. She'll be chasing me around with a big bottle of castor oil and a spoon."

Poppy laughed. "You better get on out of here. Oh, and Mrs. Jenkins said you don't need to come inside. Just wait in the parking lot. You ain't let that truck of yourn get all dirty now, have you?" Poppy called after him.

Meyer waved him off and went outside to get into the truck he kept spotless for just such a summons to the big house. He headed back in the direction he'd come, wondering which guest needed a chauffeur. He hoped it wasn't the drunk. The man was supposed to be here until the weekend and he hadn't been sober since he'd arrived. If he made it to the end of his stay without somebody having to set him down hard, it would be a miracle, and, unfortunately, Meyer Conley was apt to be the "somebody."

He parked in the Lilac Hill parking lot as instructed. His passenger came out immediately—not the drunk but the woman Bobby Ray was so worried about. He got out of the truck as soon as he saw her.

"Are you waiting for me?" he asked, glancing toward her own vehicle.

"I…don't feel much like driving," she said and he believed her. She looked pale and tired, much more so than when he'd seen her earlier.

"Okay. Where to?" he asked.

"Don't we need to discuss your rates?"

"No, ma'am. Mrs. Jenkins takes care of that—unless you want me to drive you to Cincinnati or something."

"No, just the cemetery," she said, smiling slightly.

"Right," he answered. "Your...daughter didn't want to go?"

She looked at him and he knew right away that he hadn't slipped his interest in the rest of her party past her.

"She's gone into town to do some shopping," she said, smiling again.

He opened the door for her, then went around and got into the truck. "There are several cemeteries," he said as he got it into gear.

"*The* cemetery," she said.

"Yes, ma'am. Are you here for the funeral?" he asked as he pulled onto the road and turned in the direction that would take them to the church he'd just left. *Estelle's* church.

"No, what funeral is that?"

"I'm not sure. I saw them digging a grave earlier, but I don't know who it's for. It's not like it used to be," he added after a moment. "Lot of strangers in the valley now. Flatlanders mostly. You know about flatlanders?" he asked because he was almost positive she wasn't one.

"I know about flatlanders, but my daughter doesn't," she said, and he glanced at her.

"She didn't grow up in the hills, then."

"No."

"I didn't think so."

"Flatlanders can come in handy sometimes."

"Ma'am?"

"Your place—the one Mrs. Jenkins mentioned. I would think you rent it mostly to them."

"Mostly," he said. "It keeps me in pocket change. Like

I said, Mrs. Jenkins doesn't have to worry about the competition."

"Business is good at Lilac Hill, then."

"Up and down, I guess. She does a lot of advertising, but it's still feast or famine. Depends on…I don't exactly know what it depends on. Whatever the flatlanders feel like doing that week, I guess."

"Did you ever try it? Being a flatlander?" she asked.

"Yeah, I tried it. I was in the military long enough to see the world and to find out the world isn't what it's cracked up to be."

He could feel her looking at him.

"I'm…sorry," she said.

He shrugged. "I got a college education out of it. Ma'am, would you mind if I ask you your name?"

"Maddie," she said.

He waited for the rest of it and, for a moment, he thought she wasn't going to tell him.

"Kimball," she said finally.

"Meyer Conley," he said to refresh her memory.

"Yes. I know. Do you mind if we don't talk?"

"No, ma'am." He reached to turn on the heater.

"Are you cold?" she asked.

"Me? No, ma'am."

"I'm not, either," she said, and he left the heater alone.

They rode along in silence.

"What parts of the world did you see?" she asked abruptly, in spite of what she'd just said.

"The Balkans. Korea. Two tours in the Middle East. People around here—in this valley—are a lot better off than I used to think. There are some bad places in this

old world. Of course, us folks here didn't have any idea
we were so bad off until the government sent people to
tell us."

She smiled. "You grew up here." It wasn't quite a
question.

"Yes, ma'am. Mostly. I lived in Chicago for a while
when I was young until my great-aunt Nelda came and
got me. One of the best days of my life."

"Nelda...Conley?"

"Yes, ma'am."

She lapsed into silence again, staring at the passing
scenery—a Christmas-tree farm, then another one, then
the volunteer fire department with a sign out front an-
nouncing the Brunswick stew supper next Saturday
night—one with live music. Eat in or take out.

"Interesting name," she said absently.

"Ma'am?"

"Lilac Hill."

"Well, it's on a hill and there are a lot of lilacs," he
said, and she smiled again.

"Do you have a flashlight?" she asked.

"Yes, ma'am. It's not far to the cemetery now."

The church steeple came into view, and the Garth
house halfway up the hillside. He pulled into the circle
drive in front of the church because the backhoe now
blocked the narrow drive that divided the cemetery into
two sections. The wind buffeted the truck as it rolled to
a stop.

She got out immediately, pulling her coat collar up
against the wind, crossing the road quickly. He watched
her moving among the headstones, clearly looking for
something—or someone—in particular. Sometimes she

seemed to know where she was going, sometimes not. He saw her reach out and touch one of the tombstones, then move on. It would be dark soon. She had to be cold out there.

He saw her abruptly stop at another grave, and he knew whose it was because it was the only one made of black marble. The grave belonged to Tommy Garth's son.

Meyer suddenly got out of the truck because he'd forgotten to give her the flashlight. He crossed the road and called to her, but she didn't hear him.

"Ms. Kimball?" he called again.

She looked around and he came at an easy run toward her with the flashlight.

"Here you go. You might need this," he said, handing it to her.

He made no attempt to leave, and she went back to looking. He glanced toward the church—and saw Estelle bearing down on them.

"Damn," he said and Maddie Kimball turned around.

"What's wrong?" she asked him.

"The cemetery police," he said as the woman neared.

"The what?"

"Meyer Conley, what are you doing out here?" Estelle demanded before he could answer.

"He's with me," Maddie said and he couldn't help but grin.

Estelle looked at her, clearly annoyed that a stranger would put herself forward like that, especially on his behalf. Then, she gave a sharp intake of breath. Even in the waning daylight, Meyer could see the range of emotions that crossed her face, the self-importance giving way to confusion and then to denial and, finally, to what he could only describe as fear.

"I was just looking at the graves—like that one," Maddie said to her, gesturing in the direction of the black marble headstone that bore Estelle's last name.

Estelle didn't say anything. There was only the sound of her rapid breathing, clearly audible in the stillness of the cemetery.

"You ain't supposed to be out here," she said abruptly, finally finding her voice. "We ain't wanting people who don't belong here messing with the graves—"

"Well, that's a little harsh, Estelle," Meyer said. "Ms. Kimball, there's no reason why you can't look around out here if you want to."

"No, it's my mistake," Maddie said. "I shouldn't be here. Isn't that right?"

A question formed in spite of all Estelle could do. "You ain't *that* Kimball," Estelle said, twisting her hands.

"Yes," Maddie said quietly. "I am."

Estelle began to back away. After a few steps, she turned and walked rapidly in the direction she'd come, stumbling once when she reached the edge of the road.

Maddie Kimball stared after her, the flashlight clenched tightly in her hand.

"Well, that was interesting," Meyer said after a moment.

"I...have a favor to ask you," Maddie said.

"Go ahead."

"If...Bobby Ray Isley is—if he still lives here, I'd appreciate it if you'd tell him I— Tell him Maddie wants to see him. As soon as you can."

Meyer stood looking at her. "You're not going to hurt him or anything, are you?" He was serious.

She smiled slightly. "No. I'm not going to hurt anybody. I just want to see him. It's…personal."

"Personal," he repeated. "How personal?"

"I…don't want my daughter to know anything about it. Will you tell Bobby Ray? And tell him not to come to the house. If you let me know where, I'll come to him."

"Okay. I'll tell him."

"I'm not answering any more questions, Meyer," she added when he was about to say something else.

"No, ma'am. No more questions. I was just going to say…welcome home."

CHAPTER 5

Loran saw Meyer's truck parked in front of yet another church with a cemetery. As helpful as the kitchen staff at Lilac Hill had been in telling her that her mother had found it necessary to go look at a local graveyard, nobody had bothered to mention that there was more than one.

She pulled sharply into the church drive, making no effort to repress the exasperation she felt at having to chase Maddie down. Again. And while she was at it, she was annoyed with the man who had made it necessary this time. She knew perfectly well that there was no point in being angry with Meyer, that he was the hired help and that he couldn't possibly know that her mother was ill or that it was becoming a full-time job of late just to keep up with her. Even so, he would do well not to get in her way. Maddie had to be exhausted—and hungry. And besides all that, *she* would have taken Maddie any place she wanted to go.

Her head hurt. She needed a couple of aspirins, and a long bath. Some peace and quiet just so she'd be up to cornering Maddie once and for all and finding out what this was all about. She was beginning to think she couldn't take her eyes off Maddie for a second without her wandering.

Ain't nothing but a stray-away.

She had only just heard the quaint expression while she'd been waiting in the checkout line at the little discount store where she'd bought her impromptu travel wardrobe. Two old women in sweatpants had been talking about someone's granddaughter, one who apparently frequented places where she had no business being. And it wasn't that the girl "hadn't been raised" and didn't know better, they had assured each other. It was that she apparently was just like Maddie. She knew better—but she did it anyway.

She parked the SUV behind Meyer's truck and got out. The church door was standing ajar, and she walked in that direction. The sconce lights were on in the alcove behind the altar, but Loran didn't see anyone around at first. She entered quietly and walked down the carpeted aisle toward the front, noting immediately that the place smelled like a church, even though she would have been hard-pressed to say exactly why she thought so. It was a kind of mixture of things, she supposed—mildewed hymnals and candle wax and furniture polish or something. There were candles on the altar table, but they didn't look real to her.

She turned her head at a small repetitive sound—a woman vigorously rubbing the back of one of the pews with a folded cloth. A stack of hymnals sat on the floor at the end of the row.

"Excuse me," Loran said, startling the woman so much that they both jumped. "I'm looking for…Meyer?"

"Well, he ain't in here," the woman said shortly. "And you ain't supposed to be in here, either."

"Really? I thought it was all right to come into a church—especially when the doors are standing open."

She hadn't intended to sound so confrontational, but it had been that kind of day.

"Strangers don't belong in here unless they've been invited," the woman said bluntly. "And I told you Meyer ain't in the church."

"Did you happen to see him around anywhere?"

"I've got better things to do than keep up with Meyer Conley," the woman said, going back to her pew polishing.

"Oh. Well. Thank you so much for your help," Loran said. "Such as it was."

"If you know what's good for you, you won't go getting mixed up with that Conley boy," the woman called after her. "All them Conleys is liars."

Loran gave her a look and went back outside—and she immediately saw Meyer and her mother in the cemetery across the road. She had to wait for a car to go by before she could catch up with them. The person on the passenger side waved, and Loran waved back, wondering if she'd been mistaken for someone else. Or maybe people here either waved at you or threw you out of their houses of worship.

Or gave you advice about who not to get "mixed up" with.

She walked quickly toward where Maddie and her accomplice stood, fighting the gusts of wind as she went.

Meyer and Maddie were deep in conversation about something. Neither of them saw her until the last moment.

"I don't know if he will," Meyer was saying. They both looked startled to find her so close.

"Hello, Mother. Silly me, I thought you would be resting," Loran said in spite of her inclination—feeble though it was—to at least try to be reasonable. But at the moment, it was impossible to be reasonable where Maddie was concerned, not when she'd suddenly developed this penchant for not staying where she was supposed to be.

"Yes, Mrs. Jenkins told me that was my assignment," Maddie said.

"So what are you doing out here? What's going on?" Loran asked.

The remaining edge of the sun slid behind the mountain ridge. Loran could barely distinguish the features on her mother's face. She could only suspect the degree of evasiveness there, which was every bit as aggravating as actually seeing it.

"Oh, not much," Maddie said easily.

"Well, thank heavens for that," she said, falling back on sarcasm to try to hide the tremor in her voice. "I'd hate to be doing all this worrying for a reason."

She wanted to just let it go, but her being here in the first place was all Maddie's idea and now she seemed so…devious.

"This just isn't your day," Meyer said to Maddie.

"I've had worse," she said.

"Yeah, I hear that," he answered, their unexpected camaraderie causing Loran to have to fight a sudden and ridiculous urge to cry—when she'd done enough crying for one day.

She wondered if Meyer had told Maddie that he'd had to bribe her out of weeping on the gazebo steps with a piece of candy.

"Okay, what am I missing?" she asked, looking from one of them to the other.

"Nothing," Maddie said. "I'm ready to go if you are. Meyer, thank you for your trouble and your time. I appreciate both."

"You're welcome. Anytime," he said, but he made no attempt to leave. Loran could feel him looking at her, and, after a brief moment, she looked back. He seemed…not worried exactly, but still concerned somehow, just as she was. She had the sudden impression that she and Meyer were both in a situation they didn't quite understand.

She glanced at her mother, then at the child's grave the three of them seemed to be standing around—or at least she assumed it belonged to a child, because of the lamb resting on the top of the headstone.

Her mother abruptly began to walk away.

"Ms. Kimball?" Meyer called after her and she turned to look at him. She turned, but she didn't want to. Loran could feel her wariness more than see it.

"There's an eating place on Highway 16, just before you get to the Parkway," Meyer said. "The food's good. You just take this road as far as you can, then turn right. It's on the left, before you get to the Parkway bridge. Best apple pie in the world," he added, as if he thought it would matter.

"Thanks," Maddie said. "Maybe we'll try it." She walked on.

"Are you done with the flashlight?"

"Oh. Yes. Thank you."

Loran watched as her mother returned it, still trying to understand. She was rapidly losing hope that Maddie would be answering any of the questions she'd been formulating all the way down the Blue Ridge Parkway.

Aside from her normal policy regarding inquiries, it was obvious that Maddie didn't feel up to being interrogated—or anything else for that matter.

"Don't take my mother off anywhere again," she said to Meyer under her breath as she walked by him.

"Do what?" he said, clearly surprised.

"You heard me," she said without stopping. She ran the few steps it took to catch up with Maddie.

"Did you find everything you needed to buy?" Maddie asked lightly.

"Yes."

"See anything interesting?"

"No."

She had seen a sign for a hospice agency that had been set up in what used to be somebody's brick ranch house, but that was the last thing she would have wanted to talk about, even if Maddie hadn't been sick and a prime candidate for their services.

"Are you ready to go back to the B and B now?" Loran asked the question, but she wasn't offering alternatives. She wanted Maddie accounted for and resting in a warm and comfortable place out of the cold wind, and, as far as she was concerned, it wasn't up for discussion.

Maddie looked up at the sky. "Beautiful," she said, supposedly admiring the last tinges of orange and purple in the sunset but in fact studiously trying to avoid answering Loran's question. "Look."

Loran looked. Briefly.

They walked by an abandoned backhoe and a newly dug grave, and Loran shivered as much from the dread the sight of it evoked as from the cold. She didn't like anything about this place.

"So you and Oscar are new best friends," she said as they crossed the road to where she had parked in the circle drive in front of the church.

"Oscar?"

"The guy with the truck who takes my mother off to God knows where when I'm not looking."

"Oh, that Oscar." Maddie suddenly smiled. "Oscar. Meyer. I get it. Does he know you call him that?"

"Yes, he does, and whatever you do, don't start tap dancing."

"I'm too tired to tap dance."

"Which is exactly the point, Mother. Why are we here? *What* are you doing?"

"You mean besides hoping to convince my lovely daughter to buy me a hearty meal before she locks me in my room for the night?"

Loran gave a sigh. "There is no talking to you, is there?"

"Nope. You're not going to ground me, are you?" Maddie asked, smiling.

"Oh, very funny. I would if I could, believe me. *I* would have brought you out here, you know."

"I…needed to see it alone."

"Alone—with Meyer Conley along."

"Meyer is a very unobtrusive person," Maddie said.

"It's his job to be unobtrusive or anything else the guests or Mrs. Jenkins want him to be."

"Maybe so. But somebody definitely took the time and the trouble to teach him how to behave. You don't see much of that anymore."

Loran didn't miss the not-so-subtle dig at Kent, and once again she felt the urge to cry. No. Not just cry. To throw her head back and wail, like some big overgrown child who had dropped her ice cream in the dirt, lost her nickel, torn her best dress *and* broken her favorite doll— and who was completely out of options.

"He's been all over the world, in the military," Maddie said. "I think there's something a little sad about him, too. Did you notice that?"

"Everybody I've seen here looks sad. Are you trying to change the subject?"

"Not…very," Maddie said.

"You're not well, Mother—"

"No, I'm not. So humor me. Tell me what you bought on you shopping spree."

"Deodorant," Loran said, fumbling with the remote on her key ring so she could unlock the SUV doors. She glanced over her shoulder. Meyer was standing at the same place in the cemetery where they'd left him.

"Lucky me," Maddie said as she opened the door, smiling until Loran smiled in return—in spite of herself.

"What else?" Maddie said when they were both in the SUV.

"A toothbrush and toothpaste, a three-pack of men's undershirts, a red flannel nightgown, socks, a pair of jeans, a three-pack of ugly cotton panties, some weird shoes and a shirt, royal-blue plaid, also flannel."

"Going for the Oscar look, are we?"

"Ha, ha. I didn't have much choice if I wanted to be comfortable. Really, Mother, if I didn't know better, I'd think you were making fun of him."

"I wasn't making fun of *him*. I was making fun of you and Kent. I wonder what *he* would say—if he saw you dressed like that?"

"Nothing. He wouldn't recognize me."

"I hope he's getting along all right without you."

"I hope his hair catches on fire," Loran said as she pulled the SUV onto the road. "What?" she asked pointedly, because of Maddie's startled look.

"Well, me, too, then," Maddie said, making Loran smile again in spite of her worry. Her mother might be difficult to contain, but she was blindly loyal.

"Don't ask me why," Loran warned her.

"I don't care why. If you want his pin feathers singed, that's good enough for me. I think Meyer thinks you're cute, by the way."

"I am cute."

"And so modest, too. Oh—" Maddie said, suddenly grabbing the door.

"What is it?" Loran asked, reaching out to steady her.

"I'm feeling a little…wobbly…."

"Wobbly? What do you mean, wobbly?"

"Just…tired all of a sudden. It happens sometimes." She leaned back and closed her eyes, then took a deep breath. Then another one.

Loran was already slowing down the SUV, looking for a place to pull off the road.

"No, don't stop," Maddie said, opening her eyes. "Keep going. Just take me back to the house. I can rest while you go find us something good to eat. Maybe that place Meyer mentioned."

"I'm not leaving you by yourself. This trip has been too much for you. Maybe we should find a doctor. I'll ask Mrs. Jenkins where the closest—"

"I don't need a doctor. I need to eat. Just drop me off at the B and B. It shouldn't take you long. I'll be fine while you're gone. It's already starting to pass." She took another a deep breath. "Buy something with a lot of onions, will you?" she said as if it were all settled. "And watch the road, not me."

"Mother—"

"Loran, stop worrying. Will you please just return me to my room? I'll feel much better after I shower and eat something."

"I wish I could believe you—you have no idea what it's like having such a liar for a mother," Loran said, and Maddie laughed.

"Ah, well. We all have our heavy burdens to bear."

Loran kept driving. They weren't far from the B and B now. Maddie did seem better. She was sitting up a little straighter at any rate.

"So what were you doing at the cemetery?" Loran asked after a moment.

"Just looking."

"At what?"

"Headstones mostly. There's not much else out there."

"Right. And I'm supposed to believe that, I guess."

"Well, what else would I be doing?"

"I don't know, that's why I'm asking. I just don't…" Loran gave a quiet sigh instead of continuing, mostly so she wouldn't say something she couldn't take back.

"Don't what?"

"Understand! I don't understand why you wanted me to come. And now that I'm here you're…hiding!"

"Farther along, daughter," Maddie said.

"What is that supposed to mean?"

"It's a song. About having patience because all will be revealed. Later."

"A song. Great. Do you have any idea how much I want to help you—and how am I going to do that if you won't let me!" The tremor in her voice was back, in spite of all she could do, and Maddie reached out to caress her shoulder.

"If it's any comfort to you, I don't understand what's going on with me, either. I think I'm...filled with whims, that's all. Well, actually, I've *always* been filled with whims. It's just that now I'm giving in to them. And I kind of like it, you know?"

"Like...what?"

"Like eating whatever I want to eat. Going wherever I want to go."

"Going to a cemetery in the cold with a total stranger?"

"That, too," Maddie said, looking out the side window. There was nothing to see in the dark, nothing to see in the daytime, either. Maddie was clearly avoiding the cemetery topic again.

"So what did he mean?"

"Who?"

"Meyer, Mother. The total stranger. He said this wasn't your day. He must have meant something. What was it?"

"He meant that you weren't happy about me being there. And one of the locals had just left—she wasn't happy about me being there, either."

"Why not?" Loran asked, realizing she had probably encountered that particular local herself.

"I look highly suspicious," Maddie said.

"Right. You look like everybody's idea of a graveyard

vandal. What about Meyer? I guess he's suspicious-looking, too."

"Well, the light was bad, and people here don't like outsiders."

"Tell me about it," Loran said under her breath.

"What?"

"Nothing. How do you know they don't like outsiders?"

"I've seen Mrs. Jenkins's face," Maddie said.

"She told me she was born here."

"You can be born in a place and still be an outsider."

"Maybe her feet hurt," Loran said for no other reason than to counter her mother's self-assurance.

"Maybe nobody ever asks her over for Sunday dinner. So what happened with you and Kent?" Maddie asked without warning.

"I thought you'd get around to that."

"I have to get around to it. You're my daughter. It's my duty to ask. Besides, it's an interesting concept—spontaneous combustion and Kent's designer 'do.'"

"I don't want to talk about it," Loran said.

Maddie didn't say anything else, but Loran could feel her mother waiting.

And waiting.

"All right. It's over. End of discussion."

"Because *he* said it's over or because you caught him red-handed at something?"

"It doesn't matter."

"Of course it does. Which is it? Is he moving on of his own accord or because you found out he's misbehaved?"

Loran stared straight ahead without answering.

"What did he do?"

"A woman answered the phone when I called him earlier," Loran said abruptly.

"His cell phone or the one at your house?"

"My house, Mother."

"Oh. I'm…sorry."

"No, you're not."

"Yes, I am—a little bit. I don't want you to be unhappy, Loran. Maybe you can patch it up."

"She was in my house, Mother. In my bed."

"You don't know that for sure."

"I know Kent."

"Well, you've got me there," Maddie said. She didn't say anything else. She didn't say anything for so long that Loran looked at her.

"Does Kent know he's caught?" Maddie asked as if she'd been waiting for her to do just that.

"No."

"Then there's still a chance to fix it—if you want it fixed."

"I don't want it fixed."

"Well, it could be worse."

"Oh, really? How?"

"You could be in love with him."

"How do you know I'm not?"

"Are you?"

Loran gave a quiet sigh instead of answering. How would she know if she was or wasn't? When it came to "love," she had absolutely nothing to go by. And it took everything she had not to say so.

"I'm serious," Maddie said. "It really could be worse."

"*This* feels pretty bad, Mother. I didn't think we were going to last forever, but I didn't see it coming—at least not right now, *today*. And don't tell me I should have. I know you never liked him."

"It's not that I didn't like *him*. I just didn't like him for you. He isn't good enough for you. And there's a big difference in having your heart broken and having your pride hurt. I think your heart is just fine. I think you're more worried about what people are going to say."

"And you would know all about that, I guess. Broken hearts and hurt pride."

"I read a lot," Maddie said. "Will you bring me something really good for dessert?" she asked, changing the subject once again.

"If I can find anything."

"Wonderful. You are such a good daughter."

"And a lot of good it does me," Loran said as she turned into the driveway at Lilac Hill. "You still insist on running wild."

"You know what they say—if you don't sow your wild oats when you're young, you'll sow them when you're old."

"Couldn't you have picked someplace a little closer to home?"

"Home is a state of mind, my darling."

When Maddie got out of the SUV, Loran got out with her. Maddie gave her a look but didn't say anything, apparently deciding that to do so would only prolong the arrival of the dessert.

A number, if not all, of the other B and B guests had gathered around the fireplace downstairs for some kind of celebration complete with wine-filled glasses and piano music.

"Pray, come and join us, fair maiden!" one of the men

called loudly to Loran as she walked through. He was unsteady on his feet and he lurched in her direction.

"Maybe later," Loran said, forcing a smile. She'd learned a long time ago that with most men, drunk or sober, false hope worked far better than outright refusal.

She took Maddie's arm as they walked up the stairs, and the grateful look her mother gave her brought the tears she'd been fighting close to the surface again. Maddie should have never made this trip.

Never.

She waited until her mother had showered and was safely ensconced on the small sofa in her room—a pillow at her back and a blue afghan over her legs—before she finally felt comfortable enough to set out on yet another quest.

"You're not going over the wall while I'm gone, are you?" she asked, tucking the afghan more closely around Maddie's feet.

"No. I'll be right here. If I'm asleep, wake me up."

"Mother, are you sure you—"

"Go, go, I'm *hungry*."

"I don't know what I can find. It might be a bag of chips."

"At this point, I don't care."

"I could ask Mrs. Jenkins if she could whip up a little something."

"I'd rather have chips," Maddie said.

"Okay, then, I'm going," she said. "And we're going to talk when I get back. I mean it."

She opened the door into the hallway. She could immediately hear the racket from the gathering downstairs, and she didn't want to have to fend off any more unwanted invitations. She closed the door again, cutting off yet another chorus of "Won't You Come Home, Bill Bailey?"

"I'm going to go out that way," she said, crossing the room to the door that led to the outside stairway and ultimately to a deck with a view of the mountains.

"Be careful," Maddie said as Loran fumbled to turn the dead bolt on the door. "It's dark out there."

And still windy, Loran realized as she stepped outside on the landing. She stood for a moment to give her eyes a chance to adjust, then made her way down the steps, hanging on to the rough banister until she reached the deck.

She made the trip easily to the gravel path that led to the parking area. The path was lit with dim walkway lights, and for a brief moment she was in the shelter of the house and out of the wind.

She had to pass by a window where the celebration was going on. She could see the fire in the fireplace and hear the guests' alcohol-induced laughter. No singing, though. Apparently, Bill Bailey had finally arrived.

As she crossed the parking lot, she realized that she wasn't alone. Meyer stood at the edge of the yard, talking to another man. The man had his head bowed, and, in spite of his great size, he kept shifting from one foot to the other like a contrite little boy who was being sent to the principal's office.

She kept walking, trying not to intrude. Another Lilac Hill patron who had had too much to drink would have been her first guess, given the rowdiness of the party inside. Clearly, there was no limit to the list of duties that comprised Meyer's job description, and he was welcome to that aspect of it.

She could hear snatches of their conversation as she made her way to the SUV.

"...she's not going to hurt you, Bobby Ray..."

"...she's mad at me..."

"...it's up to you. I can't tell you what to do. You wanted me to find out what her name is and I did. I told you what she said. Now, I'm done here. I don't like being in the middle of this."

"Meyer, you go tell Tommy," the other man said.

"No!" Meyer said.

"You got to, Meyer!"

"I thought you didn't want him to know."

"This is bad, Meyer. Real bad! He's got to know about it and I'm scared to go up there. You do it. Okay? You do it, Meyer."

"Whatever it is, it's ancient history, Bobby Ray. How bad can it—?" Meyer suddenly broke off and looked in Loran's direction.

She didn't say anything; she kept going.

"Who is that, Meyer?" she heard the other man say. "It's not—"

"Bobby Ray, go on home."

"No, Meyer—"

"Go on. Hey," Meyer called to her.

She took a deep breath, disconcerted because she was glad to see him. "What?"

He didn't answer until he'd crossed the parking lot to where she stood. "You going to go get something to eat?"

"Yes," she said. The man followed after Meyer, but stopped short of actually joining them. He stood in the middle of the parking area, looking as if he would bolt if either of them stamped their foot.

"Now?"

"Yes," she said pointedly.

"Is Maddie all right?"

Maddie?

"Yes, why?"

"She's not with you."

"She's very tired. I guess you didn't notice."

"I noticed. That's why I asked after her. You got time to tell me why you think I'm into kidnapping the Lilac Hill guests?"

"No."

"I don't think you understand the situation—"

Loran gave a short laugh. He had no idea how right he was about that.

"Meyer?" the other man said tentatively in the background.

"I don't think you understand the situation," Meyer said again, undaunted by the interruption. "There aren't that many jobs in these parts. I work for Mrs. Jenkins, and I need the money she pays me. If she says drive a guest around and the guest wants to be driven, I drive. You see how that works?"

Loran stared at him. Actually she did. She'd only just told Maddie the same thing. "Fine," she said.

Someone came out onto the back porch. "Meyer!" Mrs. Jenkins called. "We need some help in here."

"I think she'd better get in line," Loran said, because the man was still hovering—and growing more distressed by the minute.

"See you later," Meyer said. "I have to go referee a bunch of drunks."

"Are you any good at it?" Loran asked impulsively as he turned to go.

"Yeah, I am. Used to be an MP. Of course I have to kick it up a notch or two for some of the guests that come here. You may not know this, but drunk rich people can be a handful."

She knew it, and he knew she did. He stood for a moment, and, when she didn't say anything else, he turned away again and began walking toward the back door.

"Hey," he called when she was about to get into the SUV. "What's your name?"

"Kimball."

"No, your other name. What do your friends call you?"

"Loran—with an *a*, not an *e*," she said.

"I've known a few Lorans with an *a* in these parts—none of them were girls, though."

"I'm not a girl, either," she said, sounding exactly like one, like a junior-high-school wallflower trying to hold the attention of the most popular boy in the class after he had inexplicably looked her way.

"Well, you could have fooled me," he said. "Drive carefully, Loran. And don't take any candy from strangers—you know how you are about that."

She tried not to smile. He was teasing her as if he'd known her forever, and he had every right to do it—whether she was annoyed with him for taking Maddie off or not.

"Meyer, tell her she can't—" the other man began.

"Come on, Bobby Ray," he said, turning abruptly and clasping the man's shoulder. "You wait in the kitchen for me, okay? I might need you to help me." He walked the man toward the house, and she watched as they went inside, fully aware of how little recent events with Kent had to do with her desire to prolong a conversation with Meyer Conley.

She got into the SUV and, when she was about to pull out of the parking area, she saw the man who had been with Meyer coming out of the house. He stood for a moment, looking in her direction, then turned and walked down the lit path.

CHAPTER 6

"Bill Bailey" started up again downstairs, and there was some kind of muffled commotion that seemed to get louder then abruptly ended with the slamming of a door at the far end of the hallway. Maddie leaned her head back and closed her eyes again.

She didn't know how long she had dozed before the singers began another encore, but she did feel better, physically if not emotionally. She knew perfectly well that it wasn't just the encounter with Estelle Garth in the cemetery that had left her so drained. It was having to take Meyer Conley into her confidence, even minimally.

Now what?

All of a sudden she was barreling down a road she couldn't even recognize anymore. She couldn't get off it, and she had no one to blame but herself.

I don't know what to do.

No. That wasn't true. There was only one conclusion she could make after her conversation with Estelle. It was obvious that the woman had been afraid—which could only mean one thing. Estelle didn't want Tommy to know she was here. Even after all this time, Estelle didn't want Maddie Kimball talking to her son.

But what Estelle wanted was no longer part of the

equation. Loran was Maddie's only concern, and there was only one decision to make at the moment. Did she or didn't she want to see the father of her only child?

When she'd telephoned Loran this morning, everything had seemed so clear to her. Loran was a grown woman with a life of her own. She had the right to know where she came from. She had the right to know her mother's history—*her* history. Maddie had wanted Loran to come here so that she could tell her everything—more or less.

Unfortunately, she hadn't anticipated the possibility of having to deal with Tommy Garth firsthand—and he must be here or at least close by. She hadn't really considered that he might be. No one had ever wanted to leave this place as badly as he did, not even she herself. Together, they had made such plans. When he got out of the army, they'd go someplace exciting—like Atlanta. They'd live in a big city, born again, all shiny and new, both of them rid of the misery Estelle Garth and Foy Kimball had caused them.

She couldn't change her mind about telling Loran now. She didn't have the luxury of waiting, whether Tommy was here or not. She had never felt obligated to try to inform him that he had a daughter, and she had never told Loran anything about him. Her goal had been simple. She had wanted her daughter to believe that there was nothing the two of them couldn't handle, and the you-and-me-against-the-world concept had served them well. It was fine as far as it went, as long as there was a "you and me."

If she found out she had a father, too—if it all came to light somehow after Maddie was gone—then what?

Loran would never know how it really was and why her mother had done what she'd done, unless Maddie herself told her. Loran would only know Estelle's version—or Tommy's. Or perhaps she wouldn't know any version at all, and she'd always wonder.

How can I explain this?

The bottom line was that she had deliberately kept Loran from knowing anything about her father and now she was going to have to justify it.

Broken heart or hurt pride?

Which was it? She had only just assured Loran that there was a difference.

It was both, she suddenly decided. And more. She realized that her own relentless determination, the inner strength she'd always prized, had been finite. It had been an either-or situation for her. She had been able to put her very soul into giving Loran a good life, but she hadn't been able to find the courage to face the pain and humiliation of Tommy Garth. Perhaps she still couldn't.

She was certain of only one thing. She had deliberately constructed an emotional safe haven for herself, one filled with purpose rather than bitterness, and she wanted to stay there. The Maddie Kimball she was now had no room and no time for tears and regret. This Maddie had other, more pressing matters. She didn't want to have to rely on anyone at this late date, least of all Tommy Garth. She had personally seen to it that their beautiful daughter had everything—except the emotional independence she needed and somewhere to belong. Maddie could have given her the latter easily enough, but she hadn't, and now there was only one thing left to do.

I have to make her understand.

There was a gentle tapping on the outside door.

"Back already?" Maddie called, getting to her feet. She crossed the room and opened the door without hesitation, realizing too late that it wasn't Loran returning with the food.

She wasn't alarmed, not after the initial surprise. He had changed so little since she'd last seen him, and the memories associated with him swept into the room like the wind behind him.

"Bobby Ray," she said after a moment. "Come in. It's cold."

He didn't move.

"Come on," she said gently. "It's all right."

"Meyer, he said to wait in the kitchen," he said after a moment. "He said you weren't wanting me to come to the house."

"I've changed my mind. Come inside. I expect he'll know where you've gone."

He looked over his shoulder, then at her. "Foy Kimball ain't here no more."

"No."

"He was a mean old man."

"Yes, he was. But he's long gone. I'm the only Kimball left. Come inside out of the cold."

She stood back and he stared at her hard, as if he still didn't trust what his eyes were telling him. Finally, he crossed the threshold.

"You got your long hair cut off," he said.

"Yes."

"How come you did that?"

"I was sick," Maddie said because, unless he had

changed, the simple unanswered questions would be the ones that worried him. Her short hair would be much more of a concern to him than her long absence.

"Like when you was little and had the typhoid fever?"

"Something like that," she said, surprised that he remembered. She had been bedridden for weeks in the summertime, and someone had convinced her mother that she needed to have her hair cut off. It had been a relief to get rid of it, but the relief had been short-lived. She hadn't anticipated the teasing when school had started, and there was only one person whose teasing she hadn't minded. Almost-grown Tommy Garth had run his hand over the top of her cropped head.

"Hey, little boy," he'd said, smiling and giving her a piece of bubble gum to show her that there was no meanness in it.

"It's shorter than mine," Bobby Ray said, pulling her back into the present.

"Yes," she said again.

"Except where I ain't got any. You ain't mad at me, are you, Maddie?" he asked, suddenly pulling his ball cap off and rotating it in his big hands. He kept glancing around the room as if he expected Foy's ghost to suddenly materialize.

"No, Bobby Ray."

"You got gone and nobody ever said where you went. You never come back, Maddie. How come you never come back?"

She shook her head rather than try to explain the unexplainable. "It doesn't matter now."

"That there's what Meyer said. Ancient history, he said. That means real old, don't it? You got old, didn't you, Maddie?" He was staring at her again. "You still look like you, though. I knowed you right off when you was at Poppy's. I told Meyer I was hoping it was you—and I was hoping it wasn't. Ain't that a crazy thing?"

"Bobby Ray, is Tommy still here?" she asked instead of answering.

"I reckon so."

"I want to see him," she said, her indecision suddenly gone.

He didn't say anything, and for a moment Maddie thought he was going to turn around and leave.

"I want you to tell him that, Bobby Ray."

"I don't never talk to him."

"You said he was living here."

"Way up on Lady Ridge, Maddie. He built him a place up there. It's real hard to find, if you don't know right where it is and the apples ain't ripe. That was about the only way I could find it—smelling them apples on the trees close to where that old burnt down cabin is up there. It's a scary place where that burnt cabin is. Don't no grass grow around it. I was always scared of haints, that woman's dishes all got broke. You can see them sticking up out of the ground. Pretty pink-and-white dishes with roses. Some of them's got gold lines on them, Maddie. You can see that gold a-shining, when the sun hits them. I ain't never seen dishes like that before. Now you know she wouldn't want somebody big like me a-walking around up there, stepping on her dishes, even if they is already broke. I told Tommy that, but Tommy, he said it don't bother him none. He said weren't no dead going to bother me, neither—it was the folks what was alive you got to worry about. I never did like it around her place, though. Never did. Reckon where she went to, anyway, leaving all her stuff like that? Most times I'd just stand somewhere and holler until Tommy come and got me. Reckon she'll come back like you did, Maddie?"

"No, Bobby Ray. I think she's long gone by now."

He nodded thoughtfully. "Long gone," he said after a moment. "Like Foy. Well, Tommy, he don't show up down here in the valley much anymore. He don't even come to church, except maybe on Christmas now and again. He might get a little something at Poppy's store sometimes. Tater chips. You remember how he liked tater chips, how every time he'd go off someplace, he'd bring you and me a bag, too? Tommy, he—"

"Don't you and Tommy go hunting anymore?" Maddie asked, interrupting Bobby Ray's reverie in a blatant effort to steer him in another direction.

For the first time, Bobby Ray smiled. "Lordy, you remember about that? Naw. I ain't been hunting with him since before his daddy died. Him and me and Emlin, we used to go all the time after he come back from Atlanta. Emlin, he would sneak off from Estelle. You know how Estelle is about things," he said.

Maddie nodded. She knew only too well, because she had had the misfortune of being one of the "things" that annoyed Estelle Garth.

"Estelle never did find out about it, though, till after Emlin was in the ground. Boy, she was mad then. She come into Poppy's store and got all *over* me about it. Yelling and waving her arms, trying to make me say it weren't true. She said her Emlin didn't go sneaking off to Tommy's place when she didn't want him to. I said it was so true—my mama didn't raise me up to tell no stories. Estelle, she didn't believe it, though. She called me a liar right to my face…. Anyway…" Bobby Ray's voice trailed away as he remembered. He gave a quiet sigh then abruptly looked at her. "Tommy, he had a good pack of hounds. I was wanting him to sell me one, but he never did."

"Bobby Ray, will you tell him I want to see him?"

"It wouldn't do no good. He don't have nothing to do with people. He won't talk to nobody."

"He'll talk to you."

"No, he won't. He don't even talk to his mama."

"Why not?"

"'Cause of what she did, I reckon, when he brought his dead young-un home."

"What dead young-un?"

"His little boy what got run over by a car down in Atlanta. I reckon the boy's mama didn't care where he was put, so he brought him back here to get buried. Estelle, she didn't like that one bit. She told the preacher it weren't right on account of Tommy never did marry his boy's mama. She got to saying Bible verses at the preacher and everything. She tried to make Emlin say the boy couldn't be buried here, too, but he wouldn't. Her and Tommy got into it right on the church steps. She said she weren't having no bastard buried in the Garth family plot, and Tommy said she didn't need to be worrying about that. He'd throw that boy's body in the river before he'd let him be put over there where she was going to be. He just wanted him in the church cemetery—home—with his daddy and his granddaddy close by, so they could look after him, put flowers on his grave on Decoration Sunday. And the preacher said he could.

He said Estelle couldn't say who was to be buried in the cemetery, no, she couldn't."

Maddie folded her arms over her breasts, feeling the emotion of Bobby Ray's matter-of-fact account as if she'd actually been here.

"I think I saw his grave," she said after a moment. "Someone put some pink carnations on it."

"Weren't Estelle. I know that."

"Bobby Ray, I still want you to tell Tommy I want to see him. Then I want you to come back here tomorrow and get me and take me up there."

"Naw, Maddie, I can't tell him—"

"Then you can just take me. In the morning."

"He might not be up there, Maddie."

"I'll take the chance. I don't have a lot of time, Bobby Ray. There's nobody else I would want to ask, but you." She looked into his sad eyes. "Nobody else knows how it was then—with him and me."

He looked at her, and she understood perfectly what he didn't say.

Nobody but Estelle.

"I'm scared to go up there. And he don't *want* nobody up there, Maddie," Bobby Ray said. "If I holler now, he won't come."

Maddie gave a quiet sigh. She knew firsthand the futility of "hollering" for Tommy Garth. "I'm asking you to do this for me, Bobby Ray."

"I got to go," he said abruptly. "I got to go right now. I got to wait in the kitchen. Tommy, he ain't what he used to be no more." He put his cap on and opened the outside door. "We can't fix him. There ain't nobody to help us, Maddie. Nobody."

"Bobby Ray—"

She followed after him noisily down the wooden steps to the deck below.

"Bobby Ray, wait! Wait!"

He didn't stop and he didn't go toward the kitchen. Maddie stood on the deck, watching as he disappeared like a frightened rabbit into the darkness under the trees. She shivered in the cold wind, but she made no effort to go back inside.

"I know you're getting tired of hearing this," Loran said at the top of the stairs behind her. "God knows I'm getting tired of asking—*but what is going on?*"

Nothing, Maddie almost said, but it was too late to keep trying to avoid the truth. She didn't have the time for it and she loved her daughter.

She took a deep breath and began to climb the steps up to the room. Loran stepped back inside, still holding two white plastic bags of whatever she'd brought to eat.

"Who was that?"

Maddie still didn't say anything. She was too tired to think of an answer. Her only choice was the truth or an unconvincing lie, and she didn't have the strength for either.

"Let's eat," she said instead. "I'm starving."

"Mother—"

"We'll eat. And then I think I'll explain some things."

"You *think* you'll explain?"

"Yes. I'm not sure I can. What did you bring?" Maddie asked, taking a bag out of her hand and opening it.

"Two vegetable-plate specials with cornbread," Loran said. "Don't ask me what the vegetables are. I couldn't recognize anything."

"Is there some dessert?"

"Yes, there's some dessert," Loran said. "The famous apple pie Meyer recommended. And two coffees, if I didn't spill them trying to see why you were chasing some man out of your room."

Maddie frowned into the bag.

"I saw what I saw, Mother, and it's pretty obvious you don't think anyone in law enforcement should be involved. So you go right ahead and have your dinner and your dessert. Work on your explanation all you want. But I'm telling you right now, I'm probably not going to believe it."

Maddie smiled slightly and gave Loran a small and a large take-out box and a coffee. "Are you going to take yours to your room?"

"Nice try, Mother. *No.*"

"Then sit down and let's eat."

Loran sat, but she didn't open the box. She watched Maddie.

"Lovely," Maddie said when she opened hers. "Pinto beans with raw onions. Fried okra. Fried squash. Did you say you got it at the place Meyer told us about?"

"Yes, but I'm not sure it's edible."

"It's very edible. I haven't had anything like this in a long time. Try it, try it."

Loran finally opened her Styrofoam box, but she only took a few random samples.

"Don't you like it?"

"This is a heart attack with a lid."

"Then eat the pie," Maddie said, pushing one of the smaller boxes toward her. "So what was the restaurant like?"

"There were a bunch of old men playing music, banjos and things."

"Ah. A place with live entertainment."

"I don't think they were playing for the customers. If anything, they were playing for each other. They didn't seem to notice anyone else was there. What is that in the beans?"

"Ham hocks, probably."

"Ham hocks. I'm supposed to eat something called ham hocks."

"Eat the beans. Forget the ham hocks," Maddie said.

They ate for a time in silence. Maddie could feel how closely Loran watched her. She looked up from the box of food on her lap just in time to see Loran's furtive attempt to get rid of the tear that had slid down her cheek.

"I saw him in here, Mother," Loran said quietly. "And I saw him earlier, down in the parking lot with Meyer. Don't put me off anymore. Please."

Maddie took a quiet breath.

"His name is…Bobby Ray Isley," she said after a moment. She took a sip of coffee.

"What was he doing up here?"

"He was here because I asked Meyer to tell him I wanted to see him."

Loran stared at her, trying to understand.

"So…why did you want to see him?"

Maddie closed the box and set it on the small table in front of the sofa. "I used to live here."

"Here?" Loran repeated, clearly alarmed by the possibility that her mother had suddenly lost her mental clarity.

Or maybe not so suddenly, given the day's events.

"*Here,*" Maddie said, making a sweeping gesture with her hands.

"You mean Lilac Hill?"

"It wasn't Lilac Hill then. It wasn't much of anything."

Loran pursed her mouth to ask another question, then sighed.

"You used to live here. In this house."

"Yes. With my mother and father and my grandfather."

"So this trip of yours is a kind of…Thomas Wolfe thing. You're trying to go home again."

"Sort of."

"What does that mean?"

She sighed. "The Internet can be a terrible thing."

"The Internet?" Loran said, obviously still worried about Maddie's mental state.

"I was looking for lilac bushes—images—I wanted to see what the different kinds looked like before I tried to order some for the backyard. I might not see them bloom, but you could. I always loved lilacs. My mother planted the ones outside that window there. Anyway, I found Lilac Hill. I…recognized it right away. I told myself it was impossible, but I sent for a brochure. The house was a hovel when I lived in it, and it wasn't a happy place for me or my mother. I couldn't believe somebody could resurrect it, or would even want to. I kept thinking about it and thinking about it—maybe because I was sick. It makes you…nostalgic. Anyway, I woke up one morning knowing it was something I needed to do before I died. I needed to go home again. I needed to see if the pain was still there."

"Is it?"

"Yes. And no. There's more to it now. I want to stay for a while."

"Mother, you can't—"

"Yes, I can. I…haven't worked out all the details but I need to be here. I knew that even before I found out—"

Loran waited for her to go on, then abruptly closed the Styrofoam box.

"I have things I need to do," Maddie said.

"Like what?"

"I need to see someone. I need to see…your…father."

"What?"

"You heard me, I think."

"You mean he's *here?*"

"So Bobby Ray tells me."

"What, you didn't know?"

"No. He always wanted to get away from here. He had…plans. I didn't think he'd ever come back."

"There seems to be a lot of that going around. Whatever you're going to do, Mother, I don't want any part of it—"

"Actually, this is between him and me. You aren't invited."

"I—" Loran gave a sigh of exasperation. "You wouldn't ever talk about him! I thought he was probably dead."

"He was. To me."

"Why didn't you tell me before?"

"I didn't want to, and you never really asked."

"I never really asked?" Loran said. "I stayed in government-funded day care when I was little. *Nobody* had a father. I thought that was the way it was supposed to be.

No, you know what? I never asked because I was afraid to. I was afraid of something crazy like *this!*"

"Yes," Maddie said. "It is crazy. And it can't be helped."

"Well, this is just great. You run off to the mountains, Kent's got another woman, and suddenly I have a father—all in the same day. So what else is new? Any half siblings around I don't know about?"

Maddie didn't answer.

"There *are* some."

"Not living," Maddie said. "There's only the one boy, as far as I know. He's buried at the cemetery—"

"So that's why you went there."

"No. I didn't know about him until just now. Bobby Ray told me about that, too. I saw the headstone, but I still didn't know. I went because your grandparents are buried there. And your great grandparents. I called you this morning—I wanted you to come here—because I thought you should know about your family."

"That's the only reason you wanted me to come?"

"Yes. I didn't know Tommy was here. I was probably going to tell you about him, too."

"Probably?" Loran repeated.

They stared at each other, until Loran finally looked away.

"I see," she said after a moment. She stood up, and then sat back down again. "No, I don't see. Why are you telling me all this *now?*"

"Maybe I want you to know the truth about your father and me. And maybe you will—if I can find out what it is."

"What are you going to do?"

"I don't know what I'm going to do. I just need to see him again. That's all I'm sure about."

"He knows about me, I guess."

"No."

"*No?* Are you sure? Do I look anything like him? I got some pretty strange stares when I went into at that little store down the road."

"That's because you're a flatlander in a big car. I never told him about you. I never told anyone here. I left and I never came back until yesterday."

"So I'm not the only one in for a big surprise."

Maddie didn't say anything. Neither of them did for a time.

"His name is…Tommy. Are you going to tell me his last name?" Loran said finally, clearly still trying to get her mind around the revelation.

"Garth. Tommy Garth."

"And nobody here knows? About me."

"Nobody."

"Meyer doesn't?"

"No."

"This Bobby Roy person?"

"Bobby Ray. No. I'm really—" Maddie began.

"Don't you dare drop all of this into my lap and then say you're sorry!"

"I wasn't going to. I was going to say I'm really tired. I'm going to bed now. We can talk some more in the morning."

"Mother—"

"In the morning, Loran."

"How many more secrets are there? You can tell me that, at least."

"That's pretty much it, as far as I know."

"Mother—"

"Good night, Loran," Maddie said pointedly. She handed Loran the Styrofoam box. "Toss this someplace, will you? I'll keep the coffee and the pie. If you meant what you said about wanting to help me, you won't ask me anything else. I love you and I'm doing the best I can. We've been through a lot together, you and I. We can get through this. Trust me a little, okay?"

She stepped into the bathroom and closed the door and leaned against it, hoping with all her heart that when she came out again, she would be alone.

CHAPTER 7

Beloved and…illustrious father…

Loran lay in the dark, trying to remember where she had heard that particular phrase. It had come from another time, of course, another century, when loyalty and respect for one's male parent were required of a child, whether it was deserved or not. She was very sure that this Tommy Garth wasn't illustrious, and she had never had the chance to make him beloved.

It was incredible to her that he might be somewhere close by and that she might actually, at some point, see him.

What did he look like, this wayward father of hers? Like the men she'd seen at the small store where she'd stopped to buy gas this afternoon? Like Bobby Ray? Like Meyer?

It was certain that he wouldn't look like Kent.

Kent.

She still had that ordeal to face. She exhaled quietly in the darkness. The only good thing about her mother's startling revelation was that Kent's offense didn't seem nearly as daunting as it had initially. She couldn't be bothered with his peccadilloes at this point. She wouldn't call him again. He'd be too preoccupied with his business dinner at first to even notice, but then it would occur to him that she hadn't telephoned. He'd immediately blame it on some unforeseen technical or logistical circumstance beyond her control. Then he'd remember how resourceful she was and he'd realize that there must be another reason for her not having called. With a little effort, he might even figure out what that reason could be—and he'd start working on his big she-just-came-by-to-drop-something-off explanation.

Or maybe not.

He could just as easily feel relief that it was all finally out in the open. Maybe he'd been longing for his freedom and he was happy that it had suddenly fallen into his lap.

She closed her eyes and tried once again to sleep. Part of her wanted to think that all this craziness was some aspect of Maddie's illness. But most of her believed every word of it. It was the look in her mother's eyes, the kind of look she'd never seen there before.

She turned over in bed, trying to push the image out of her mind, trying to find some position that would make sleep possible.

Beloved…and illustrious…father…

She still couldn't remember the source. There had been at least one more adjective, but she couldn't remember what it was.

Mary…Celeste.

No.

Maria Celeste. That was it. Maria Celeste. The devoted daughter of the astronomer, Galileo.

Maria Celeste had written him the letters with the simpering salutations from a cloistered Italian nunnery. Loran didn't even remember why she had attended the feminist lecture where the young woman's life and her relationship to her father had been discussed. All she remembered was that Maria Celeste was no enigma to her. She had understood immediately how a father could take on an extremely dazzling persona in the eyes of a daughter who was kept locked away from him. It was especially true in her own case, where the daughter had never even seen her father.

But whatever notion Loran might have had about him, she had never imagined him coming from a place like this.

Never.

It had been a long time since she had bothered entertaining the idea of what he might be like, but when she had, he'd always been, if not prominent, then worthy of prominence. She imagined that his accomplishments would be such that he could actually choose whether or not he wanted to be in the limelight. She saw him educated and informed, kind, witty, handsome and honorable. Not so much like Robert Young on *Father Knows Best* as like Gregory Peck in *To Kill a Mockingbird*. What a standard for fathers Mr. Peck had set with that performance. She had immediately wanted a father like Atticus. Perhaps she still did.

Sometimes she imagined that her mystery father had money, especially in the early years when she and Maddie had had to struggle financially. But aside from that, it had never really mattered to her whether he was wealthy. Mostly, he had to not mind having a daughter.

Maria Celeste.

And now she remembered why the young woman's name and her circumstances had been filed away somewhere in the back of her mind. Maria Celeste had had a father who'd loved her, advised her, worried about her—and she had been born out of wedlock.

Loran abruptly sat up, then lay back down again. She was exhausted beyond sleep. Every time she closed her eyes she could feel the motion of the SUV, see the winding Parkway. It was too quiet here. There was no human activity inside the house or out. She longed for the sound of conversation, of D.C. traffic. Even a wall-rattling rendition of "Bill Bailey" would have been welcome. *Anything* to impede the thoughts scurrying around and around in her mind and the terrible sense that things were only going to get worse.

She turned over to face the window. The moon was shining. She could hear the wind whistling around the eaves. Maybe her mother had once lain sleepless in this house on the hill, listening to the wind.

And what was *he* doing tonight?

Loran closed her eyes, determined not to cry.

I don't need a father now!

The phone on the bedside table rang suddenly. She reached for it, fumbling in the dark.

"Hello?" she said tentatively.

"It's me. Meyer."

She closed her eyes tightly, but she felt a tear slide down her cheek anyway.

"Loran?"

"What?" she said, her voice husky.

"I…just wanted to see if you and Maddie were okay."

She could hear voices in the background, a woman's and a man's. The man's she thought she recognized—the

Bobby Ray person. She took a deep breath and tried to sound in control.

"Don't you ever sleep?" she asked.

"Not much, no. Are you all right?"

"I've…been better," she said because she suddenly didn't mind telling him this. "Maddie is sleeping. Is…that man there? The one who was in the parking lot with you."

"Yeah."

"He sounds upset."

"Yeah," Meyer said again. "I want to give you a phone number."

"Why?"

"In case you need anything. Find something to write on."

She hesitated, then fumbled to turn on the lamp and find the Lilac Hill pen and scratch pad. "What is it?"

He gave her the number. "This is my aunt Nelda's phone. She knows you…might need to call. You can leave a message with her and she'll get it to me."

"I don't think—"

"Just keep it, in case you need it. You don't have to use it if you don't want to. It's just a contingency plan."

"Contingency plan. Is that some kind of military thing?"

He laughed softly. "Yeah. It is. Go to sleep now."

"I will if my phone stops ringing."

"Maybe…I'll see you tomorrow."

He hung up and she lay there holding the receiver. She put it back and turned off the lamp.

Sleep finally came, without her realizing it, and when she opened her eyes again, it was to bright sunlight. She sat up and snatched her watch off the bedside table. It was after eleven. How could she have slept so long—she had given the stray-away a huge opportunity for a head start, and who knew what Maddie might have done with it?

She dressed quickly, in her scratchy new clothes, leaving torn-off tags wherever they fell. As an afterthought, she put Meyer's aunt's phone number into her purse.

When she stepped out into the hall, she saw the door to her mother's room standing ajar. A woman and a giggling girl were making the bed.

"I'm looking for my mother, Ms. Kimball," Loran said.

"She left out early, honey," the woman said.

"Did she say where she was going?"

"No, she didn't. We run into her in the hall, and she just said she'd get out of our way. I told her we don't never mind working around people, but she said she had to go out for a while."

"A while."

"That's what she said. 'A while.'"

Great, Loran thought.

When she reached the bottom of the stairs, Mrs. Jenkins called to her.

"I was just about to bring this up," she said, handing Loran a small envelope. She stared at her name scrawled on the front. It wasn't her mother's handwriting.

She hastily opened it and took out a small sheet of lined paper.

Maddie is with me, it said tersely—in pencil. *Don't worry. Meyer.*

"Easy for you to say," Loran said under her breath.

"Pardon?" Mrs. Jenkins said.

"Nothing," Loran said. She stood there, trying to decide who to be angry with, and what to do.

"Your mother thought you needed to sleep after your long drive yesterday," Mrs. Jenkins said. "You must be hungry. Breakfast is over, but I've made you a tray. I'll bring it up to the Rose Room, or you might like to have it down here in front of the fire. It's chilly this morning. I think it feels like snow, but Meyer says no. Something about a 'mackerel' sky and no 'mare's tails' or something. I'm not sure what that means, but he's right as often as the meteorologists on television are."

"I think I'll just go into town," Loran said. "Thanks anyway."

"Well, actually, your mother and Meyer took your SUV."

Loran looked at her, but she didn't say anything. She was too busy fighting the impulse to race to the window to look for herself. Instead, she quietly opened her purse to verify that the keys to the SUV were indeed gone. Maddie must have pilfered them while she'd been asleep, and unless Loran could hot-wire her mother's car, she was stuck here. Whatever Maddie had planned today, she'd meant it when she'd said that Loran wasn't invited.

Obviously, today wasn't going to be any better than yesterday had been.

"Would you like the tray?" Mrs. Jenkins asked.

"No," Loran said. Then added, "Yes." It had been a long time since she'd eaten and she really was hungry.

"Down here by the fire? No one will bother you," Mrs. Jenkins said, apparently alluding to the "Bill Bailey" crowd.

"That would be nice," Loran said, because she wanted to be able to watch for Maddie's return.

"Just have a seat, then, and I'll get it," Mrs. Jenkins said. "Would you like coffee or tea?"

"Tea," Loran said absently. "Do you—?"

"Yes?" Mrs. Jenkins prompted when Loran didn't go on.

"Nothing," Loran said. "Never mind."

She wandered over to the small table in front of the fireplace and sat where she could see the door, dividing her attention between it and the crackling fire. She had actually been going to ask Mrs. Jenkins if she knew Tommy Garth, but she lost her nerve.

So, she thought. Meyer apparently hadn't taken Maddie off this time—she had taken him.

She looked around the room. If this had once been Maddie's house, or even if she'd only *thought* this had been her house, the experience had to be, at the very least, unsettling.

Mrs. Jenkins came with the tray—a basketful of warm muffins and scones, a plate of fresh fruit, orange juice, a pot of hot tea, and a choice of cream cheese, lemon curd, orange marmalade or butter for the muffins and scones.

Loran ate listlessly at first, then realized how good it all was. She even managed to be gracious and tell Mrs. Jenkins so when she wandered through to assess the degree of Loran's enjoyment.

Clearly satisfied, Mrs. Jenkins disappeared upstairs. Almost immediately Loran could hear someone singing in what she assumed must be the kitchen area. The melody was familiar, but not the words. It was a song about trying to entice "the wagoner's lad" into staying when he wanted to go, and what the singer lacked in polish she made up for in earnest emotion, especially on the last line.

"…I am just a poor girl and my true love is gone."

Loran abruptly got up and put on her coat, leaving the meal she'd actually been enjoying and going outside. She kept expecting Mrs. Jenkins to call her back for an interrogation every step of the way.

But Mrs. Jenkins was apparently occupied elsewhere, which Loran was beginning to prefer. She stood on the porch looking around the grounds for a moment, then began walking up the path toward the gazebo, and then beyond. She had no idea where the path led. She didn't really care. She just wanted to do something, anything, to keep herself occupied until Maddie came wandering back—hopefully not with more stellar news.

The air felt much colder and damper than yesterday, but the wind had died. She looked up at the sky, wondering if the bumpy arrangement of clouds that actually did remind her a little of fish scales was Meyer's mackerel sky.

The path lost its manicured look and wound deeper into the woods. She didn't find it the least bit inviting, but she kept walking. She could smell the dead leaves and rotting tree limbs as she carefully made her way, and then the sharp, pungent odor of newly cut wood somewhere nearby. Meyer must have been cutting it for the Lilac Hill fireplace—Meyer, who was suddenly taking up far too much space in the middle of her life and her mother's. She still couldn't believe he had called last night. No. What she couldn't believe is how much it meant to her that he had.

Eventually, the path ended in a wider track that meandered off to her left and seemed to go up the mountainside. She walked down it, dodging the saplings that grew in the old ruts, stepping over what remained of mud puddles from time to time. The sun didn't reach this part of the old narrow road, and the way seemed gloomier and gloomier. A startled bird flew up from the underbrush at her approach. She didn't like it here; it made her feel even more forlorn than she already did, and, after a short distance, she turned around and headed back toward Lilac Hill.

When she reached the gazebo, she saw the SUV in the parking area, and Meyer walking up the gravel path toward her.

She breathed a quiet sigh of relief and stood and waited.

Halfway up the slope, the young couple she'd seen carrying out the trash yesterday intercepted him, both of them talking at once. Meyer stopped and tried to listen, then shook the boy's hand. After a bit more conversation, he waved goodbye and started up the slope again, until the girl suddenly burst into tears. The boy tried to put his arm around her, but she jerked free and moved several steps away from him. Meyer went back and said something to her, bending down to make her hear him, because she'd covered her face with both hands. After a moment, she took her hands away. Meyer kept talking. Then she and the boy walked away arm in arm, her head on his shoulder. Loran watched as they disappeared into the house.

Meyer took his time coming the rest of the way up the path, and when he reached the place where Loran stood, he was clearly in no hurry to initiate the conversation. He stopped in front of her and he looked as unsettled as she felt.

"What's wrong with them?" she asked. "Lover's quarrel?"

"Not…really. His army reserve unit's been called up. He's on his way to the Middle East."

"The army reserve takes little boys?"

"He's nineteen. That's old enough, believe me."

"He doesn't look old enough to drive."

She had been avoiding looking into Meyer's eyes, and when she finally did, he didn't look away. She felt the sudden urge to cover her face and bawl the way the young soldier's girl had just done.

"I'm going to go talk to my mother," she said abruptly.

"She's not here," he said as she stepped around him.

"What do you mean, she's not here? Where is she?"

"She's over at my place," he said. "I showed you where it was yesterday."

"I remember," Loran interrupted. "What is she doing there?"

"She's decided to rent it."

"Oh. Well. She didn't waste any time, did she? Let me guess. She rented it, and then she stuck you with bringing the happy news to Lilac Hill."

He looked up at the sky. She could see a jagged scar on his neck. "Actually, she bribed me with the chance to drive your vehicle some more."

"Wonderful," she said, meaning anything but that. "That can't be all. What's the rest of it?"

"She wants you to pack up the stuff in her room and bring it to her."

"Oh, she does. Did she say what she'll do if I don't?"

"No. But I don't think it'll slow her down for long."

Loran looked into his eyes again. He did have a certain sadness about him. It was all she could do not to ask him point-blank whether Maddie had gone to see the man who was supposed to be her father.

"Are you going to tell me where she went this morning, or are you sworn to secrecy?" she asked, rephrasing the question at the last moment.

"You know, I asked her about that. She said no."

"No what?"

"No secrecy."

"Then where did she go?"

"She went to see a doctor."

"Oh, God—" Loran said because that was the last thing she'd expected.

"No, she's not feeling bad or anything. She wanted to contact a doctor here in case she needed one and so you wouldn't worry. So she went and made arrangements for the one in town to get in touch with the doctor she sees in Arlington."

"And?" Loran said because she was certain there had to be more.

"That's pretty much it."

"I *hate* this," she said, feeling close to tears again. "I hate that *you* know more about what's going on than I do. You do, don't you?"

"Probably."

"Are you going to tell me?"

"No."

"Then what was the telephone number for? I thought you wanted to help."

"What I want to do is stay out of the way and not make things worse. Even if it doesn't look like it, I'm trying not to meddle."

She gave a heavy sigh and looked off toward the mountains.

"Sometimes..." he said.

"Sometimes what?" she asked when he didn't continue.

"Nothing. Forget it."

"Sometimes what!"

"Sometimes you just have to get with the program."

"I don't know what that means."

"It means I think you're fighting a losing battle here."

"You don't understand how sick she is."

"Maybe not. But I think *she* does."

Yes, Loran thought. And that was at the heart of all this craziness.

"So why don't you go get your mama's clothes and take them to her? Tell her I'll bring her car the first chance I get."

"Why don't you mind your own business!"

"I told you. I'm trying to. The thing is, Maddie's a pretty determined kind of woman—just like you are. I expect the two of you will be butting heads from here on out if you're not careful. But the way I see it, you don't have much say in all this. I'll tell you the same thing I just told Mary Ann about Clay. You can make it hard for somebody to do what they have to do or you can make it easy, and if you care about them, you suck it up." He reached into his coat pocket. "Your keys—nice set of wheels."

She took the keys, eventually. His logic was infallible, and she hated that, too.

"How do I get up there?" she asked, looking off toward the place he'd pointed out to her yesterday.

"Just turn right, go down the highway a little ways. You'll see a mailbox with Conley on it. Don't turn where that is. That road goes to my aunt Nelda's. Go on down a little further to another dirt road. Turn there. The SUV will make it up to the cabin all right, but be careful. You don't want to go rolling into a holler."

"What, you think I can't drive?"

"I think you're not used to driving up narrow dirt paths in the mountains," he said with his maddening reasonableness. "It's not like big-city traffic, but it's just as dangerous. The shoulders are soft and it wouldn't take much to turn over that big SUV of yours."

She gave a quiet sigh. She couldn't quite make herself thank him for his concern. Gratitude wasn't at all what she was feeling.

"I'm sorry," she said instead because that was closer to the truth.

"For what?"

"For your…inconvenience. None of this is your problem, even if you do work for Mrs. Jenkins. I just—"

She didn't go on. She turned and walked toward the house, then abruptly stopped.

"Meyer," she said. "Did my mother used to live here at Lilac Hill?"

"I think it was before my time," he said. "People around here still call it the Kimball place."

The Kimball place, Loran thought as she walked away. If that was true, then the rest of it could be true as well. Her father could actually be here.

CHAPTER 8

Meyer watched Loran walk away, hoping she'd look back one more time. He didn't know as much about her situation as she suspected he did. He was still trying to work it all out. His best guess was that she was the reason Maddie wanted to see Tommy Garth. On the other hand, it might not have anything to do with her at all. Either way, he could see Maddie wanting to keep her daughter out of it. The only thing he was reasonably sure about was that Tommy Garth didn't seem like the kind of man who would abandon a child of his—not after the fight he had put up to get his boy buried here. If Loran Kimball was his living daughter, Meyer thought he would have wanted to claim her.

That is, if he knew about her.

Meyer exhaled sharply.

Maybe Tommy Garth was out of the loop, too. It was looking like whatever details came to light were strictly on a cornered and no-way-out basis. Nelda wasn't talking, and Bobby Ray was no help whatsoever. He was scared of the "haints" up on Lady Ridge, and he was scared of Estelle Garth, and he was scared of Tommy, too, while he was at it. What with all the *other* things he was afraid of, he didn't have enough room left in his brain to concentrate on answering questions.

Bobby Ray's biggest fear at the moment seemed to be giving Tommy Garth the news that Maddie Kimball wanted to see him. The pile of distressed people was definitely growing. As far as Meyer knew, Tommy was up on his mountain ridge oblivious to all of it—and that was about to change.

Meyer hunted in his jacket pocket for the cheap digital watch he used to keep himself on the Lilac Hill schedule. It was possible that he would soon have more information to work with than he did now. It was probable that he would be a whole lot better off if he just stayed ignorant.

He found the watch, but he didn't look at it. He stood watching Loran as she went inside the house. He did feel sorry for her. Maddie was asking a lot of her—especially if she wouldn't tell her what was going on. If he had any sense, he really would mind his own damn business. He would walk away from the whole mess and tend to his own worries. He could do that easily enough—if she didn't have that leave-me-alone-no-help-me way of looking at him. He had always been far too interested in trying to fix things that weren't fixable, and he should be over that by now.

He glanced at the watch.

Okay, Bobby Ray.

He started walking toward the woods. He was going up on Lady Ridge. He didn't have much choice if he ever wanted a minute's peace again, and it didn't hurt Bobby Ray's powers of persuasion that Meyer was already as involved as he was.

He had never been on the ridge—nobody went tramping around on Estelle's land—but, from what he'd always heard, it was an odd place up there, some kind of natural meadow on the mountaintop that had been settled and abandoned a long time ago. No one knew why the people who had started the homestead had left. The Garths had claimed the land as long as anyone could remember, and these people must have been part of the family. At any rate, *someone* had lived on the ridge long enough to build a cabin and, according to Bobby Ray, they hadn't taken their household belongings with them when they'd abandoned it. They had left their iron pots and skillets, the fireplace hooks and andirons, and the ploughs to rust. *Necessary* things were completely disregarded. And the ground around the place was supposedly littered with broken dishes. The cabin had fallen to ruin—but nothing much grew there or, it was believed, ever would. So the valley inhabitants created their own myths about it, and the real or imagined woman of the cabin evolved into a handy scare tactic to use on little children when they got to running wild.

The lady'll come and get you if you don't mind!

It wasn't much of a leap for them to believe that she wouldn't like people who didn't know how to behave. She had left all those pretty dishes behind and maybe it was rambunctious children who had broken them.

He didn't know where Tommy Garth's cabin was exactly. As far as he knew, no one had been up there but Bobby Ray and Tommy's daddy. When he was a boy, Meyer and his braver friends had always *said* they wanted to go up on Lady Ridge—and would one of these days—but they never had. He, for one, had never had the free time to make the trek. Nelda had believed that idle hands were the devil's Gatlinburg amusement park, especially when it came to boys, and she wasn't about to let the devil get a hold of Meyer Conley if she could help it. He really didn't have the time now. All he had was a certain curiosity and a grudge because Estelle Garth used to pick on him all the time.

And a more than passing interest in Loran Kimball. She was every bit as scared by recent events as Bobby Ray was, no matter how hard she tried not to show it. He could recognize the look easily enough, thanks to the United States Army. Maddie was afraid as well.

It had been a long time since he'd been this involved in anything. Ever since he'd given up his military career and come back home, he'd been functioning in the same kind of oblivious way Bobby Ray did, taking comfort solely from mindless routine. His social life was nonexistent. He didn't even go and play bluegrass with the old men at the café or at Poppy's store anymore. Their prying questions had driven him off.

"You ain't having nightmares, are you, Meyer?"

"You didn't go looking them dead ones in the face, did you, Meyer? You ain't never going to get shed of them bad dreams if you did."

He gave a sharp sigh and looked over his shoulder. He hadn't cleared his upcoming segment of personal time with Mrs. Jenkins, but so far so good. She wasn't yelling out the back door for him.

He went deeper into the woods, down the winding path, trying to ignore the cold. After a while he could see the old logging road, and Bobby Ray's truck was parked and waiting.

He didn't say anything when he got into the truck,

regardless of the host of questions that needed to be asked.

"This old truck'll make it," Bobby Ray said, as if Meyer had voiced one of them. "I know the way…just about."

"Yeah, and it's the 'just about' that's worrying me."

"We ain't lost yet, Meyer," Bobby Ray said optimistically.

"You haven't started the truck yet, either, Bobby Ray. Let's go, damn it, if we're going. I've got things to do."

"I ain't got nobody else to ask, Meyer," Bobby Ray said, coaxing the truck engine into turning over. "Just like Maddie didn't have nobody but me. I only got you."

"Drive, will you?" Meyer said.

"I seen Estelle at Poppy's," Bobby Ray offered as they bumped along. "She was a-looking for me, Meyer. Reckon what she wanted?"

"Didn't she tell you?"

"Naw, I hid, Meyer. Took off out the back door and went down by the river till she was gone. I ain't wanting to talk to that woman anymore than I have to. I ain't wanting her to lock *me* up. Nor you, neither."

Meyer looked at him. "Just drive, okay? Don't talk. Watch what you're doing. Drive."

"Okay," Bobby Ray said as the truck hit another hole.

Meyer tried to find something to hold onto.

"Whup!" Bobby Ray said, slamming on the brakes.

Meyer came close to banging his head on the windshield. "Damn it, Bobby Ray!"

"I was about to miss the fork, Meyer. See yonder? It's about all growed in. I like to have missed it."

"You liked to have cracked open my head."

"Maybe you better hold on harder than you was, Meyer. I might have to do it again."

The truck wobbled and bounced in and out of the old wagon and sled ruts. From time to time, the ruts disappeared, only to reappear again farther ahead. About the only good thing Meyer could say about the road was that no flatlander had bought up the land it crossed and closed it off. Somebody still used it enough to keep it from getting completely overgrown.

Bobby Ray seemed to know where he was going, turning down fork after fork without the drama of the first one. They had gone downhill for a time, but now they were heading upward again.

"How much farther, Bobby Ray?"

"Truck can't go much farther—then you got to walk."

"What are you going to be doing while I'm walking?"

"I'm going to wait till you get back," he said reasonably.

"You better wait."

"I will. 'Lessen I see a haint or something."

The terrain flattened for a short distance; the road disappeared again, and this time for good. Bobby Ray turned off the engine and let the truck roll to a stop. He opened his door and got out, motioning for Meyer to come, too. Then he stood staring into the deep underbrush to his left.

"I wish them apples was ripe," he said.

"What apples?" Meyer asked, looking in the same direction.

"The ones so's you can find Tommy's place. Now what you got to do, Meyer, is walk yonder way until you run

into a big old flat rock. You just stand on that and holler for Tommy and he'll come and get you."

"If he's up there. And if he don't shoot me first,"
Meyer said. "Are you sure that's the way?"

"Yeah, I'm sure. Just about," he added.

Meyer shook his head, resigned. He put his hand into
his pocket. "You stay right here with the truck. Don't you
make me have to look for you."

"Okay, Meyer. I'm staying right here. If there ain't no
haints."

"I don't care if you see the whole of Hell's Jubilee Chorus. You stay here, you hear me?"

He pulled a military compass out of his pocket to get
his bearings. "How long is it going to take me to get to
the flat rock?"

"Not long—if you walk hard."

"How big is the rock?" Meyer asked, fighting the urge
to show his aggravation about the lack of detail, expected though it might be.

Bobby Ray looked at him blankly.

"Big as the table Nelda uses when she's making a
batch of pies?" Meyer asked.

"Bigger than that."

"Big as the truck bed?"

Bobby Ray looked at it, considering. "I reckon so.
Only it's flat."

"What about a path?"

"Ain't none."

There was no point in dragging this out. Meyer began
walking in the direction Bobby Ray had indicated. And,
damn, it was cold! Bobby Ray was right about one thing.
There was no path now—if there ever had been—and

Meyer had to fight his way through the laurel and the fallen trees. After a few yards, the terrain went nearly straight up. There were large outcroppings of rock, none of them flat.

He struggled along and eventually stopped long enough to check his compass again. He was surprised that he hadn't strayed all that much from his initial direction. His old sergeant would be proud.

He continued the climb, growing more and more out of breath as he went. His legs were beginning to shake from the strain of trying to keep his footing and he grabbed onto a nearby tree so that he could relax the muscles for a moment. The cold air cut deep every time he took a breath and came back out in little white puffs. He couldn't hear anything beyond what he expected to hear.

He pushed on. When he was all but ready to give up, he saw the rock. It was indeed as flat as a tabletop, and huge, sticking out like a giant spearhead impaled in the side of the mountain.

He crawled up on it and he had to rest a minute before he tried to summon the lion from his den. When he had enough wind, he whistled loudly, the earsplitting kind he'd learned as a boy. The piercing noise sent something scurrying in the underbrush, but there was no answering call. He whistled again, and again, then cupped his hands around his mouth and gave a yell, the kind that mountain neighbors once used to check on each other every morning, long before there were ever telephones.

He waited for a time, then tried again, wondering if Bobby Ray could hear him and hoping he would know that it was him and not one of the ghosts he was so worried about.

Meyer had left the army—but the army hadn't left him. He realized that when every nerve in his body suddenly told him that he wasn't alone. He couldn't see anyone, couldn't hear anything out of the ordinary, but he still knew.

He stood waiting because that was all he could do.

"What do you want?" someone said off to his right.

He looked in that direction as a tall bearded man stepped out from behind a tree.

"I'm looking for Tommy Garth," Meyer said.

"Who are you?" the man asked.

"Meyer Conley."

"Kin to Nelda Conley?"

"She's my great-aunt."

"How is old Nelda?"

"About like always. Got some aches and pains, but she's still doing all her own work," Meyer said, as if they'd run into each other in Poppy's store grocery shopping and one of them didn't have a hunting rifle in the fold of his arm, resting but ready.

"She still preaching at the church?"

"Sometimes."

"Estelle send you?" the man he took to be Tommy Garth asked, apparently getting to what he really wanted to know.

"No. Bobby Ray Isley."

The man gave a short laugh of disbelief.

"What the hell does Bobby Ray want?"

"He wants me to tell you Maddie Kimball is back and she wants to come see you."

Meyer saw no reason to beat around the bush about it. The man looked away.

"Well, she's about forty damn years too late," Meyer thought he said.

The man stood for a long time, his mind clearly someplace else.

"Don't you bring her up here," he said finally.

They stared at each other across the rough terrain between them, until Tommy suddenly turned to go.

"She's a stubborn woman, but I don't think she could make the trip even if you wanted her to," Meyer said, just loudly enough so that Tommy Garth could hear him.

"Then I reckon we're having this conversation for nothing, ain't we, boy?"

"You...want me to tell her anything?"

"No, I want you to get your ass back down the mountain where you belong."

"Be glad to," Meyer said, walking to the edge of the boulder in preparation for getting down. "I reckon I ought to tell you I don't think you have a lot of time to decide what you want to do about her."

"I don't want to *do* anything. She can go back to wherever the hell she come from. And you can tell her that."

"No, I think I'll pass on that one. I've done my good deed for the day." He climbed down from the rock and began to make his way back the way he had come. He could feel Tommy Garth's eyes on him—he was sure it was Tommy Garth, now—as he went.

"Hey!" Tommy yelled when Meyer hadn't gone far.

Meyer stopped and looked around.

"Estelle know she's here?"

"Yeah."

"Did she—?" Tommy broke off. Even from as far away as he was, Meyer could see the struggle the man was having to maintain his former oblivious state.

"Maddie say why she wanted to come up here?" he suddenly asked—as if he didn't want to, but the question had gotten away from him somehow.

"No. I guess she didn't think you'd come to her."

Tommy gave him an odd look, then frowned. "She's...not..." He didn't finish the question, and Meyer didn't attempt to prod him into it. His task had been to deliver the message. Period.

Tommy Garth suddenly made up his mind. Apparently, he had ventured out on this limb from the past as far as he intended to go. He turned and disappeared into the trees, leaving Meyer standing.

Well, that's that.

He waited a moment, then began his slow descent, tree to tree, to keep from falling headfirst and rolling the rest of the way.

Bobby Ray was waiting where Meyer had left him, sitting in the truck he'd turned around for the return trip. He couldn't resist banging on the side of the truck to make him jump.

Bobby Ray was still grinning when Meyer got inside.

"You see Tommy? You tell him about Maddie?"

"I saw him. I told him. But I don't think he much cared."

"He cared, Meyer. I know that."

"Well, I'm done here, either way. You and Maddie wanted him told, and I told him. She'd never make the trip up there anyway. It was all I could do to make it."

Bobby Ray started the truck. "She could if she went the other way."

Meyer looked at him. "What other way?"

"By the fork that goes up yonder to the cabin."

"There's a fork that goes to Tommy Garth's cabin?"

"Yeah," Bobby Ray said. "Right up there to it."

"Then why the hell did you make me go climbing through all that brush and stand on a damn rock!"

"That fork, you got to go right by Estelle's house to get there, Meyer. We ain't wanting to do that. We ain't wanting Estelle to see us. She'd make me tell her what we was a-doing, and that wouldn't be good. No, sir."

"Damn it, Bobby Ray," Meyer said. "As soon as I rest up, I'm going to jerk your arm off and beat you with it."

"Aw, you ain't, neither," Bobby Ray said, grinning again.

"You watch me. And don't go getting us lost on the way back. I mean it."

At one point, they cleared the trees and Meyer could see a long way off—to the far hillside where his own cabin was. He wondered what Maddie was doing, and whether or not Loran had packed up her clothes and taken them to her.

Bobby Ray hummed to himself, happy at last. Mission accomplished. And Meyer had gotten to see a little something of Lady Ridge with his own eyes.

He took a quiet breath, wishing that some of Bobby Ray's merry mood was catching. He'd tell Maddie he'd seen Tommy Garth—but he wouldn't tell her the word-for-word truth about it.

CHAPTER 9

"I told you a long time ago—when you asked about your father. I told you he couldn't be a part of our lives. That was the truth."

"Your truth."

"Yes. My truth. For the most part."

"For the most part? You see? There's always something you don't say!"

"What I didn't say is that he didn't *want* to be a part of it. And I didn't say it because it would hurt you."

"Last night you told me he didn't even know about me."

Maddie sat down on one of the straight chairs. She'd seemed steady enough on her feet but she held on to the edge of the table as if she thought she might fall. "You're not a child," she said, but it was more to herself than to Loran.

"I feel like a child. Betrayal always hurts, Mother."

Maddie looked at her in surprise. "Betrayal," she repeated. "If that's what it was, I can't apologize for it. Believe me, the betrayal wasn't mine. I did the best I could."

"So when are you going to see him?"

Her mother started to get up from the chair, then didn't. "I don't know."

"Why not? Won't he talk to you?"

"I'm not sure where he is. Exactly."

Loran suddenly remembered Maddie chasing Bobby Ray Isley down the stairs, and the light dawned. "People here stick together, don't they?"

"Sometimes."

"Well, I don't think I want to wait around here on the off chance my long-lost father wants to meet me."

"I don't want you to. You have to work and I don't know how long this will take. I want you to go home. I mean it. I didn't plan any of this," Maddie said, as if suddenly needing to defend herself. "It's just that I...saw the house."

"Yes. The house. If someone had burned it to the ground instead of turning it into a B and B, we'd both be better off," Loran said, but Maddie wasn't listening to her. She was clearly in some other place, a place where Loran couldn't go even if she'd wanted to.

"I want you to leave today," Maddie said. "I mean it."

"All right then. I don't want to fight about this anymore."

"Have you got a road map?" Maddie asked. "Maybe there's a quicker way back than the way we came."

"I don't need a map. I've got the navigation system."

"Ah," Maddie said. "Yes. The navigation system. I forgot."

If she had, it was the only thing that had slipped her mind, Loran thought. Maddie had already addressed every objection Loran could possibly make. Food, shelter, transportation, clothing, medical care—even a certain companionship. She'd even bought a charger for her cell phone, so she could recharge it in the cabin. She'd taken care of all of it.

Loran stood for a moment, looking around. It was a nice enough place. More rustic than shabby. Before the argument with Maddie, she had gone to the bookshelf and taken note of some of the titles. *John Burroughs: Naturalist. A River View and Other Hudson Valley Essays. Hudson River Memories.* Did Meyer actually read those? she wondered.

She opened the door and went out onto the porch. A rocking chair made out of bent tree limbs with the bark still on them moved slightly in the wind.

Maddie came to stand behind her.

"Are you going to call me if you need anything?" Loran asked, trying to keep her voice from quivering. "Or are you just going to disappear into this place and never be heard from again?"

"I don't plan on disappearing. And I will call— whether I need anything or not. If the cell-phone reception is bad, I'll find a pay phone. I've got a car."

And a terminal illness, Loran thought but didn't say. She looked toward the long winding road that led down to the highway.

"As soon as I see Tommy, I'll be home and we can talk. I love you very much, you know."

Loran did know, but she couldn't bring herself to say so. She stood for a moment, then stuffed her anxiety and aggravation far enough down to be able to offer Maddie a parting hug. They stood for a moment with their arms around each other. Her mother felt so frail and her skin seemed hot.

"Have a good trip," Maddie said, stepping back from the embrace.

Loran turned and ran down the steps before she cried,

or worse. She got into the SUV, but she had to sit for a moment before she started it.

I hate this!

Maddie remained on the porch, as if she didn't think Loran would actually leave if she didn't.

Loran abruptly started the SUV and drove down the sharply curving drive and eventually onto the highway— without registering any of it.

The sudden appearance of Lilac Hill as she rounded a curve took her by surprise. She turned into the B and B driveway slowly. Her mother's car was still there, but not Meyer's truck.

She parked and went inside. Mrs. Jenkins looked up when she walked to the desk, tense and ready to "help"— only not quite hiding the look that said she dearly hoped she didn't have to.

"I'd like to leave Meyer a note," Loran said without prelude. "Do you have something I can write on?"

"Oh, yes," the woman said. "Or I can tell him for you."

"No, thanks," Loran said.

She waited while the woman reached under the desk and brought out a sheet of paper with the Lilac Hill logo on it.

"Do you have an envelope?" Loran asked, and Mrs. Jenkins produced one and a pen, as well.

She took all three to the nearest table, in case Mrs. Jenkins was adept at reading upside down, then wrote the note and put it into the envelope, sealing it and scribbling Meyer's name on the front.

"Would you see that he gets this, please? As soon as possible?"

"Yes, all right," Mrs. Jenkins said, taking the envelope. "I don't think he'll be here until tomorrow, though."

Loran stood for a moment, looking around the interior of the waiting area.

Maddie had lived here. The Kimball place.

"Mrs. Jenkins," Loran said abruptly. "I need the envelope back."

Mrs. Jenkins handed it to her without comment, and Loran took it and went upstairs. She wasn't worried about causing Meyer any problems with his employer. Mrs. Jenkins was lucky to have him.

There was no one around that she could see, but she could hear muffled voices farther down the hall. She went to her room and quietly closed the door, standing for a moment before she made up her mind. She had told Maddie she wasn't waiting around for an audience with Tommy Garth. She had planned to check out now and be on her way.

But she wasn't going to do either.

She stuffed the envelope into her purse and went back downstairs again, leaving Mrs. Jenkins to stare quizzically after her as she left the house.

She got into the SUV and drove out onto the highway, heading in the direction that would eventually lead to the Parkway. She began to slow down as she neared the little store where she'd bought gas when she'd first arrived. She parked at the gas pump and waited for someone inside to flip the switch. It was cold standing in the open, and she kept switching hands as she pumped the gas so she could flex her fingers. From time to time she scanned the mountain ridges that rimmed the valley, wondering what Maddie felt when she looked at them. Nostalgia? Sadness? Longing for a lost love?

There were a number of vehicles parked this way and that in the dirt parking lot and one or two along the road.

Good, she thought.

In spite of the number of cars and trucks, she didn't see anyone when she first went inside to pay. After a moment, she realized that they had all congregated around a stove at the back. There was a group of six or eight men, solving the world's problems from the seats of dilapidated wooden straight chairs. She came and stood at the edge of the group, behind the man who was expounding on the "mess" in Washington. After a moment, he realized that he'd lost his audience and that they were all looking at something behind him. He turned to see.

"Afternoon, gentlemen," Loran said, smiling the smile that most men found pleasing.

These seemed to be no exception.

"I need to pay for my gas and I need some directions," she said, looking around at them.

The man she'd been standing behind stood up. "Yes, ma'am," he said, taking the money she held out to him. She recognized him as the storekeeper she'd seen before.

"Where are you wanting to go?"

"Tommy Garth's place," she said, still smiling. And the gorilla she'd dropped into the middle of their political discussion was apparently of considerable poundage.

She pretended she didn't notice, taking a ballpoint pen and the envelope she'd meant for Meyer out of her purse and waiting expectantly.

"Well, now," the storekeeper said. "Well, now—" He frowned and looked at the others, who looked elsewhere.

"Are you sure you got the name right?" one of the others asked.

"I'm sure," Loran said.

"Maybe somebody from Asheville is looking for him," another one said, as if she weren't standing right there. "I heard tell he shows them college teachers how to make things the old way sometimes. You know, wagon wheels and the like."

"Naw, it ain't no college teachers. It's them movie people, I reckon. Louise said she seen his name at the end of a picture show not too long ago where they say who did what to make it. 'Tommy Garth.'"

"Might not a-been him."

"Now how many Tommy Garths have you ever heard of?"

"Excuse me!" Loran interrupted. "Could I get directions?"

"You planning on going in the car you're driving?" the storekeeper asked.

"Yes," she said.

"It won't make it up there. You got to have four-wheel drive."

"It's got four-wheel drive," she said, which sparked another, entirely different discussion.

"I need to see him," she said in the middle of it. "As soon as possible. It's important!"

They all looked at her.

"It's important," she said again.

"Ain't no landmarks to speak of. You ever drive on a

road you had to make up as you went along?" the store-keeper asked.

"Yes," she said, thinking of the narrow lane up to Meyer's cabin. She had told a lie, but not much of one.

"You might get lost."

"I know. That's why I'm asking you for directions."

"Tommy in trouble?" somebody asked.

"Not that I know of," Loran said, looking at the man in bib overalls who had posed the question. "Is anybody going to help me or not?"

They all looked at the storekeeper.

"Honey, you ain't wanting to go up there by yourself. Even if you could find it, Tommy, he don't take much to strangers. Ain't no telling what he'd do if somebody he don't know just walked up on him."

"I'm going one way or the other. If I have to get the law involved, I will." If that threat made any impact, she couldn't tell.

"She'd have to go by Estelle's," one of them said.

"Estelle don't own the damn road."

"Them logging roads back there she does, if it goes over her land."

"It might not go over *her* land. It might be through what Tommy's daddy give to him."

"That don't matter. Estelle's going to think it's hers. She thinks she owns the damn church and graveyard, don't she?"

One of the other men got up from his chair and edged around Loran as if he thought she might tackle him to the floor if he tried to make a break for it. "I got to be going. My old woman's looking for me by now. Makes her mad as fire if I'm gone too long."

"More like it makes her mad as fire if you come back," someone said, and they all laughed.

"Yeah, I reckon I ought to be going, too," another one said.

Yet another one stood up to go, nodding his goodbye and offering no explanations for his departure.

"Where does Estelle live?" Loran asked the ones remaining. "I'll ask her. If she owns the road, she must know which way—"

"Naw, honey, you ain't wanting to go bothering that one."

"Look," Loran said. "I told you. It's important. I need to talk to him."

The storekeeper shook his head and walked off toward the cash register. One of the remaining men opened a fiddle-shaped case sitting on the floor beside him and took the fiddle out. He began to tune it, his eyes closed. Loran had never felt so utterly dismissed in her life. She abruptly turned and followed the storekeeper.

"You're really not going to help me," she said as he counted out her change.

"I reckon not," the man said.

"Then thanks for nothing."

He looked at her, then walked to the back of the store. After a moment, the fiddler started to play, something mournful and lost-sounding.

Loran went outside. She could still hear the fiddler.

She got into the SUV and started it, but when she reached the edge of the highway, she abruptly stopped. She put her head down on the steering wheel, trying not to cry. She had given up too easily, and she had to get herself together if she was going to go back inside and try again.

Someone rapped sharply on the window and she jumped. Meyer stood peering at her through the glass. He made a cranking motion with one hand.

She took a deep breath, then hit the button to lower the window. "If you offer me a piece of candy, I'll punch you right in the nose," she said. "MP or no MP."

"No candy," he said.

"What do you want?"

"I want to see if you're all right."

"I'm just fine."

"You don't look fine."

He glanced over his shoulder. All the old men left in the store were gathered at the window watching.

"What happened?" he asked, looking back at her.

"They won't help me," she said. And she sounded every bit as miserable as she felt.

"Help you what?"

"I'm looking for...someone," she said.

"Who?"

"Tommy Garth. I want to see him. Maddie won't leave here because of him and I'm going to hurry things along. And I'm not giving up!" she said, leaning forward so she could see the old men, hoping they could read lips.

"Wait a minute," Meyer said. He walked toward an old truck parked at the side of the store. There was a man in it she couldn't quite see, one who kept shaking his head "no" to whatever Meyer asked. Meyer kept talking and the man finally stopped shaking his head. After a little more one-sided discussion, Meyer came walking back.

"I'll take you," he said.

She stared at him.

"Changed your mind?" he asked.

"No. Get in."

He looked at her doubtfully.

"It's supposed to go off road," she said. "I think this trip qualifies."

He came around and got in. "It might go off road, but it's not going to look as good as it does now."

"Yeah, well. Had to happen sooner or later. Who is Estelle?" she asked, and he looked so startled, she thought he must have completely misunderstood what she said.

"They said the road to Tommy Garth's goes by Estelle's. I got the impression she wouldn't be happy if I drove on it. Who is she?"

He was frowning instead of answering.

"Say something so I'll know you're conscious," she said.

"I'm just the guide here," he said finally. "That's all."

"You're not going to tell me anything."

"Nope."

"Is that because you don't know anything or because you think I don't know enough?"

"Yes," he said pointedly.

"Maddie said Tommy Garth is my father. Is that enough?" she said quietly, relieved to finally say it to somebody—to him. He didn't look surprised.

"Let's go," he said. "Before Poppy starts selling tickets. Turn that way."

She hesitated, then turned in the direction he indicated.

"Which one is Poppy?"

"He owns the place."

"Are they going to be mad at you for taking me to see…him?"

"Did you offer them money?" he asked instead of answering.

"No."

"Good."

"I threatened them with the law," she said, and the startled look was back. She couldn't help but smile. A little.

"So are they going to be mad at you or not?"

"Not," he said.

"Are you sure?"

"I'm sure. I've just relieved them of any responsibility for whatever happens. Now they can just sit back and enjoy the show. If we can get by Estelle without her seeing us, the only person who'll be mad is Tommy. I've already seen him once today."

"You what?"

"Bobby Ray Isley and I went up to see him. I told him Maddie was here and she wanted to come talk to him."

"And?" Loran said when he didn't go on.

"And…he didn't shoot me. But he wasn't what I would call thrilled. You might want to rethink this."

"Yeah, well, I'm not exactly thrilled, either," she said. "I want to take Maddie home, and the sooner she deals with him, the sooner I can do that."

"What about you? Are you planning on dealing with him?"

"I'm not planning on anything. He's nothing to me."

She could feel Meyer looking at her.

"Are you married?" she asked abruptly.

"No, why?"

"I didn't want to drag you into something dangerous if you've got a wife and ten children."

"No wife," he said. "Not sure about the ten children." He was smiling that half smile of his and she couldn't keep from responding to it. He was so…reassuring somehow, and he didn't have to *do* anything. She wondered if it was something he'd learned in the military or if it was just his personality.

"There's the church," he said. "You need to turn into the little road there on the right, the one that goes up to the house back there."

"Is that where Estelle lives?"

"Yes."

"Are we trespassing?"

"Probably."

"We're not going to ask her for permission?"

"*No.*"

She kept looking at him as she drove. He didn't seem particularly worried.

"No," she repeated. "So how's Nelda?" she asked as she slowed to make the turn.

"Fine as far as I know. But then she doesn't know about *this*," he said, but his attention seemed to be taken by the house on the side of the steep hill. "I'll take you to meet Nelda if you want."

"Would there be any point in asking her about my…situation?"

"She knows a lot about everything—the history of the valley, the customs. She can tell you how to cure what ails you with the plants that grow around here, how to live off the land, how to make wine out of blackberries.

There's a good chance she'd know something about Tommy Garth."

"Would she tell me if I asked?"

"Don't know. I wouldn't offer her money or threaten her with the sheriff, though."

Up ahead, there was a car parked on the narrow road that led up the mountainside.

"Can you get around it?" Meyer asked.

"Yes," Loran said. And did so. So far, the SUV was living up to the salesman's hype.

"Don't stop," Meyer said as they neared the house. "No matter what, keep going. Bobby Ray says there aren't any forks. This goes straight up to Tommy's place."

"Not nearly so complicated as the men at the store made it sound."

"As long as we can tell where the road is," Meyer said.

The house was bigger than she'd first thought and in better repair than others she'd seen.

"Estelle's place, I take it," she said.

Meyer made a sound that could have been yes or no.

"She may be the one to call the sheriff," he said as they moved past the house and continued into the woods.

"Oh, why not?" Loran said. "Being arrested ought to top it off just about right."

She didn't see anyone around the house as she drove past or a face at the window. The way grew steeper and Loran shifted into four-wheel drive. The SUV immediately responded, lumbering over the rough terrain with the purposeful bouncing grace of a giant beetle.

Meyer kept looking behind them.

"Any sign of her?" Loran asked.

"Not yet. I wouldn't hang around, though."

She had no intention of hanging around. She kept her foot firmly on the gas pedal, adjusting for the difference in traction as the SUV climbed upward. It was only when she could no longer see the house in the rearview mirror that she let herself relax.

But only for a second. It was like when she'd first woken up this morning, that brief instant when everything had seemed all right, before she'd suddenly remembered that it wasn't.

"How much farther, do you think?"

"I don't know. Just keep going. Bobby Ray says you'll know when you get there."

Loran looked at him doubtfully. She was beginning to think there was no such thing as "directions" in this place.

"You actually saw Tommy Garth today?" she suddenly asked.

"Yeah."

"What...does he look like?"

"Tall. Thin. Beard. Hunting rifle."

She could feel Meyer looking at her and she gave a quiet sigh.

"Are you sure you want to do this?" he asked.

"Want has nothing to do with it. I have to get Maddie out of here."

"Why?"

"She's sick. She needs to be home."

"Maybe, for her, this is home," he said. "Maybe she's happier here."

Before she could respond to that, the stand of trees

suddenly ended and they were entering a grassy open place. She could see a cabin to her left and numerous outbuildings. To her right stood a stone chimney and a foundation—what was left of another cabin, she thought.

She stopped not far from the ruins, where anyone in the remaining cabin or any of the outbuildings could easily see the SUV.

"I don't want you to come with me," she said.

But he opened the car door when she did and got out.

"I mean it, Meyer. I don't want you to come with me." This was a moment she had imagined all of her life and, given the circumstances, the last thing she wanted was a witness to it.

"I'll wait here," Meyer said. "I just want him to see who's with you."

She looked at him and nodded. And took a deep breath. Then she began walking toward the porch. She kept looking around herself, expecting a dog to come tearing out from someplace.

Or a bullet to fly over her head.

Beloved illustrious father…

There was no dog and no gunshot. She looked up at the sky. The fish-scale clouds were still there, and some long wispy ones as well.

Mares' tails, she thought suddenly.

But she had forgotten what it was supposed to mean, or if Mrs. Jenkins had even explained them. Maybe it was going to rain after all. But it was too cold to rain.

Just keep going.

She couldn't keep from shivering as she made her

way to the cabin, and she was aware that it didn't come entirely from the cold.

She knew Meyer watched as she stepped up on the porch. She didn't hesitate, maybe because he was watching. Maybe because he might not be the only one.

She knocked on the door. Hard. Then she waited. She was in the shade now and even colder. After a moment, she knocked again and then stepped into a triangle of sunlight at the edge of the porch. She couldn't hear anything from inside the house. No movement. Nothing.

But then she did hear something—a kind of long, whispery scraping sound that repeated, and repeated.

Then there was nothing. She moved to the door, intending to knock again, but it abruptly opened.

The man standing there completely filled the doorway. Tall. Thin. Bearded. She couldn't see a rifle.

"My name is Loran Kimball. I'm looking for Tommy Garth," she said.

They stared at each other. He didn't give her a chance to say anything else. He turned and went back inside, but he left the door open. She stood for a moment, then followed after him, fighting the urge to look over her shoulder at Meyer because he might think she wanted him to come along—which she desperately did now, and it was bound to show.

The cabin was one big room and smelled of coffee and bacon and wood smoke. There was a fireplace directly in front of her, but the heat source seemed to be a wood cookstove on the far wall. She could see three mostly intact Blue Willow plates—none of them the same size—standing on their edges on a makeshift mantelpiece. Or maybe it wasn't so much makeshift as primitive. The bark had been left on the wood of the mantel like the rocking chair at Meyer's cabin.

The man she feared was her father went to a kind of bench in a patch of sunlight by the window. He sat down astride the bench and picked up a long blade with a handle on each end of it, and began to drag it toward himself, down a piece of wood held firmly by a vise at the other end of the bench.

"I'm—" she began.

"I know who you are. Close the door. It's cold."

She hesitated, then did as he asked—ordered.

"You can't possibly know who I am—"

"You're Maddie's girl," he said. "You've got her look about you."

"I don't look like her at all."

"I didn't say you looked like her. I said you've got her look about you, the one she always had when she was mad about something. And scared."

Loran opened her mouth to say something, then didn't.

"I reckon you come up here to get a look at me," he said. "So look."

All the time, he never broke the rhythm of shaving long strips of wood off the piece held in the vise on the bench. After a moment, he stopped and released the screw clamp holding it, so he could rotate it and begin shaving the strips off again.

Loran stood watching him, and if having her attention bothered him in the least, it didn't show. His hands were lean and strong, long-fingered—and battered from the kind of work he was doing now, she supposed. His hair was dark. There was some gray in it and in his beard.

He was seriously in need of a good barbering. She stared at his profile. If he really was her father, then she'd obviously gotten very little of her outward appearance from either of her parents.

She looked around the room. There were three tables. One was for eating—two places had already been set.

How odd, she thought. That he would set his table with such care. Had he done it anticipating a visit from Maddie?

The other two tables seemed to be for ongoing projects in addition to whatever he was doing now—wood carving and some kind of silver jewelry that was set with bits of china plates that had been shaped into hearts and circles and ovals—for pendants or bracelet charms, she supposed. They were quite pretty.

"It's the story that people buy," he said.

"What?" she asked, not understanding.

"Them pieces of porcelain come from that old homestead out there. Nobody knows what happened to the people that used to live there—or why all their fine dishes got broke."

"And you just sell it off?"

"I don't reckon *they* need it."

"Kind of like grave robbing, isn't it?"

"Got to eat."

She moved away from the jewelry and looked at the wood carving—an intricately designed plaque or sign of some kind with carved flowers and leaves and curving vines that flowed into the words, Samuel's Daughter's House.

She frowned, wondering what it was for, but she wasn't about to ask. She saw a picture in a cheap frame nailed to the wall, so she went to look at that. A group of laughing men more or less in uniform. Some of them were shirtless. One or two held weapons. All of them were lean and sunburned and dirty.

There was only one place left to look, and so she looked at him. He kept glancing out the window.

"He's worried about you. You better tell him to get in here before he turns wrong side out. Well, go on, sis," he said when she didn't immediately comply. "It's cold out there."

"My name is Loran," she said—but she went and opened the door again. "Meyer!" she called and motioned for him to come. She saw immediately that Tommy Garth had been right. He was worried about her.

"There's some cups over there on the shelf," Tommy said behind her. "Pour us some coffee. There's some sugar around somewhere. Try that can over there, if you want any."

She didn't. She didn't want the coffee either, but she needed something to do, so she got the cups down. The splatter-ware coffeepot sat on a stove on the other side of the big room.

"Do you always give people orders?" she asked as Meyer came through the door.

"Who come to see who, sis?" he asked, still working with the wood. "So here you are again, Meyer Conley," he said as Meyer stepped inside.

"Yes, sir," Meyer said. "Again."

"Might be some would wonder how a body could go so long without ever running into a single solitary Conley—and then there's one everywhere you look. Not me, though. I reckon I know how hard it is to say no to a Kimball woman."

"Yes, sir," Meyer said and both men laughed.

"This is just great," Loran said under her breath. She poured the coffee. She had no intention of serving it, too, but Meyer saved her the trouble. He came and got his and Tommy's.

She stood awkwardly while he sat the second cup on the windowsill where Tommy could reach it.

"What did your mama tell you about me, sis?" Tommy asked, the suddenness of the question belying the calm rhythm of his work.

"I never heard your name until yesterday," Loran said.

"I don't think you answered what I asked you."

And she had no intention of doing so. She merely looked at him. God, this was *not* the father she'd dreamed of having.

"Maddie know you're here then?" he asked next.

"No."

"Didn't think so. What do you want?"

"I want to take her home. And she won't go until she's talked to you."

"She's waited a long time to get around to that. I reckon she can keep on waiting."

Loran set the cup she was holding down on the table. Hard. The coffee sloshed over the edges.

"You know what? My mother was right never to have spoken of you. You can't possibly be of any help to her. I'm going," she said to Meyer.

She headed for the door, not realizing until she stepped off the porch that Tommy Garth followed her.

"What do you mean—help? What kind of help would Maddie be wanting from me?"

She walked on a few steps before she turned and looked at him.

"I don't know," she said. "All I know is she's dying."

CHAPTER 10

Loran nearly drove past Poppy's store. She made a sharp turn into the parking lot, remembering at the last moment that Meyer was with her and that he had left his truck parked under the trees. She stopped well away from the gas pumps, half expecting to see Poppy and what few men she hadn't scared off with her demand for directions to Tommy Garth's hermitage still standing in the front window—all of them waiting for Act III of the Kimball-Garth Dog and Pony Show.

She sat staring out the windshield at nothing. Meyer made no attempt to get out.

"You want to go talk to Nelda?" he asked finally.

She looked at him. "Is this you not meddling again?"

"I know you've got…questions. Maybe she'll answer them. Nelda keeps the things she knows private, if she thinks that's the way it ought to be, but it won't hurt to go ask her. Now is as good a time as any."

Loran didn't say anything. Her only choices were making the long trip back home in her current state of mind or going back to Lilac Hill and dodging "Bill Bailey."

Or bawling her head off.

"Yes or no?" Meyer said. "If you want to go talk to her now, I need to buy some snuff."

"What, you think talking to me is going to make her fall off the wagon?"

"Yes," he said bluntly.

"Why?"

"A lot of people are...upset."

Loran couldn't argue with that—she herself being one of them. She gave a heavy sigh. "Okay. I'll go talk to her."

"Outstanding," he said, opening the door.

"Maybe you better buy me some snuff, too," she said, and he grinned.

She waited, envisioning Poppy jumping all over him for the details the minute he walked in the place. But he wasn't gone long enough to have imparted much information beyond, "We saw Tommy Garth. He didn't shoot anybody."

When he got back into the SUV, he had two cans of snuff, one of which he tossed to her.

"You did know I was kidding," she said as she caught the can.

He grinned again. "This is for you to remember me by. I'm betting no guy *ever* bought you snuff."

She smiled in spite of the misery she was feeling.

"Yes, well, you'd win that one."

"Let's go. You know where it is."

"What about your truck?"

"Later," he said.

"Oh, I get it. You think I won't go if you're not right here to make me."

"I think you could talk yourself out of it between here and there," he admitted.

The old men were back in the store window.

She started the SUV, then pulled onto the road in the direction of the Conley mailbox, her thoughts as scattered as the dry, dead leaves that blew and swirled in the wind.

Tommy Garth.

That man was her father. The woodwright. The... jewelry-making recluse. Did he realize she was his daughter?

No.

No.

"What did he say to you?" Loran asked abruptly, because Meyer had lingered for a moment after she'd rushed out of the cabin and left them both standing.

"He asked me about your name," Meyer said, not pretending that he didn't know what she meant.

"Kimball?"

"No. Loran—with the *a.* I don't know why," he added to head off her next question. "Maybe it meant something to him."

"Like what?"

"I don't know. Maybe it's a Garth family name. Maybe it's something he and Maddie talked about one time."

Surely not, Loran thought. Surely the man Maddie had never even mentioned didn't matter enough to influence what name she'd chosen to give her only daughter.

"You remember where to turn—"

"I remember, I remember."

"Just checking," he said. "So how old are you?"

"How *old* am I?" she said incredulously.

"Yeah."

"I'm thirty-nine," she said. The SUV bounced

through the turn at the Conley mailbox, and, rough ride and distracting passenger or not, she couldn't keep from glancing at the hillside where she thought his cabin would be. There was still enough daylight, but the sun was in the wrong place for her to see a reflection on the tin roof through the bare trees.

Maddie, I hope you know what you're doing.

She herself had lost all sense of control of the situation. She was just ricocheting from one emotional catastrophe to another.

She maneuvered the SUV down the rutted narrow road and into some woods, expecting Meyer to give her some unsolicited driving tips.

"How old are *you?*" she asked.

"Forty-one."

"You don't look that old."

"I didn't expect to get this old."

"So why aren't you married?"

"You need to quit being so bashful, Kimball. Just ask me a personal question, why don't you?"

"People ask women—*me*—that all the time."

"You'll be okay," he said, completely changing the subject. They weren't talking about him or being married anymore.

"Easy for you to say. You don't know anything about it."

"I know you don't take any crap—from life or anybody in it. And nothing bad lasts forever. You'll be okay," he said again as the patch of woods ended and they came into a clearing. Not the situation. Just her. He sounded as if he actually expected her to come through this upheaval in her life reasonably unscathed. He sounded very much the way he had when he'd found her bawling on the gazebo steps.

She sighed. She was much too old to need generic re-assurances. But she was still grateful for the effort.

"You'll like Nelda," he said. "And she'll love you."

"She doesn't even know me."

"You're Maddie's girl. That's enough for her. You belong here. That pretty much makes it a done deal."

She didn't say anything to that. She didn't feel as if she belonged anywhere.

She could see a big L-shaped, weathered house off to her right. It was a two-story rectangle with a long wrap-around porch and a single-story wing on the back. There was a barn and a number of small outbuildings, all of which must have served some purpose—and mountain ridges all around. They bounced past a fenced-in corn-field. The fence posts, large and small, still had the bark on. Bundles of corn stalks stood upright in rows, making her think of frosts and Halloween.

As soon as she parked the SUV, the front door of the house opened, and a woman wearing an apron and a baggy beige sweater came out onto the porch and down the steps to meet them. She was plump and round, and she wore her hair parted in the middle with a bun at the nape of her neck.

"You called her and told her I was coming," Loran said, realizing the real reason he'd gone into Poppy's store and the reason he was making sure she got here. This woman meant enough to him that he didn't want her disappointed, on any level.

"Yes," he said.

Loran looked at him. She didn't know how to deal

with a man who took responsibility for his behavior and his choices without apology. She sighed and got out of the truck when he did, wishing all the while that she hadn't come.

"This is Loran Kimball, Nelda," he said. "This is my great-aunt, Nelda Conley."

"Bless your sweet heart," Nelda said to her. "Come on in the house. I'm so proud you come to see me. I'm a-making apple pies for the church this evening."

"Maybe this isn't a good time—"

"No, honey. Now you're here, you can help me."

"I've…never made an apple pie," Loran said.

"You ain't?" Nelda said, clearly incredulous.

"No," Loran said.

"Well, you ain't too old to learn, is she, Meyer?"

"No, ma'am," Meyer said, trying not to smile. "She's been up to see Tommy Garth, Nelda."

Nelda received this information without comment. "Meyer, I'm needing some more wood cut, honey. Before it gets too dark."

"Yes, ma'am," he said, and he walked around the side of the house out of sight.

Nelda reached out and took Loran's cold hand in her rough warm one.

"Thank you, honey," she whispered, looking in the direction Meyer had gone.

"For what?"

"For getting Meyer here. It's a-coming down on him again, I can see it."

"I don't understand."

"Oh, it's that darkness what comes from being over there in all that fighting and killing like he was. He just weren't cut out for it. Liked to have broke his heart—he always was tender-hearted, even when he was a little boy. He got home from over there in one piece, but he really reckoned he ought to have stayed longer. Signed up again, you know, because he knowed how to do what them generals wanted done and he's used to looking out for the younger ones. He just ain't the same as he was, and now here's Ransome Smith's boy a-going. Clay, he ain't nothing but a young-un and that's the truth. I reckon he only joined the army because he saw Meyer do it and get to go to college from it. It's going to make Meyer get all sorrowful again. It worries me when he don't sleep and he don't eat—but maybe you and me can get him back on the sunny side. At least for a little while.

"Now. Come on in and you can tell me how your mama is," Nelda said as they walked up onto the porch and into the house. "Go right down yonder and wash your hands," she said, pointing Loran toward a door at the end of the long central hallway. "Then we'll get us to baking."

Loran washed her hands and stared at herself in the mottled mirror over the bathroom sink. How could she be confronting a father she'd never even known about one minute and baking pies the next?

When she came out, she immediately discovered that Nelda had been perfectly serious about the pies. The kitchen was huge and warm, and there was a long wooden harvest table in the middle of it, covered in various stages of pie making. Before Loran could turn around twice, she'd traded her coat for a brown-and-white gingham checked apron with cross-stitched embroidery on the bib and along the hem, and she was measuring flour and cutting solid shortening into it as if she knew what she was doing.

"There, that's right," Nelda said, praising her efforts. "Now, how's your mama?"

Incredibly, Loran told her. Everything, including Maddie's notion to stay alone in Meyer's cabin and how worried she was.

"She won't be alone, honey," Nelda said. "There's plenty of folks what knowed your great granddaddy and your grandmaw Adeline still around. And don't none of us hold Foy against her."

"Foy?"

"Foy Kimball. That's your granddaddy. Maddie's daddy—Adeline's husband. He was a hard-hearted man, and that's about the best a body can say for him, but you ain't got to worry about that. I reckon everybody's got a 'Foy' in the family somewhere if they look hard enough.

"Anyway, we'll all be seeing to Maddie, making sure she don't want for nothing. You don't have to worry none about that."

Loran looked toward the window suddenly at a sharp sound from the outside.

"That's Meyer, honey. Chopping that wood. I don't reckon I need it, but it does a man good to get hisself busy when something's bothering him. My husband, Delman—he was the same way. He was a good man, too, like Meyer is, but it gets hard for men sometimes. Delman used to work so long in them fields out yonder, sometimes he couldn't hardly make it back to the house when the sun went down. Couldn't hardly walk, and that's the Lord's truth. I used to keep me a big old pot of water a-boiling, and when he'd come in like that, I'd put him right in that big old tub we had—the one we used for a bathtub. I reckon you seen it hanging on the wall out there when you come in. I ought to throw it away, but I just can't part with it.

"He'd come home all used up and full of misery, and I'd make him get in it. I wash him myself, because he didn't have the strength left to do it—his back and shoulders would be a-hurting him so bad. Now I know young women these days would be thinking that's a terrible thing—me wanting to do for him like that and acting like I was his servant—but I loved that man to death. He wouldn't never let me work in the fields with him, I was sickly when I was a girl. His family told him he ought not marry me because of it—but here I still am, and he's the one gone.

"He was my sweetest friend. Them tub baths was just a little something I could do for him, and Lord, he appreciated it. And I appreciated him, yes, I did. He's been dead nigh on to forty-two years, and I still love that boy like the day I first set eyes on him."

"How did you meet him?" Loran asked, trying to follow what Nelda was doing with her batch of pie dough.

"Oh, it was when we was both about sixteen years old. He come a-visiting the church when we was having the Decoration—you know about Decoration Sunday?"

"No."

"Well, it's kind of like a Sunday set aside to remember who you come from and where you're a-going to—and to enjoy the company of your kin and your neighbors. Different churches do it on different Sundays, so's you can get around to all of them if you've got people buried other places. There's lots of food and' preaching and singing. And flowers. You wouldn't believe the flowers, honey. All the graves is cleaned up and the weeds pulled and flowers put on them. It's real pretty. *Real* pretty—and it makes you feel good to remember all them ones that's gone before you—letting them know you ain't forgot them and you're carrying on as best you can. If they can still see us, it's got to be a comfort to them, and it's a comfort to us here, too.

"Anyways, Delman, he had some family buried in the cemetery here, and him, and his mama and daddy, and his brothers come that Sunday. Oh, it was hot that day, lordy, it was hot. He got stung by a bunch of yellow jackets when he went to get a drink of water from the well, and I got my daddy to put some chewing tobacco on the places for him. I took one look in them blue eyes of hissen and I went just as silly in the head as I could go. If that boy hadn't been interested in me, too, I believe I would have put a rope around him and dragged him off someplace and kept him all tied up till he said he'd marry me." Nelda threw her head back and laughed out loud, clapping her hands together, and Loran laughed with her.

"It sounds like you had a good marriage."

"Well, we had our ups and downs, honey, I can tell you that. I learned what the two secrets was, though, afore I married him. Old lady Graham, she told me. You know what the first secret is?"

"No," Loran said truthfully.

"Well, when young folks first get married, they're all crazy about one another and everything, so they think they ought never disagree or get mad—but that just ain't so. You're going to get mad—ain't no woman on this earth can live with a man and not get mad at him, I don't care who she is. And him, too. I hear tell we're exasperating creatures," she whispered, making Loran smile.

"But now here's the first secret. It's all right for you to get mad at him or him to get mad at you. But when you both get mad at the same time—*that's* what causes all the trouble. Makes you say hurtful things you can't take back or hit one another with the first thing you pick up. You got to watch that getting mad at the same time business. That's what worked for old lady Graham, and that's what worked for me.

"I can't understand about these marriages now—all that *money* for wedding dresses and honeymoons and showing off. Prideful things don't make the marriage work no better as far as I can see. Marriage is a funny doing, if you want my verdict. Some of them have all that fancy stuff, and it still don't make it take. And some don't have nothing at all, but they got a marriage as true and binding as if the good Lord Jesus hisself come down and tied the knot. Like your mama and daddy," Nelda added quietly.

"They weren't married," Loran said.

"Not with all that going down to the courthouse and buying a license and signing papers the government makes you go through, no. But their hearts were married. Anybody that ever seen them knew that. That's why Estelle got so—"

Nelda abruptly broke off. Loran waited for her to continue, but she didn't. They worked for a time in silence. She could hear the wind against the side of the house. The chopping noises outside had stopped.

"I came to ask you to tell me about Tommy Garth," Loran said as Nelda gave her some apples to peel.

"I reckoned you did, honey. Does he know who you are?" she asked bluntly.

"He knows I'm…Maddie's girl. Maddie says she never told him…anything."

"You favor the Garths some—one of Tommy's daddy's sisters—but she died way before Tommy was born. We'll get around to him, but right now, I'm wondering if you might would go out there and see what you can do for Meyer. He should of been back in here by now."

Loran hesitated. "All right," she said, mostly because of the way Nelda was looking at her.

"Here," Nelda said, getting something out of a glass dish with a lid on a shelf by the sink. "Give him some of these—so's he'll know we're understanding him."

She put several peppermint candies into Loran's palm.

"Put your coat on. You might have to walk around the place to find him."

Loran couldn't hear anything when she stepped out on the porch. She went around to the side of the house, in the direction he had gone earlier. The ax and chopping block and some newly split logs were there, but he wasn't. She stood for a moment, listening, then walked toward the barn.

She could hear his voice, hear him talking to someone as she came closer.

"Meyer?"

"In here," he said. "Come meet Pearl."

She had no idea who—or what—Pearl might be, but she went. The inside of the barn was deep in shadow and dusty-smelling—among other things. She could see

Meyer at the far end, pitching hay into a stall—for a white mule.

"Pearl, Loran. Loran, Pearl," he said.

Pearl was clearly unimpressed.

"Well she's…interesting looking…."

"She's mean as a snake is what she is," Meyer said, hand-feeding her a clump of the hay. "She bites, kicks, bucks, tramples, elopes. You name it, she does it. Except when she doesn't want to do anything at all. Man, I hate mules."

The mule leaned out to push him with her nose.

"But you're crazy about *her*," Loran said, smiling.

"Yeah, well, there's that. I've got a weakness for block-heads, I guess."

"That must have been a really big help in the army."

He smiled and went back to pitching the hay. "Nelda tell you anything?"

"She told me a lot of things, but not much about Tommy Garth."

"Well, don't give up yet."

"I'm not. She says we'll get to him. She sent me out here. I think she's afraid I'm going to wreck her pies."

Meyer smiled again, but the smile quickly faded.

"Did you get the wood chopped?" she asked to keep the conversation going.

"Yeah. I figure she's got enough now to last her until 2175. Did she…say anything else?"

"I think she thinks you might be feeling…down and misplaced." She reached into her pocket and handed him the pieces of candy.

He looked at them for a moment, then took them,

his fingers warm against the palm of her hand in spite of the cold.

"You…want to go for a walk? See a little bit of the place?" he asked, his tone suggesting both that it was hard for him to ask, for some reason, and that he fully expected her to say no. She realized suddenly that he was making an attempt to divert her from her current distress and perhaps his, as well.

"Why not?" she said. Anything to keep from thinking about her brand new father.

She followed him out of the barn and toward a narrow rutted road that led upward into a field of broom straw. Grass grew in the ruts and it was still green in places, the last remnant of Indian summer, she supposed.

"Where does this road go?"

"It's not a road. Some of the old men around here say it was a buffalo trail."

"There were buffalo in the mountains?"

"Well, not lately."

The wind grew sharper as they moved toward higher ground. He slowed his pace so that they could walk side by side. She kept watching him, wondering how much he was like Nelda's Delman. Did they have the same build, the same quiet strength, the same sense of humor? She had to admit that her own idea of marriage had more to do with what she'd seen in slick bridal magazines—the lavish ceremony, the gowns and the flowers and the rings—and not the real-life aspect of it. But she had no difficulty whatsoever understanding how Nelda could have wanted to "do" for the husband who'd worked so hard for her. A sudden image rose in her mind—the long galvanized tub she'd seen hanging on Nelda's porch, filled with steaming soapy water and an exhausted Meyer Conley. In her mind's eye, she could see herself touching him, trying to make him feel better....

She abruptly pushed the image aside.

Meyer was looking at the rolling hills around them, and savoring the sight of them, she thought. And she could see a certain sadness in him, the sadness Maddie had mentioned, if not the full-blown sorrowfulness that Nelda seemed worried about.

"Do you read John Burroughs?" she asked.

"Yeah, why?"

"I saw the books in your cabin."

"'The peace of the hills is about me and upon me....'" he quoted. "He was talking about the Hudson Valley, but it's the same here—look over there," he said, stopping and pointing into a stand of trees. She could just make out the ruins of some building.

"What's that?"

"It was a school."

"Why is it so far out of the way?"

"They built it there so it would be halfway between two settlements. The river's not too far on the other side of that hill and there used to be a bunch of families up that way. The kids from the valley and the ones from across the river met at the closest place to both."

"When was that?"

"I'm not sure. Long enough for most people to forget about it. Bobby Ray would say it was full of 'haints'— ghosts."

"Is it?" she asked.

"If somebody thinks it is, it is."

"Does Nelda own this land?"

"Yeah. It's been in the family about a century and a half. So what do you do for a living?"

"Me? I work for a bank."

He smiled. "I'm guessing there's more to it than that."

"I'm...it's investment banking. Corporate stuff, mostly."

He made a small noise. "Pays good, I notice."

"Yes," she said, slightly offended without knowing why. She certainly hadn't been handed the job. She'd studied long and hard for the necessary credentials, then worked an equally long and hard apprenticeship to get the high-pressure position she had now and the reputation to go with it. She'd worked so hard that there had been no time for anything else—except for an occasional man like the faithless Kent.

Kent.

She'd all but forgotten about Kent.

They walked for a time in silence.

"Are you going to go talk to Clay?" she asked abruptly.

"Do what?" he said, clearly startled by the inquiry.

"If he's being deployed, maybe you should talk to him."

Bringing up the topic of Clay Smith's departure was ill-advised at best. She could almost see him shutting down.

"I don't need to talk to him."

"I wasn't thinking about you. I was thinking about him. You could tell him things—"

"He wouldn't want to know the things I could tell him."

She stopped walking. "Things that might help," she said pointedly. "Things that might make him feel better."

"Nothing's going to make him feel better, believe me. He's already given me his letter. The one I'm supposed to give Mary Ann if he gets killed over there. I'm holding on to that for him. That's enough."

She stood looking at him. "I'm…sorry. I didn't mean to overstep."

"It's okay."

They started walking again.

"There's something you should know," he said after a time.

"About what?"

"About you. You should know you're a good-looking woman."

She frowned. "Thank you."

"And I appreciate every opportunity I get to look at you. *But*—there's not going to be any kissing."

"What?" she said, stopping dead.

"You heard me. And you need to know that."

"Oh, really."

"No kissing," he repeated. "We aren't going to be doing any of that."

"I see. Any…particular reason?" she asked, knowing he was teasing her again in that taciturn yet droll way he had and trying not to let him get the best of her.

"Yeah, you might like it."

"*I* might—!"

"See, I'm already pretty sure I'd like it. And if you liked it, too, well, we'd be in a hell of a fix then, wouldn't we?"

He started walking again, leaving her to follow or not.

"Yes!" she called after him.

He laughed and stopped walking. "Well, come on!" he said. "You want to see the back forty, or don't you?"

She stood for a moment, then grinned. "You are a decidedly conceited person, you do know that."

"Yeah," he said. "But you like me anyway."

She caught up with him, and they began walking again. He gave her one of the pieces of peppermint.

Yes, she thought. She did.

CHAPTER 11

"What do you want?"

Maddie heard the question plainly, but she made no attempt to answer it. She stared at him, taken completely by surprise. She had opened the door expecting to see Meyer on the porch, or perhaps Bobby Ray. Not for one moment did she think that Tommy would come to her. She thought she'd have to negotiate a face-to-face meeting with him or even have to corner him someplace. She kept looking at him, knowing she could have passed him on the street and not realized it—unless she happened to look into his eyes. The eyes were the same. The eyes were Tommy, the boy she had loved.

"What do you want?" he said again, the hard edge to his voice surprising her, as well. He was behaving as if *he* were the injured party here.

"Well, I used to want you to marry me, but I got over it," she said.

"Don't play with me, Maddie. You been asking after me. Now I want to know what for."

She stood looking at him, feeling the anger rising in her—after all this time. She felt suddenly as if she had split in two somehow, and she was both participant and observer.

"What could I possibly want from you?"

"Damn it, woman! You're the one stayed gone—"

"*I* stayed gone? *You* left *me*. You knew what living with Foy Kimball was like, and you knew I loved you. You still walked off and left me. It takes a cruel man to do what you did. It takes a man just like Foy—"

"I ain't like your daddy!"

"What's going on?"

The question made both of them turn. Loran stood at the end of the porch.

"Nothing. He was just leaving," Maddie said.

"Maddie, *you* are the one started this—you sent your girl after me—"

Maddie gave Loran a look. Her girl was more enterprising than she'd imagined.

"I've changed my mind," Maddie said. "You know how that is."

"Maddie—"

"All right!" Maddie said suddenly, the anger flaring up white-hot now, and there was nothing she could do to stop it. "You wouldn't marry me—maybe you can bury me, instead. I want you to make my coffin, Tommy. I want you to dig my grave. I want you to sit up all night with my body, like they used to do. You owe me that much, don't you think? We could say it's just for old time's sake."

She abruptly turned and walked back into the cabin because she knew she was going to cry. She hadn't cried over Tommy Garth in—she couldn't remember when—but she was going to cry now. The tears were already spilling down her cheeks. She walked blindly to the window on the far side of the room and stood there, trying to regain control.

She could hear Loran say something to him, then come inside. Loran hesitated behind her, then took off her coat and walked to the kitchen area to fill the kettle and put it on the stove to heat.

"Mother?" she said when she'd finished.

"Is he gone?"

"No. Yes. Mother—"

"I thought you were going back home."

"I changed my mind."

"I see."

"No, you don't. We can both go now. I've seen Tommy Garth and so have you. It's obvious you can't talk to him. We can leave as soon as you—"

"No. I'm not ready to go yet."

"Why, for God's sake!"

"I told you before. I don't really know."

Maddie kept looking out the window, staring at the trees, at the ridge, at nothing.

"Then I…want to stay, too. For a while anyway. I can't just go off and leave you here. I thought I could, but I can't. If you'd rather I didn't stay here, Nelda said I could stay with her. I've already called them at work and asked for some more time off."

Maddie didn't say anything, couldn't say anything.

"Mother, are you all right?"

Maddie shook her head, then put her face into her hands, crying openly now. Loran came closer to her, hesitating at the edge of her anguish. Finally, she stepped forward and put her arms around her, their roles reversed suddenly for the first and only time in both their lives. Loran didn't say anything. She just stood there, holding on, crying with her, Maddie, the observer, realized.

The kettle began to whistle, and Maddie took a wavering breath and moved away. "I'll make us some tea," she said, her voice husky from crying.

"No, I'll make it," Loran said. "You sit down."

Maddie let her make the tea. She sat down heavily on the sagging but comfortable pull-out sofa, pulling her knees up, trying not to cry anymore.

"You went to see him?" she asked after a time.

"Yes. Meyer took me."

"Poor Meyer. Did you see…Estelle?"

"I saw where she lives. Why?"

Loran stood looking at her, the kettle in her hand, waiting, but Maddie couldn't begin the sad tale with Estelle Garth. She waited until Loran had made the tea and brought them both a mug. Loran sat down on the couch at the far end.

Maddie wiped her eyes with her fingertips. "I…was fourteen when—" She abruptly stopped. She had been about to say, "your father," but he wasn't that, except in the strictest biological sense. This was going to be much harder than she'd anticipated. She took a quiet breath and began again. "We couldn't let anyone know that we were…together."

"Nelda knew," Loran said.

Maddie looked at her, surprised by the revelation.

"Yes," she said after a moment. "Nelda would. Not much gets by her. But my father didn't—"

"That would be the hateful Foy— Sorry," Loran said. "I don't mean to make light of any of it. It's just that I'm…floundering."

So am I, Maddie thought.

"Please, don't stop," Loran said. "Tell me."

Maddie took a quiet breath. "Foy…didn't…couldn't know about Tommy and me—and neither could Estelle."

"She's Tommy's…mother."

"Yes."

"Why couldn't they know?"

"My family wasn't good enough, thanks to Foy. I was his daughter, so I wasn't good enough. Foy lived to make everyone around him miserable. It was like a game with him, finding someone's weakness and taking advantage of it. I never understood why my mother loved him so." Maddie stopped, remembering the cruelty.

"You were so young," Loran said.

"Yes. Fourteen going on ninety. And Tommy was in the army. He was my…knight in shining armor. It was hard for me to trust him—because of Foy—but I did. He came home on leave—the last the lucky ones got before they were shipped off to Vietnam. We were going to get married—elope—by driving down to a county seat in South Carolina. I was going to lie about my age. You didn't have to have blood tests to get married in South Carolina. He was supposed to wait for me on the logging road behind the house, behind Lilac Hill. I was all ready. I had everything I owned in a big grocery bag, and there was no one at home but me. It was going to be so easy this time, getting out of the house. Except that he didn't come. I waited and waited—but he…just…never came. I couldn't find out where he was or what happened. People said he went AWOL so he wouldn't have to go to Vietnam, that he'd taken off to Canada. He wasn't like that. He might have run away from me—he *did* run away from me. But he wouldn't have dodged the army.

"Of all the things that could have gone wrong that

night, I never once thought he wouldn't show up. Never. I believed him, I believed *in* him. It was a terrible waste."

She stopped. She was so tired suddenly.

"I...never saw him again—until today." A single tear slid down her cheek without her even knowing it. "I'm...sorry," she said, brushing it away. "I thought it wouldn't mean anything to me now, but I—"

"He just didn't show up," Loran said, more to herself than to Maddie.

"It wasn't because of you," Maddie said. "He didn't know I was pregnant. *I* didn't know I was pregnant."

"But didn't you try to find out what happened?"

"Why should I? I thought I knew. He'd...changed his mind. I didn't want to make him marry me, and I had enough pride not to go chasing after him. A person's pride—it's important here."

"Then what happened?"

"I asked a teacher for help, the only one who ever seemed to have...hope that I could become something. Foy kicked me out of the house. She made the arrangements for me to go into a home for unwed mothers about a hundred miles away. I worked on my GED while I was there, learned to budget money, learned how to take care of you, learned I wasn't stupid and I wasn't a...bad person." She suddenly smiled, remembering. "The director was a man. Every year they had a Halloween party, and every year he came as one of us—in drag and pregnant. We loved it."

They sat for a time in silence.

"So can I stay?" Loran asked suddenly.

"You shouldn't be away from your job."

Loran shrugged her indifference to the obligation. "I want to be here—with you. Can I?"

"Of course, you can stay here," Maddie said, and she realized the moment she said it that Loran had been by no means sure she would be welcome—a clear indicator of how unsettled the situation was for her.

"I…need to go get the SUV," Loran said after a moment. "I walked up here the back way—a path Meyer showed me. You'll be all right while I'm gone? You don't think he'll come back?"

"No. I think once every forty years or so is about it for him."

Loran smiled at the very feeble joke. She seemed about to say something else, then didn't. She finished her tea and put on her coat.

The walk back to Nelda's was easier, almost all downhill. Loran had enjoyed the leisurely morning stroll up to Meyer's cabin, but now she barely noticed her surroundings. It was cold in the woods. Her feet tingled with it and her breath came out in short white puffs. She kept thinking about Maddie, about how hurt she must have been, how scared. No wonder she'd never trusted another man.

I don't want to know anything else, Loran thought as she reached the edge of cleared land that was Nelda's "back forty." She didn't even want to know Nelda's second secret for a successful marriage. Nothing mattered now, except getting Maddie out of here.

Pearl was out of her stall and browsing the fenced-in pasture, still unimpressed by Loran's presence. As Loran drew closer to the house, she could smell the remnants of the breakfast she'd been invited to share with Nelda and Meyer earlier—coffee, biscuits, country ham. It had been...pleasant. More than pleasant. It had been comfortable. She'd felt completely at home—as if she'd known them both for years, as if she belonged. It was a new experience for her, belonging, one she had longed for as a child and had long since abandoned. She realized as she made her way past the outbuildings and around Nelda's vegetable garden that perhaps it was worth the wait.

Meyer's truck was still in the yard. She saw it, and then she saw Meyer. He was deep in conversation with Tommy Garth.

She walked up to them both.

"It's supposed to be a lot warmer tomorrow," Tommy Garth was saying. He had just broken her mother's heart all over again and, incredibly, he was talking about the weather.

She waited until he realized she was standing there. "I know I set this all in motion by coming to see you," she said. "That was a huge mistake on my part, and I regret it. Don't bother my mother again. I mean it."

Meyer started to say something and she turned on him.

"You stay out of it!" she said, not because he was guilty of anything, but because she'd never seen Maddie cry in her entire life, and he was standing much too close to the reason for it.

She looked from one man to the other, realizing she'd be crying herself if she didn't get out of there. "Tell Nelda I said goodbye—and thanks—for everything."

She turned on her heel and walked away, but Meyer caught up with her.

"Loran, wait," Meyer said. "Talk to him—he's here. Go talk to him."

"No," she said. "I don't want to talk to him. I'm done—with him, with all of it. I'm going to get Maddie out of this place and we're going home."

"Does your mama know that?" Tommy Garth had the nerve to stroll up and ask.

"*That* is none of your business! Or yours, either," she said to Meyer. She got into the SUV and drove toward the highway, without once looking back. She went to Lilac Hill and checked out, and she realized as she did so that all of them, from Mrs. Jenkins to the teenage girl, Mary Ann, knew that Loran Kimball was no ordinary guest. Clearly, the valley people were now aware of her connection to the reclusive Tommy Garth, and there was nothing she could do about it.

Except ignore it.

She continued ignoring it after she returned to the cabin. She didn't press Maddie for any more details. She didn't tell her she'd had yet another run-in with Tommy when she'd gone to get the SUV or that Meyer had been caught in the fallout. She spent the time trying to develop some kind of plan—without success. There was no plan for a situation like this, beyond out-and-out kidnapping.

The only thing that came to mind was something Maddie had told her when she was a little girl, and they'd been literally struggling to survive.

Sometimes all you can do is try to outlast the misery.

CHAPTER 12

What is that?

Loran opened her eyes, startled by her strange surroundings and by the fact that it was morning already. It had taken her forever to fall asleep on the pull-out sofa in the main room of Meyer's cabin, and for a moment she had no idea where she was. The deer head over the mantel came into focus, and the insistent tapping on the window off the front porch continued as her brain tried to right itself.

What time is it?

Not as early as it felt, she decided.

She sat up on the side of the sofa and forced herself to be awake, glancing toward the door to the only bedroom where Maddie was sleeping in a bottom bunk—but not for long if Loran couldn't stop whoever was knocking on the windowpane. She stood up, dragging the blanket with her because the room was cold.

She staggered to the front door and opened it. Tommy Garth stood on the porch.

"What!" she said, with no attempt at politeness.

"Give these to your mama, sis," he said, thrusting a bouquet of flowers at her.

"You have got to be kidding," she said, swatting the flowers away.

"No, I ain't," he said. "Give these to her and tell her to get herself ready. I'll be back in a little bit to pick her up."

"Well, I don't think she's going to fall for *that* line again," Loran assured him. She expected him to be offended, or at least surprised that she was privy to his feckless past, but he smiled slightly instead.

"You're a lot like your mama."

"So you've said."

"You ain't quiet like she is, though. You can't let that quiet of hers fool you. She never let nobody beat her down, not even Foy, so I reckon you probably know this already. Ain't no way in hell she's going to sit still for you making her decisions for her. And I wouldn't want to be in your shoes, sis, when she finds out you tried."

"Don't call me *sis*."

"Can't help it. It suits you."

Loran looked at him, then at the flowers.

"Go on," he said. "They won't bite you."

She snatched the flowers—a supermarket bouquet from the look of them—out of his hand.

"She won't go," Loran assured him.

"You just tell her what I said, sis, and keep your opinions to yourself."

He stepped off the porch, leaving her standing in the chilly air, struggling to hold on to the blanket and the bouquet.

"Damn," Loran said under her breath, trying to make a dignified retreat in case he'd stopped somewhere to watch. "Damn, damn, damn!"

She slammed the door hard behind herself, remembering too late that she was trying to keep Maddie from being disturbed.

She tossed the flowers on the nearest piece of furniture and dragged the blanket back to the sofa. The door to the bedroom opened before she could sit down.

"Who was that?" Maddie asked.

"Dear old dad," Loran said, thinking, *I am too old for this*. "The flowers are for you."

Maddie picked them up. "What? No card?"

"I'm the card. He says to tell you to get ready. He'll be back to get you."

She expected Maddie to be insulted. Or angry. Or something.

But Maddie wasn't saying anything. She stood holding the flowers.

"I'm going to get dressed," she said after a moment.

"Mother, you're not going off with him—"

Maddie closed the bedroom door without answering.

"Mother!"

Maddie said something, but Loran had no idea what. There was nothing left to do but get dressed, too—in the one remaining set of clean clothes she had. She put them on and rounded up the rest of her wardrobe, tossing everything into the stacked washer-dryer she found behind a louvered door in the kitchen area, knowing she was likely going to end up with dingy blue underwear.

The washing machine sloshed behind the louvered door, and, eventually, Maddie came out. She was wearing jeans and an oversize pale pink sweater. Her cropped-off hair made her look young and vulnerable—and beautiful, Loran suddenly realized. Otherworldly, somehow.

But that didn't stop her from saying what she wanted to say.

"At least you won't be alone this time."

Maddie looked at her, but made no comment.

"When he doesn't show up again," Loran added in case Maddie missed the point she was trying to make.

"That's right," Maddie said.

Loran wasn't quite sure if her mother was being sarcastic or not—if she was, Loran deserved it. She felt like a petulant child, one deliberately shut out of the adult events swirling around her and trying to pretend otherwise.

"He shaved," Loran said after a moment.

"What?"

"Tommy. He shaved. Looks like he had a haircut, too. Maybe he means it this time."

"Is the coffee ready?" Maddie asked, ignoring Loran's second not-so-oblique remark.

Someone knocked on the door before Loran could pour it.

"I'll get it," Loren said. "You need to play just a *little* hard to get, you know."

Maddie gave her a be-my-guest gesture and Loran crossed the room to open the door. Tommy Garth stood on the threshold.

"It's him," she said by way of announcement.

"You ready?" Tommy asked Maddie, as if there were no one else in the room.

"Yes," she said, putting on her coat.

"All right, then."

They both walked outside.

"Wait a minute!" Loran said. "Where—what— Mother!"

"We'll be back in a while," Tommy said.

"Where are you taking her?"

"None of your business, sis. Be ready, though. When we get back, we're going again. You, too."

"In your dreams," Loran said.

"That young-un of yours needs her legs switched," he said to Maddie.

"Too late now," Maddie said. "See you later," she said to Loran, giving her a clear I-know-what-I'm-doing look.

Loran stood on the porch, completely incredulous as her mother walked to the old truck parked on the narrow rutted road leading to the highway. Tommy Garth actually opened the door for her and she got inside, giving Loran a little wave through the window as the truck pulled away.

"You take good care of her!" Loran yelled after the truck.

She went back inside, tossed the flowers into the garbage can, then fished them out again. She took the wrapper off, cut the stems shorter with a good deal more force than was necessary, found a water glass tall enough to put them in, muttering to herself all the while.

This is crazy!

Where could he be taking her? And why on earth would she go?

Besides that, Loran had no idea what that remark about her needing her "legs switched" meant—except that it was disparaging.

It suddenly occurred to her that Maddie might be telling him about *her*.

Great.

She was far too keyed up to stay at the cabin, but she

finished the load of laundry, made up the sofa and left it open. Then she picked up her purse and headed for town and the discount department store where she could buy some more clothes she didn't want and hoped not to need.

She shopped. She ate some reasonably edible French fries at a fast-food place. And when she returned to the cabin, Tommy's truck was parked near the porch. She braced herself and got out, taking her time about getting her bag full of rustic clothes out of the SUV—just in case Tommy wanted to avoid a face-to-face encounter with his newly revealed love child.

He didn't, apparently. He was sitting by himself at the table under one of the windows when Loran opened the door, drinking coffee and staring at the view. A shaft of sunlight angled through the windowpane and warmed a patch on the floor. She could see the motes of dust floating in the light.

He glanced at her when she came in, but he didn't say anything.

"Where's my mother?" she asked.

"Resting up."

"*Why?*"

"She's got a big day ahead of her, sis."

"No, she doesn't—and don't call me *sis!*"

He gave her a look, but he didn't respond to what could only be described as an invitation to annoy each other.

"Is…she all right?" Loran asked after a moment.

"She's a little tired," he said. The word *tired* sounded like it should have been paired with *and feathered*. "She's all right, though. I think she's looking forward to seeing people."

"What people?"

"Can't say, for sure. She's been asleep about a half hour or so. I'm to wake her up in about fifteen minutes."

"*I'll* wake her. You can—run along."

"You ever heard tell of a truce, sis? I'm thinking you and me ought to declare one. For your mama's sake," he added, before she could tell him what she thought of his truce and where he could put it.

"You care about my mama's sake these days, do you?" she asked instead.

He didn't dignify the loaded question with a response—or not the one she might have expected. "I'm glad to see her again," he said simply, which was hardly the tune he'd been singing yesterday.

"I can't imagine that you'd have much in common now."

"We don't," he said, still not allowing himself to be insulted. "Never did, if you want the truth. She was too good for a misbegotten son of a bitch like me."

Loran gave a quiet sigh, the need to quarrel with him dissipating suddenly. She was satisfied for the moment that Maddie hadn't told him he was her father. She poured herself a cup of coffee and sat down at the counter that divided the kitchen area from the rest of the cabin. She glanced at him from time to time, but she had no intention of talking to him, which apparently suited him. He went back to looking out the window.

"Might be you ought to ask me one of those questions you've got stewing—before they get up and start walking around the room," he said.

"I don't have any questions *you* could answer."

"Suit yourself," he said.

After a time, the door to the bedroom opened and Maddie came out. She looked…fine. Refreshed. Almost happy.

"Mother—" Loran began, getting up from the stool she'd been sitting on. Maddie held up her hand.

"Now don't fuss over me. I don't need it."

"Are you ready to go?" Tommy asked for the second time today. "You, too," he said to Loran.

"Oh, I think we'll pass," Loran said, and he gave her a look that reminded her that she was on dangerous ground usurping her mother's right to accept and decline her own invitations.

"Actually, I want to go—and I want you to come along," Maddie said to her.

Loran looked at them both for a moment, then capitulated. She had no choice. Earlier, she'd pleaded with Maddie for a chance to help her in some way, and clearly Maddie remembered the offer. Loran shrugged her acceptance.

"Good," Maddie said.

"Are you going to wear that?" Tommy said.

"Are you talking to me?" Loran asked pointedly.

"Yeah. And you'd know it if I could say *sis* without making you mad."

Loran decided it was better just to ignore him. "Mother, I don't—"

"He's teasing you. You look fine."

She glanced at Tommy Garth. Incredibly, he *was* teasing her. And he was good at it, just like Meyer was.

She frowned. "If we're going…wherever we're going, let's go."

"I'll be along directly," Tommy said to Maddie as they walked out onto the porch. "*She* knows the way."

But even if *she* hadn't, *she* wouldn't have given him the satisfaction of letting him know it.

Loran gave an inward sigh and wondered when it was she'd become a petulant five-year-old. Nothing about this situation brought out the best in her.

"So where are we going?" she asked once she and Maddie were in the SUV.

"Up to his place. On Lady Ridge."

Loran swallowed a barrage of protests. "Okay," she said instead. "You'd better hang on. We have to go by Estelle's house to get there. Meyer said we don't stop no matter what."

"Good advice," Maddie said.

"Oh, God," Loran said suddenly.

"What?"

"This Estelle everybody's afraid of. She's my *grand-mother*."

Maddie reached over and patted her on the shoulder in commiseration.

Once again, Loran managed to get past Estelle's house without incident.

"Do I get to know why we're going up here?" Loran asked as they bumped along the logging road.

"It's a get-together. People I haven't seen in a long time."

"Mother, did you tell him? About me?"

"No. Not yet."

"Then what did you talk about?"

"This and that. The changes in the valley. What I've been doing in Washington. Where I put my hillbilly accent."

"Where did you put it?"

"I left it in a class on how to lose one's regional dialect and succeed in the job market—don't you remember? I used to practice on you all the time."

"No. And he's happy with…chitchat?"

"He has to be. It's one of my ground rules. No resurrecting the past."

"I wish I could see a point to all this," Loran said. "If you aren't even going to make him explain why he…did what he did, then—"

"It's too late for explanations. And I don't want to be burdened with what-ifs and if-onlys."

"I still don't understand."

"I don't want to hate him anymore," Maddie said simply.

Other people had arrived at Tommy's place ahead of them—a lot of other people. Children were running and playing in the open field. There were a number of trucks parked here and there. And a Jeep. Some men were piling up wood for what looked like a potential bonfire. Several women were on their way toward the cabin carrying cardboard boxes with towels draped over them.

"Bigger turnout than I thought," Maddie said of the activity.

Loran saw Meyer coming out of the cabin. The man, Bobby Ray, walked with him, warily, his eyes on the ruins of the old cabin off to their left.

"He's afraid of haints," Loran said, more to herself than to Maddie.

"What?" Maddie said, smiling suddenly. "Don't tell me you're picking up the dialect."

"Bobby Ray," Loran said. "He's afraid of the old cabin."

"Meyer and Tommy will take care of him."

Loran watched Meyer join the other men, helping to drag a log and heave it onto the pile. Clearly, he was doing exactly what she'd demanded he do. He was minding his own business.

She realized suddenly that she had Maddie's undivided attention.

"He was engaged to be married," Maddie said. "Meyer," she added for clarity.

Loran frowned, but she didn't pretend that she wasn't curious. Yes. That was the right word. Curious. "Was?" she asked.

"She died."

"Who told you that?"

"He did."

Loran felt a pressing need for additional information—the direct result of the curiosity she admittedly had—but she didn't say anything.

"Have you talked to Kent yet?" Maddie asked, apparently determined to hit *the* topic Loran would rather avoid.

"No."

"You're leaving your house and worldly goods in his care then?"

"I wouldn't say that. If he knows what's good for him, he won't still be there when I get back."

"Men aren't good at taking hints, you know. You better tell him."

Someone rapped sharply on the SUV window on Maddie's side, a woman Maddie apparently recognized. Maddie opened the door and she was all but pulled out of the SUV, where she was immediately surrounded by more women who inundated her with welcome-home hugs.

"Loran—come on!" Maddie called over her shoulder, because the women gave her no time for introductions. "My daughter," she said to one of them, who smiled and motioned for Loran to follow as they swept Maddie along toward the cabin.

Loran sat for a moment, then shored up her determination and got out.

"Wait a minute," Tommy Garth said as she shut the SUV door.

She hadn't seen him arrive, and she sighed. "What?"

"I want you to do something," he said.

"What?" she said again.

"Just for today, I want you to let go of all that worrying you're doing about Maddie—"

"You don't know anything about my worrying." She tried to walk off, but he caught her arm.

"She needs this, sis," he said. "Let her have it. Don't let her see how scared you are."

Loran stopped trying to get away. She wanted to protest, to lash out, but she couldn't. It was true. She was scared, so much so that a complete stranger had seen it. The sand was running through the hourglass, and all she could think about was how little was left.

"Meyer's going to come over here and take you around to meet everybody in a little bit," Tommy continued. "People here think a lot of him. It's good for him to be the one to help you speak to everybody—especially if your mama's going to be staying a while. Maddie raised you, so I know you know how to behave. Now don't go getting all mad again," he said to head off another of their running disputes. "I'm just telling you. Today, you want to be acting like you take after her, not me."

She looked at him a long time. He didn't look away, and neither did she. She stood there, as stubborn as he was, fully aware that whatever she said—or didn't say— would verify what still might be only a suspicion.

No, she suddenly decided. He knew, and he wanted her to know it.

"Who told you?"

"Nobody told me, sis. I'm not as dumb as I look. For one thing, your mama gave you a family name. My family. That don't mean anything to you, but it does to me. Here comes Meyer," he said, and he walked away.

Meyer had indeed left the preparations for a bonfire and was coming in her direction.

"Hey," he said as he walked up.

She forced herself to look at him, to pay attention.

He smiled slightly. "That bad, huh? Come on. Let's work up to this. Go over that way." He pointed toward the ruined cabin. "I've been wanting to get a good look at that place since I was ten years old."

She walked with him. She was only too happy for a respite, however brief, before she had to face the crowd of strangers.

And her newly informed father.

"So why didn't you ever look at it?" she asked, but she was wondering what the woman he'd wanted to marry had been like.

"Nobody was living up here then. Lady Ridge was one more scary place if you happened to be a ten-year-old boy. None of my friends would go, and I never could get away from Nelda's watchful eye long enough to sneak up here by myself. Not that I would have. The lady was still up here as far as us kids were concerned. I didn't think you could bother her and live."

He walked her around what was left of the old structure, kneeling down from time to time and using his pocketknife to show her some of the broken dishes just under the dirt. She could see what was left of the cooking utensils still in the stone hearth.

"Nobody knows what happened to her—the woman who lived here. Nelda says she was a Garth and she stayed up here all by herself, maybe around the time of the Civil War. Her man was gone and then she disappeared, too. People around here supposedly looked for her, but they never found a trace except for the family Bible. Her name was marked out of it. Anyway, she left everything she owned, and this stuff—all these iron pots and candleholders and things—would have been valuable and necessary."

Loran bent down to look at one of the broken pieces of china. She could just make out the pattern. Bluebirds. The bluebirds of happiness on a pink-blossomed bough—with a gold-trimmed edge. The kind of piece Tommy used to make the pins and pendants and charms he sold as jewelry. It was the story they bought, he'd said, and she imagined that he would be very good at telling it.

The area around the cabin wasn't all grown up like the old school had been, she suddenly realized. There was broom straw, but nothing else seemed to grow here—except some kind of green, narrow-blade grass, a few tufts of which had thus far survived the frosts.

"I think we're worrying Bobby Ray," Loran said because she could see him standing among the assorted vehicles, looking in their direction and all but wringing his hands.

"Yeah, that's his worried face," Meyer said.

"What's the bonfire for?" she asked, still looking in Bobby Ray's direction.

"In case more people come than will fit in the cabin. The men will come out here and swap lies. You ready to walk into the lion's den?"

"Is it going to be that bad?" She tried to make the question light.

"No. It's not going to be bad at all. You'll see. All you have to do is be yourself. Smile every now and then, if you feel like it. Eat a lot. Dance a little. And sing."

"Sing?" she said with a certain alarm.

He grinned, and she didn't know if he was teasing her again or not.

More people were arriving. She and Meyer stood and waited as yet another truck bounced over the ground in a wide circle and parked.

"This must be driving Estelle crazy," he said.

"Is she invited?"

Apparently not, she decided, because of the look he gave her.

"I thought Tommy was a hermit," she said as they walked toward the cabin.

"He is, that's part of the big interest in coming up here. He went around inviting people yesterday, and once they got over the shock, they definitely wanted to see what he's been up to. The other part is Maddie coming home again—with you. Besides that, we like to eat."

A burst of music suddenly came from inside the cabin—a banjo and a mandolin or…something.

This was going to be more of an event than she'd realized.

"Warming up," Meyer said. "You like bluegrass?"

"I…don't know," Loran said truthfully. She had some vague notion of the sound but she couldn't really say she'd ever deliberately listened to any.

"Today, you like it," he assured her, and she smiled.

Meyer began the introductions with the very next person they encountered—several persons, actually—rowdy little boys who suddenly grew bashful in her presence and all but toed the ground.

"She sort of works for a bank," Meyer concluded.

"Do you get to take the money home?" one of them asked.

"Nope. Not a penny."

"I wouldn't work there, then," he said.

The introductions continued as she and Meyer made their way toward the porch, and she marveled at his faultless recall of each of their names. There were men and women who had gone to school with her "mama" or with her "Grandmaw Addie," and old men who used to go hunting with her "great grandpap." And men and women both who teased Meyer mercilessly by trying to make him say how pretty he thought Loran was. But no one mentioned Estelle or Foy, not even once. Loran could only conclude that she was the product of families with two very notable bad pennies.

"Is Nelda coming?" she asked as they walked inside the cabin.

"Soon as the pies finish baking," Meyer said. "Pies are her thing, so eat a big piece. And help her keep an eye on the holy box."

"What holy box?"

"The box she's bringing the pies in. If she loses her pie box, we'll never hear the end of it."

Tommy's cabin was different from before. All the woodworking tools and jewelry projects had been moved out of sight and the furniture pushed back against the walls. The inner doors on each side of the chimney had been opened and there was a circular flow of traffic into the far reaches of the cabin and back again. Laughing and talking women unpacked food and tried to carry it to the tables next to the windows without running over the numerous children underfoot.

Meyer kept introducing her to people until the faces and names became one long blur. Some of the quaint given names were often quite beautiful, names that had come into being solely because somebody somewhere had cared enough to take the time and trouble to compose one of their very own.

She could smell coffee and hot bread and fried ham. She looked for Maddie in the bustle to set out the food, but she didn't immediately see her. She saw her brand new father, however. He stood in a group of men on the other side of the room—with a fiddle under his arm.

"This is definitely my day," Meyer said, nodding in Tommy's direction. "I always wanted to hear Tommy Garth play. People say he's one of the best."

"Here comes Nelda," Loran said, moving to help her

carry her cardboard box full of still warm pies. She didn't
want to talk about Tommy Garth's musical skill.

"Thank you, honey," Nelda said. "Just put them pies
over yonder on the table for me. Now, where's that sweet
mama of yourn?"

"She's in here someplace—"

"There she is!" Nelda said, leaving Loran with the
box.

Loran carried it to the table and began to place the
pies on what she thought was the dessert end. The music
started up in earnest behind her, and when she looked
around, she was surprised to see Meyer in the musician
corner with a banjo in his hands. The song was lively and
some of the guests began to dance—clogging, she supposed—several children and two of the old men, all of
whom were surprisingly good. More and more people
joined in. Bobby Ray came and got Maddie by the hand.

The floor vibrated with the stomping of feet. The
music escalated until the room grew hot and everything
became a blur of motion and faces and sound. Someone
threw open the cabin door. Loran watched Maddie from
the sidelines, both delighted and incredulous. Dancing
Maddie. Happy Maddie.

Loran moved around the edge of the room to get a
better view, aware suddenly that Tommy Garth had been
right. Maddie needed this.

Loran looked for him at the other end of the room.
He wasn't playing with the others. He was watching
Maddie just as she was, the fiddle still under his arm. The
sadness she saw on his face at that moment might have
been heartbreaking—if she'd been inclined to forgive
him for abandoning the young and trusting girl he was

supposed to have loved. But she didn't forgive him. She would have to care about him in order to do that, and she didn't. Still, she would do as he asked. She would try to hide her fear—because it was the best thing for her mother, not because he wanted it.

The image of Maddie's neighbors, the little girl and her father, rose in Loran's mind. There was nothing about this stranger with a fiddle that would make her even remotely consider the possibility that he might have been a loving and delighted father like the one Sara Kessler had.

The music ended and Meyer stepped forward to get everyone's attention.

"Glad you all could make it," he said to a round of applause. "Now you know why we're getting together today—but in case you don't, this is a big 'welcome home' for Maddie Kimball. And for her daughter, Loran. Now, I didn't meet Loran until a couple of days ago, and Loran—I was worried about Loran," he continued, gesturing to where she stood. "She didn't know what to make of me—she didn't know whether to kiss me or chain me to a porch."

The crowd whooped with laughter, and Loran laughed with them. Clearly, she was getting used to this kind of backwoods banter.

"We're going to have a good time, a lot of music and dancing, lot of good eating, lot of good company. But first I'm going to ask Poppy to give us a word of prayer."

The room grew quiet except for a fussy baby, and Poppy began his prayer with the practiced ease of a man who was used to speaking to God in public. Loran's mind began to wander—to Maddie and how to persuade her to go back to Arlington—until she realized that he'd said her name.

"...she weren't born here," Poppy was saying, "but she got here as quick as she could—and we thank you for getting her safe home."

Loran stood there, head bowed, not daring to look up. *Safe home.*

She wasn't home or safe. She didn't belong here. She didn't want to be here. All she wanted was for her and Maddie to leave. Didn't they realize that? She took a deep breath, and the prayer ended.

The musicians conferred for a moment—except for Tommy—then started a song about the devil wearing hypocrite shoes. Loran especially enjoyed the part about giving up snuff and the pointed looks the musicians sent in Nelda's direction.

Nelda swatted the air at them and Loran crossed the room to where Maddie stood after all that exertion.

"You're going to have to teach me some of those moves," Loran said to her and Maddie laughed.

"I think I'll pass," she said. "But I expect a little clogging would do wonders for the investment bankers' Christmas party."

They sat down on straight chairs in the corner with a group of women who had clearly been waiting for the opportunity to interrogate them both. Loran answered everything she was asked, even the questions about whether or not she was married, had ever been married or, in lieu of that, if she had a "sweetheart."

"Nelda says she's looking for a sweetheart, but she ain't," one of the women said.

"I'm a-looking," Nelda insisted. "You know how these

old men are. They're always a-wanting somebody thirty years younger'n they are—and I'm a-telling you, a man a hundred and ten years old is *hard* to find."

Loran laughed out loud with the rest of the women, and the music in the background changed to "Keep on the Sunny Side," apparently the place where she and Nelda were supposed to maneuver Meyer. That song ended and another one began, one which required serious support from a banjo—Meyer's. She kept glancing in his direction, impressed by his ability to play. Once, he had the audacity to wink, as if he were fully aware of her unabashed amazement.

Someone tapped her on the shoulder, one of the little boys she'd been introduced to earlier, the one who thought she should give up banking.

"Your car's a-ringing," he told her.

"Oh, thanks. My cell phone," she said to Maddie. "We must be in a place with reception."

She quickly left the cabin—in the company of the little boys who wanted to see whatever there was to see. She was surprised by how long the shadows had gotten. The sun would be gone soon, and the temperature had fallen. Three of the men had lit the bonfire and were standing around it.

Loran got to the SUV just in time to hear the phone stop. She reached in to get it so she could check the caller ID.

Kent.

She hesitated, then laid the phone in a cup holder in the console. She had no wish to talk to Kent. More importantly, she had no need to talk to him.

"Well, get in," she said to the boys hovering around

her—and was nearly trampled for her trouble. She waited until they had stopped scrambling for seats, then gave them the full sales pitch, demonstrating everything the SUV could do, down to a short test ride around and around the cabin. When she finally stopped and they all got out, she had the distinct impression that she'd made four friends for life.

Someone had declared it time to eat when she and the boys returned to the cabin. She found Maddie again and got into line with her and the rest of Tommy Garth's impromptu guests, surprised by how hungry she was in spite of her current state of mind. Maddie didn't ask her about the phone call. She was busy looking at the musicians, at Meyer, who suddenly put down his banjo and went outside.

Loran had never seen such an array of food on what had to have been very short notice—fried chicken, ham, potato salad, cornbread, biscuits, jam, beans, corn, apple pie, blackberry pie—and the things she still couldn't recognize. Everything tasted wonderful. She kept looking for Meyer, but he didn't return, and Tommy supervised the celebration from afar, still holding the fiddle.

"Do you think he's ever going to play that thing?" she asked Maddie.

"Maybe after we eat," Maddie said.

But Tommy didn't wait until after. He waited until everyone had a piled-high plate and a place to sit. Then he stepped over the children clustered around on the floor and moved into the middle of the room. Without prelude, he placed the fiddle on his shoulder and bowed a long and perfect solitary note. He looked at no one, and the note slowly evolved into a melody, into a three-

quarter-time waltz, one filled with wistfulness and longing, a melancholy yearning for something unattainable
and unnamed.

It was haunting. It was beautiful. No one spoke. No
one ate. They listened. Loran could see Maddie's face. It
betrayed nothing of what she must be feeling. Was it a
love song? A plea for forgiveness? A farewell? Loran had
no idea. She only knew it was something Tommy Garth
was telling Maddie Kimball—as if they were the only two
people in the room.

After a time, one of the old men picked up his guitar
and began to strum a soft accompaniment, underpinning
the melody with a sorrow of his own. Loran could feel
the prickling of tears behind her eyelids, and she took a
deep breath and then another.

There was an awkward silence when the song ended,
then a burst of applause from the people who understood
that they had witnessed a rarity, something to be savored and talked about for years to come. Nelda was
dabbing her eyes with the corner of her apron.

The uneasy moment passed because Tommy suddenly launched into a lively, foot-tapping tune, one
which immediately elevated the mood. When the song
ended, he put the fiddle away and got his own plate of
food, taking it to join the men on the other side of the
room.

The conversations and laughter rose and fell as people shared some remembrance with each other and with
Maddie. Loran watched and listened. She had never experienced such a sense of community. She hadn't known
that this kind of event even existed. It wasn't the party
concept as she understood it at all. It was simply a happy

occasion—with no hidden business agenda whatsoever as far as she could tell.

The children got together to sing several songs, "Do, Lord" and "I'll Fly Away" and the one Maddie had mentioned, "Farther Along." Meyer still hadn't come back. At one point, Loran could hear a commotion—voices—coming from the direction of the bonfire. It seemed to her that everyone looked toward Tommy, who immediately went outside.

"Maddie, honey, are you ready to go?" Nelda asked quietly.

Maddie looked at her for a moment, then nodded. "Loran?"

"I'm ready," Loran said, but it wasn't quite the truth. She had been enjoying herself here, and far more than she would have ever imagined.

Maddie went around the room to say thank you and goodbye to each person who had come. Her sudden departure seemed to surprise no one—except her daughter. It was obvious that the homecoming celebration was now over. The women began packing up the remnants of the food and putting Tommy's cabin back into order. Some of the men moved a table or two, the rest wandered outside.

Loran walked into the next room with Nelda's now-empty pie pans, intending to put them in the cardboard box Nelda had brought.

"You remember how your grandpap used to wrap you up and bring you to me when things got bad between your mama and daddy?" Nelda was saying to Maddie. "Sometimes in the middle of the night, here he'd come with that sweet Maddie, all swaddled in one of Adeline's pretty quilts and looking like she was a present on Christmas morning."

"I remember," Maddie said.

"Well, you come home with me now, honey. Like you used to when you was little. We got a lot we need to talk over, you and me."

Maddie didn't answer her, and for a moment she looked as if she were going to cry. She also looked too tired to talk, and it was all Loran could do not to point it out to both of them.

"All right," Maddie said in spite of her obvious fatigue. "You come ride with us."

"I been hoping to get me a ride in that big car," Nelda said. "Let me find my box—the pies fit in it good and I'm right partial to it."

Loran gave Nelda her pie tins and waited, working to keep her questions and her objections to herself. She realized, too, that more than one person had taken to looking out the window.

"Let's go," Maddie said when Nelda was ready.

"Why do I feel like a bum being rushed to the curb?" Loran asked as they walked to the SUV.

"We're just trying not to cause anybody...trouble," Maddie said. "That's all."

"Anybody who? What kind of trouble?" Loran asked, but Maddie had shifted into her nonanswer mode.

"You did fine," she said. "Everybody liked you."

"I...had a good time," Loran said truthfully.

She let Maddie and Nelda into the SUV and looked toward the bonfire, but she still didn't see Tommy or Meyer.

Maddie and Nelda chatted on the way down the

mountain, both of them falling silent as they neared Estelle's house. The house was dark and stayed dark as Loran drove past.

It suddenly occurred to her that there might be more to Maddie's visit with Nelda than nostalgia and that she might want to talk to her about things that would be painful for her daughter to hear.

"I think I'll just leave the SUV with you and walk up the path to the cabin," she said. "It's not that far. You can drive back when you're ready."

"I…might stay the night," Maddie said, confirming Loran's suspicion that there was more to the visit than catching up.

Maddie waited in the SUV for a moment after Nelda had gotten out. "Are you all right?" she asked.

"Me? Yes. Why?"

"Well, today was a little…unusual."

"Compared to the previous one or two, it wasn't."

Maddie smiled. "I'm glad you're here. You're not afraid to stay in Meyer's cabin, are you?"

"Not yet," Loran said. "See you in the morning."

CHAPTER 13

The fog lay among the trees and rolled into the hollows as Loran made her way quickly up the path. She knew which direction to take well enough, but the sun was nearly gone and she didn't want to get lost.

The fog grew thin and patchy the higher she climbed, and the temperature dropped noticeably, making Meyer's cabin a welcome sight when it finally came into view. She went inside quickly and closed the door behind herself. She found the wall switch and flipped the lights on, considerably cheered by no longer being outside in the near dark.

The room was cold enough for her to see her breath. The cabin had two chimneys, one with a flue and a woodstove—about which she knew nothing—and the other with propane gas logs in a fireplace. She didn't know anything about those, either, except that they'd been burning earlier. The only thing she knew how to operate was a thermostat—which she didn't see anyplace.

She left her coat on and filled the kettle. She could at least make something hot to drink, and then she'd try to find a way to turn on the logs. It was so quiet, except when the wind whistled around the cabin, making her look expectantly toward the door or the windows from time to time. She thought suddenly of the woman who had lived alone up on Lady Ridge, her man gone and no one to rely on except herself. Had she been afraid?

Of course she had, Loran decided, if she'd been in touch with reality at all.

The kettle whistled eventually, and she turned off the burner. She made tea and was about to drink it when she heard a small sound outside, a swishing through the fallen leaves she couldn't attribute to the wind.

Deer, she thought as she moved to the window to look out—she hadn't heard a vehicle. She couldn't see anything—anyone—but then she realized someone was standing near the edge of the porch. Someone else stood beyond the yard in the trees.

She waited, her heart beginning to pound. There was no reason for whomever it was not to just come up and knock on the door. The lights were on. She was obviously at home. When one of them finally did knock, she wasn't at all certain whether to feel relieved or panicked, because she couldn't remember whether or not she'd locked the door.

"Who is it?" she called.

"It's me," Meyer said.

She frowned and opened the door. Meyer stood there—with Poppy from the store. She looked from one of them to the other, wondering why they both looked so…doubtful.

"What's wrong? Is Maddie—?"

"Maddie's fine," Meyer said. "We're just…"

"We was wanting to make sure you weren't needing anything," Poppy said.

"Like what?"

Neither of them answered, but Meyer gave Poppy a look.

"Well, I reckon, I'll just be going on. My old woman will be a-looking for me," Poppy said in a way he clearly hoped was convincing.

"Poppy," Loran said as he was about to step off the porch.

He turned and looked at her.

"Thank you."

"What for, honey?"

"For the prayer you said for me today."

"You're as welcome as can be, honey," he said. "It was the least I could do after not helping you when you needed it, when you was just trying to get up there to see Tommy. Sometimes we stick together a little too much around here. Sometimes when we don't need to—and sometimes when we ought not."

He stood for a moment, then gave her a smile and a nod and walked down the steps toward the long drive.

Loran turned her attention to Meyer. "What's wrong?" she asked again.

"We...sort of misplaced Estelle," he said. "After she tried to crash the welcome-home party."

"Is that good or bad?"

"Not so good when she's all fired up."

"Is she looking for Maddie?"

"No."

Loran sighed and asked the obvious. "So what does she want with me?"

He didn't answer the question. He looked off into the distance, then up at the night sky. "You want to go for a walk?"

"What, again?"

"Yeah."

"In the cold and the dark with Estelle on the loose?"

"Yeah."

Loran looked at him. He was trying not to smile, and he had no idea how endearing that was.

She shrugged and closed the door behind her. "Okay. Where are we going?"

"Down to the road to get Maddie's car. I was going to bring it up here, but I…"

"Didn't want Estelle to hear you coming," she said.

"You're pretty quick, you know that?"

"Oh, yeah." She fell into step with him as they reached the winding dirt road that led down to the highway. It was much colder now, and she pulled the jacket she'd never taken off closer. "Don't we need a flashlight?" she asked to show him just how quick she was.

"Got one."

One he wasn't using.

"How worried should I be—about Estelle?"

"Well, she's not dangerous. She's just loud and mean—like a drunk, only she doesn't drink. Poppy can set her down, though. He followed me in his truck, in case Estelle happened to be up here."

Loran stepped in a hole and would have stumbled if Meyer hadn't caught her arm. He let go as soon as she'd righted herself.

"That was a good thing—what you did."

"What thing?" she asked.

"Thanking Poppy for the prayer. He appreciated it."

"I meant it. I don't know that I've ever been mentioned by name in a prayer like that before."

"Well, you'd best get used to it."

She stopped walking suddenly because of a rustling in the underbrush. "What's that?" she whispered.

"Something nocturnal that doesn't hibernate," Meyer said. "Of the four-legged, not-dangerous persuasion."

"You're sure?"

"I'm sure. Probably wouldn't eat people anyway."

"Oh, very funny."

They started walking again, into the fog now.

"Why did you want me to come along if you're not worried about Estelle?"

He waited so long to answer, she thought he wasn't going to.

"I was thinking you'd want me to leave as soon as I brought Maddie's car up the hill, and I'm trying to stretch the visit out."

She frowned, trying to decide if he was teasing again or not.

"Give me your hand," he said.

"Why?" she asked warily.

"So I don't lose you in the fog."

She smiled. Now he was teasing. She held her hand out and he took it, his fingers warm and strong around hers—and rough from all the outside work he did. He tucked both their hands into his coat pocket.

"Nothing like walking to make distances real," she said after a time, mostly to stop thinking about how much she liked this—holding his hand in the dark.

"I hear that," he said. "So what do you think of the high country?" He slowed their pace as they rounded yet another curve. She realized that perhaps he had meant it when he'd said he wanted to stretch his visit out.

"It's different," she said without hesitation. "I'm a stranger in a strange land."

"You don't look down on us." It was a statement of fact, not a question.

"I was in government-sponsored day care when I was little—while Maddie was trying to get an education and a good paying job. She and I started out at the bottom. I can't look down on anybody, even if I wanted to. And if I did want to, Maddie would box my ears."

"Or switch your legs. You know about leg-switching?"

"Only that Tommy told Maddie I needed it done," she said, and he laughed.

"So what is it?"

"Mostly it's a threat of corporal punishment with a very thin limb from the nearest shrubbery reserved for bad little girls and boys. You never got your legs switched, I take it."

"Never. I never even heard of it. Maddie didn't talk about anything that had to do with her childhood. I didn't even know where she grew up. She has a way of answering your questions without answering. I learned pretty early on that she was only going to tell me what she wanted me to know—period."

"Whatever happened between her and Tommy must have been really bad. This is a hard place to forget."

"You sound like you've tried it."

"I have. So has Tommy Garth. Looks like all three of us emigrated in a circle."

"I like Nelda," she said after a time.

"Nelda walks the walk," he said.

She could see the highway now, and Maddie's car parked near the road that led up to the cabin.

"You want me to take you home?" she asked.

"That would be up there," he said, pointing in the direction they'd just come. She had forgotten for the moment that she and Maddie had taken over his main residence.

"Somewhere else then?"

"No. I'd rather you took me home."

They stared at each other in the dark.

"I want to make one more sweep—in case Estelle's around," he said.

"Okay."

He handed her the keys. "You drive."

"You're going to trust me on this mountain track in the dark?"

"Yeah, I am," he said. "You are going to turn on the headlights, right?"

"I thought I would."

"Okay, then. No problem."

She got in and drove them back up the steep and curvy road to the cabin.

"Are you coming in?" she asked when she'd parked the car near the porch.

"I wouldn't mind getting in out of the cold."

"I take it Estelle knows I'm yet another one of Tommy's illegitimate children," Loran said as they went inside.

"No, I don't think she does—or she won't admit it. What she thinks is that you and Maddie are lying."

"For what purpose? She doesn't have anything I want. Tommy, either."

"You've got Tommy's attention. That's enough to put you on her wrong side."

"They're that...close?"

"Close? They're not close at all. I doubt he's even spoken to her in years."

"Why not?"

"I don't know. But I do know from personal experience it doesn't take much to get her all stirred up—it's cold in here." He walked to the mantel over the fireplace and adjusted a small thermostat she hadn't had time to locate earlier.

"You okay?" he asked as the flames leaped up in a very authentic way around the fake logs.

"Fine, except for wondering why people keep asking me that."

He looked into her eyes, smiled a little, but then the smile faded.

"This is not a good idea," he said.

She made no attempt to feign ignorance. She knew exactly what he meant.

"Maybe...you should tell me to leave," he said.

She took off her jacket and moved to stand closer to the fireplace.

He came closer, too.

"We both know what's what and where this is heading. It's just going to cause us both a lot of trouble and heartache."

She thought he had defined their situation perfectly, but she still didn't comment. She gave a quiet sigh.

"It would be good if you said something right about here," he said.

She turned around and looked directly into his eyes again. Beautiful eyes. Kind eyes.

Sad eyes.

"Don't go," she said.

"Okay," he said agreeably, making her smile. Somehow he had the knack for doing that, for making her feel better whatever the situation—and what a novel experience it was.

She stepped closer to him then and rested her forehead against his shoulder. He stood for a moment before he put his arms around her and gathered her to him—as if she were something long awaited and highly prized. His cheek against hers was rough with beard stubble, and he smelled of soap and sunshine and the out-of-doors. She could feel the tremor of desire in his body as she leaned against him and slid her arms around his waist.

"People are going to talk," he said. One last warning as they stood on the brink.

"Ah, well. Can't be helped."

She lifted her mouth to his. The kiss was sweet and gentle—at first—but the warm rush of desire made her grip the back of his coat and press her body into his.

Nothing but trouble and heartache. That was the best they could hope for, and, at that moment, she didn't care. She wanted to forget everything. She wanted to feel something besides worry and sorrow. She wanted to hide. Just for a little while.

In him.

He stepped away from her to turn out the light, to lock the door, to rummage in a drawer and find the protection he kept there. She waited for him by the made-up sofa, wondering who else had been here, like this.

"Is this where you sleep?" she asked.

"Yeah."

"Good," she said. She wanted to be in his bed. And she wanted him to remember.

He took off his coat.

"I don't know if Maddie's coming back tonight," she said.

"I don't think Nelda's going to let her leave."

He reached for her then. She went into his embrace, but she wanted to look at him for a moment, and she leaned back to touch his face gently with her fingertips and to stare into his eyes.

"What?" he asked, trying not to smile.

She didn't answer. She hugged him instead, hard, smiling to herself and thinking of the remark he'd made at the welcome-home gathering. It was true. She hadn't known whether to kiss him or chain him to a porch.

She began to unbutton his shirt, slowly, painstakingly, until he grew impatient and helped, until they were undressing each other, hurrying now to be rid of the last barriers between them, to lie down, to slide close, skin to skin and breath to breath.

"I...haven't done this in a while," he said.

"It'll come back to you," she whispered, making him laugh.

When he kissed her again, there was nothing tentative about it. He knew how to do this, how to kiss and touch and taste, regardless of the dry spell. She closed her eyes and gave herself up to the sensation of his hands and his mouth and to the first stirring of pleasure. Her breath caught as the pleasure intensified.

Desire.

It diffused through her body. So acute and so...sweet. She had experienced desire before, but this was different somehow. She had felt the hunger, the need, but this time, amid all of that, she felt…safe.

Suddenly it wasn't enough just to receive. She moved closer to him, stroked his body, returned his kisses, quickly learning what he liked just as he had with her.

There were no words between them, only the wanting. Hers. His. There, in the flickering light from the fireplace, she felt herself open like a flower to the sun, vulnerable but not afraid. Whatever she was, whatever the very essence of Loran Kimball might be, she offered to him, without reservation, in spite of the consequences.

Trouble and heartache.

For them both.

But they tumbled together, and their bodies joined, until she could feel nothing but the soul-piercing ache of her need for him. It grew, soared and peaked, made her cry out, until at last she lay spent and sated and amazed.

"So much…for the no-kissing…thing," he said, his body lying heavy and still welcome on hers.

She closed her eyes when he moved away from her to lie on his back, drifting on the edge of sleep.

It wasn't until he reached down to hold her hand that the question formed in her mind.

"What was her name?" she asked in the semidarkness. "Maddie told me," she added. She thought that he wouldn't be coy, wouldn't pretend not to understand what she wanted to know. She had never asked any other man about his previous loves. She had never cared enough to ask.

She could hear him draw a quiet breath before he answered.

"Jolie. Her name was Jolie."

"What was she like?"

"She was…a good soldier."

"What happened to her?"

"Mortar attack on the base. She was in the wrong place at the wrong time."

His fingers tightened around hers.

"You remind me of her. You don't look anything like her, but you're strong like she was. Can-do, all the way. She wanted to be a teacher—she really liked that commercial on TV—the one that says if it wasn't for teachers, where would the doctors come from? She was from Iowa and she joined the military to get money for college like I did. I went out there to see her mother when I got back, Jolie didn't get along with her old man. I thought I could at least tell her mom about her, answer questions, you know? Her old man didn't want to hear anything I had to say, and he wouldn't even let me talk to her."

"It's his loss," Loran said, turning her head to look at him.

"Yeah. I guess." He drew a long breath. "Are you sorry we did this?" he asked bluntly.

"No."

She hesitated, then slid close to him, pressing her face into his shoulder. How could she be sorry? Because of him she was beginning to understand what had been missing in her life. If anything, she was afraid.

"Loran—"

"I'm not sorry, Meyer," she said.

He didn't say anything else for a time. She thought he had fallen asleep, but he hadn't.

"You and—"

"What?" she asked when he didn't continue.

"Nothing. I was thinking about you and Tommy, and it's none of my business. I can't be mixing how you feel about your father with how Jolie felt about hers."

She rose up on her elbow to look at him. "He's not my father. He's—I don't know what he is."

"It's still a waste. Life is too short, believe—"

She pressed her fingertips against his lips to stop him and he stared into her eyes. She kissed him then, with growing urgency, the invitation very clear.

He wrapped his arms around her, but not to follow in the direction she was leading. "Do I get to ask any questions?"

"About what?"

"About the guy who made you cry—the day you got here."

She sighed. "No. This bed is only big enough for the two of us, and we have other things to do." She kissed him again, and this time, he held back only for a moment before he returned it, before he let desire win over curiosity.

"I'm going to take it slow this time," he whispered.

CHAPTER 14

Maddie watched as Meyer had Loran kneel down beside him in front of the woodstove so he could show her how to build a fire.

"Turn the drafts clockwise until they're open enough to give the fire an air supply," he was saying. "Turn them the other way until they're closed tight when you want the fire to go out." His hand rested briefly on her knee as he moved on to explain the fine points of opening and closing the damper. At the same time, he had her listening to the Blue Ridge FM radio station, one that played bluegrass music.

"Hear that?" he said when a song lamenting abandonment, dark skies and high water, came on. "If you're going to appreciate bluegrass, you've got to know how to suffer."

"Be down and misplaced," Loran said, smiling into his eyes.

A lover's smile, Maddie realized. A smile that made her think of the way she'd once smiled at Tommy Garth. She wondered if she and Tommy had been as obvious. Apparently so. Nelda had certainly noticed it.

Meyer looked up when he remembered they had an audience.

"Okay," he said. "You're all set. I've got to go to work.

Try not to burn the house down. Maddie, anything you need?"

"Nothing," she said truthfully. She was feeling good today—mentally if not physically. She felt more at peace than she had...ever, she suddenly realized, and these two were at least partially responsible for it.

Loran's cell phone rang suddenly, and she hunted it down to answer it. It was a call from work apparently, and Maddie watched as her daughter shifted into executive mode, her side of the conversation direct and incisive and full of investment jargon. Loran was clearly in her element—something that was not lost on the man who had just been teaching her how to light a woodstove.

Meyer and Loran.

The ex-soldier and the investment banker. The hillbilly and the flatlander. Maddie took a moment to consider the viability of such a relationship. Stranger things had happened, she supposed, but she had no expectations. Relationships were difficult enough when backgrounds matched. She and Tommy Garth were proof enough of that. The best she could hope for was that both of them would be happy while it lasted and that neither of them would get hurt.

She gave a quiet sigh. She hadn't felt like eating at lunchtime. She didn't feel like eating now. She felt like lying down somewhere and going to sleep, but she wouldn't do that, either.

"Meyer, Nelda said something about there being a gazebo up here like the one at Lilac Hill."

"It's down that way," he said, pointing toward the area in back of the cabin. "There's a path. It's not that far. It's rougher than the one at Lilac Hill, but it's a nice place to enjoy the view."

Meyer hesitated, but Loran was still engrossed in whatever the call was about. He left without saying good-bye to her, and Maddie put on her coat.

"I'm going to walk down to the gazebo behind the cabin," she whispered to Loran, who nodded and continued her phone conversation.

Maddie walked slowly so as not to tax her waning stamina any more than necessary. It was good to be out in the sunlight. She felt better as she made her way down the path. She didn't realize until it was too late that the gazebo was occupied. Tommy sat on the railing, whittling on a piece of wood.

"I thought you'd wander out this way sooner or later," he said.

"And why is that?"

"Because this is the kind of high lonesome place you like."

"Used to like," she said, in spite of the fact that she was indeed here.

"Not too bad there in the sun," he said, going back to the whittling.

She stood for a moment, then sat down on the sunny bench he'd indicated. Neither of them said anything. There was just the sound of nature around them—a rustling in the dead leaves from time to time and the call of birds. She stretched her legs out and closed her eyes, savoring the warmth of the sun on her face. She could hear the faint noise his knife made against the wood.

"I thought she was younger," he said after what seemed a long while. "She don't look as old as she is—

takes that after you, I reckon. It took me a while to figure out she was mine. I didn't guess till I asked Nelda
about her real daddy. Nelda, she looked like a coon dog
caught in the chicken house. That, and you giving her
the Garth family name we always talked about using for
one of our young-uns."

Maddie opened her eyes. He seemed to be waiting for
her to do just that.

"I reckon you had your reasons for not telling me."

"Yes," Maddie said, closing her eyes again.

"She's…a pretty thing."

"Yes."

"Smart, I reckon."

"Yes," Maddie said again. "Very."

"She wouldn't give me air in a jug, though."

"I wouldn't, either." She opened her eyes again and
found him smiling. In spite of herself, she smiled in return.

"Are you…scared?" he asked.

She looked at him, trying to decide what he was asking. It was a test, she suddenly realized. He wanted to see
if she would tell him the truth. And he wasn't asking if
she was afraid of being here with him. He was asking if
she was afraid of dying.

"Yes," she said.

He looked away.

"I hunt in these woods. I reckon you'll be seeing me
around now and again."

She didn't say anything to that, and he suddenly got
off the rail and walked away, taking a different path from
the one she'd come down. She watched him until he disappeared into the trees.

* * *

Loran laid the cell phone down on the counter and looked around the cabin, vaguely surprised that she was alone. She had been so engrossed in the call that she'd barely registered that Maddie had said she was going… somewhere. And Meyer…

She stood there, remembering the taste and the feel of him and marveling that she had no regrets about last night. None. In fact, she was already missing him.

But clearly she was missing her real life, as well. She had enjoyed handling the sudden problem with a client's investment portfolio, assessing the information available and devising a strategy. Even now, her mind was eager to formulate a plan B in case the initial one didn't work.

She gave a quiet sigh and decided not to go looking for Maddie. She was clever enough to know that there would be times when Maddie would want to be alone and times when she would need company, even if she didn't say so. The trick would be trying to tell which was which.

She straightened up the cabin, folding the pull-out sofa back into a place to sit instead of make love. She and Meyer had been up and dressed and quietly eating breakfast by the time Maddie had returned this morning. Loran had no idea whether or not she realized that he had spent the night.

Loran washed the breakfast dishes, washed a load of laundry, paced.

Great, she thought. She had cabin fever already.

She looked at her cell phone lying on the counter, then picked it up and dialed her home number. Surprisingly, or perhaps not, Kent answered.

"Loran, where the hell are you!" he said by way of greeting.

"North Carolina," she said.

"Well, when are you coming back?"

"Kent, I know about Celia," she said instead of giving him her itinerary.

He didn't say anything. For a long time. She could hear him breathing.

"Kent?"

"Loran...I'm sorry. I don't know what else to say—"

"I'm sure you are. But it doesn't really matter in the long run."

"Look, can we talk about this when you get back? It's not what you think, not really."

"Of course it's what I think, Kent. There's no point in talking."

"I don't know what you expect—"

"I expect you to move out," she said before he could give her a laundry list of justifications for his misbehavior. "As soon as possible. Give the key to my personal assistant. I'll be calling her to see if she's gotten it."

"Loran—"

"Goodbye, Kent."

She ended the call and walked to the window to look out. She could just see Maddie standing on the side of the path, her hand stretched out and resting on the trunk of a large tree.

She looked away to pick up a coffee mug she'd missed when she'd washed the dishes, and when she looked back, Maddie was still standing there.

Loran watched for a moment longer, until she realized suddenly that something was wrong. She put the cup down and ran to the door and out of the cabin, hurrying down the path in Maddie's direction.

"Mother?" she said when she reached her.

Maddie looked at her. She was so pale and tears were streaming down her face. "I can't—make it," she managed to say.

"What?" Loran stepped forward and took her by the arm. She was trembling.

"I can't make it—up the hill—"

"Okay. I'll help you."

She put her arm around Maddie's waist to support her. When Maddie tried to take a step, her legs nearly buckled. She clung to Loran hard and, after a moment, they tried walking again, slowly, painfully.

Loran had to all but carry her, trying to keep them on a steady course, one wobbly step at a time.

"I hate this," Maddie said, weeping openly now. "I *hate* it."

"You want to rest a minute?"

"No. I want to lie down, and I don't want to do it here."

"Okay. Let's keep going."

Loran looked around at a sound, a man walking through the trees.

Tommy Garth.

"What are you doing hanging around?" Loran asked as he came toward them.

"You better be glad I am, sis. Here—"

He pushed his way in between them and picked Maddie up bodily, carrying her up the steep path toward the cabin without protest from either of them.

"You get too big for your britches again, Maddie Kimball?"

"Yes," she said, her head resting against his cheek.

"You always was bad about that. She folded up one time when she was getting over the typhoid," he said to Loran. "You ever tell her about that?"

"No," Maddie said.

"I carried her all the way home that time. Me and Bobby Ray Isley. She come into Poppy's store when she didn't have no business doing it and fell out right by the loaves of Merita bread. Got a big goose egg from where that hard head of hers butt the shelf—didn't you?"

"I did," Maddie said.

"And didn't learn a thing from it, neither," he said as he carried her inside. "Where?"

"On the sofa," Maddie said.

He set her down gently, in spite of Loran's hovering, and knelt by her.

"Anything else I can do for you?" he asked, looking into Maddie's eyes.

Maddie stared at him for a moment. "You can take the bunk beds in the bedroom apart—Meyer said they stack. Sleeping on the bottom one makes me claustrophobic. Take them apart and put one of them by the big window so I can see out."

If he was surprised—or offended—by what amounted to a work order, it didn't show.

"You any good at lifting?" he said to Loran, who was waiting to put a quilt over Maddie's legs.

"Yes," Loran said, not knowing if she was or not.

"You rest easy, woman," he said to Maddie. "If she ain't tall enough, I'll get Bobby Ray." He took the quilt out of Loran's hands and gave it to Maddie, letting her cover her legs herself.

"Mother, maybe you should see the doctor."

"No. I'm going to…rest easy."

She leaned back in the corner of the sofa and closed her eyes.

Loran watched her for a moment, until she realized that Tommy was watching them both. "The bedroom's in there."

She followed him and stood back while he inspected the beds.

"Not much to it," he said. "If you can hold up your end high enough to get the legs off the pins."

"Don't worry about me," Loran said, and he chuckled to himself, not because the retort was witty, but because it was apparently exactly what he expected.

"You got a sweetheart, sis?" he asked as he pulled the top bedspread and mattress off.

Loran didn't answer the question, and she didn't protest his use of *sis*, either. She guided the mattress to the floor and pushed it across the room to get it out of the way.

"I'm only asking because I hear somebody's been calling up at Lilac Hill for you."

"And how would you know that?"

"People talk. Ain't much else to do around here. You make a good topic even on a busy day—come around down here and get that slat. So what do you do for a living anyway?"

"Investment banking," she said.

"In Washington, D.C.?"

"Yes."

"How come you're not working on Wall Street? That's where the big money is. An investment banker's career don't begin till he's on Wall Street."

"It's not that easy—and I like—Washington."

"Kimball women don't give up, sis. Might give out, but they don't give in—get down there on that end. You got to lift the frame straight up and then set it on the floor, understand?"

"I understand," she said, her annoyance growing. If she had a problem with this, it would be a lack of physical strength, not a lack of brain power.

The task wasn't so difficult, once Loran managed to lift the bed frame high enough to clear the pins that kept it in place. They set it on the floor, then moved the other bed next to the window.

"Wait a minute," Tommy said. "Turn your end around. She's going to want to be where she can see the hills."

Loran didn't argue with him—because her cell phone rang again. She hurried to answer it, half expecting it to be Kent.

But it wasn't. It was a relatively new member of the investment team with more questions, a junior employee whose name she could never remember but who was apparently going to be handling one of their most involved and volatile clients—*her* client. She moved to the far side of the room next to the window so as not to disturb Maddie, eventually sitting down at the table as the discussion became more complicated. She backtracked him through the decisions the client had made and her response to them, explaining her rationale and waiting for him to take notes. The client was difficult at best, a man who made it his life's work to be offended daily by what he perceived as someone else's stupidity. There was no such thing as being too knowledgeable when it came to responding to the many irrelevant questions he would have regarding his company's portfolio.

"Hey," she said when the junior investments counselor was about to hang up. "You can do this."

"Thanks, Loran. From your mouth to God's ear."

She ended the call, realizing suddenly how relaxed and uncharacteristically non-possessive she felt about the account. It hadn't been an easy acquisition and she had been proud to have accomplished what no one else could.

She looked around because Tommy stood by the front door. He motioned for her to come there because Maddie looked as if she might be sleeping.

"Ask your mama if she wants the bed raised higher," he said. "I can make some blocks for it if she does."

Loran started to say something then didn't.

"It'll be easier for her to get in and out," he said.

Only if she stays here, Loran thought.

She opened the door to usher Tommy out, surprised, actually, that he went, and she stood for a moment watching to see which direction he took.

But she was thinking about Maddie.

What if she won't go? What if she intends to die here?

Loran braced herself against the fear that threatened to overwhelm her again. She took a deep breath and turned around to find Maddie awake after all.

"I think you should see the doctor," Loran said.

"I don't need to."

"Mother, it may be something...new."

"It isn't. He told me when I should come in to see him.

If I run a fever. If I can't eat or can't keep anything down. If I'm in pain. A weak spell wasn't on the list and it's nothing new."

Loran sighed and didn't say anything more. She needed to talk to the doctor herself. She didn't trust Maddie's version of how her illness should be managed.

"Someone from…hospice will be coming," Maddie said. "It's the doctor's idea."

"What hospice?" Loran said. But she suddenly remembered. She has seen the sign—the brick house—when she'd gone to buy clothes. "I don't—"

"I know you think I shouldn't be here. I know it would be easier for you if I went back to Arlington, but it wouldn't be easier for me."

They stared at each other, until Loran looked away.

"I…think I'll go for a walk," she said lightly to change the subject, to keep from starting an argument she couldn't possibly win. "You want some tea or anything before I go?"

"No. I think I'll go to bed and try to sleep for a while. I stayed up too late talking to Nelda. You got the bunks apart all right?"

"Yes, why?"

"I thought I heard squabbling."

"Imagine that," Loran said, making Maddie smile. "Tommy wants to know if you want blocks for the bed, to make it higher. So you can…see out the window better."

Maddie held out her hand for Loran to help her to her feet, but she refused any help walking into the newly arranged bedroom. Loran was surprised to see that Tommy had remade the other bed while she'd been on the phone.

She helped Maddie to take off her shoes and lie down. The window was large and with the shade up it provided a clear view of the mountain ridges around them.

"I like this," Maddie said. "And I think the blocks would be good. You can tell him yes, if he asks again."

"Okay, but we won't hold our breath, right?"

Maddie smiled again without answering. She closed her eyes, leaving Loran to deal with Tommy Garth without her.

Loran had thought Tommy was gone, but she caught a glimpse of him through the window when she came out of the bedroom. He was sitting on the porch in the sun—whittling.

She took a deep breath and stepped outside.

"She all right?" he asked immediately.

"She's...resting."

"Are you up to all this? Your mama being so sick?"

Loran looked at him for a moment, trying to find the strength to maintain the "truce." It was a question he, of all people, had no right to ask. "I...don't have a choice."

"No. Don't reckon you do. So you live in Washington." It wasn't really a question. It was an opening—and she could take it or leave it.

Loran hesitated, then sat down on the step—not too close. "Yes."

"I reckon you live in one of those apartments."

"No, I have a house."

"You own it?"

"Me and the bank," Loran said.

"You put your name on it somewhere where people can see it?"

"No."

"You need to get your name on it. Women don't own houses all that much. It needs showing off."

Loran didn't know what to say to that, so she didn't say anything.

"You been to the Vietnam Memorial?" he asked after a moment.

"Yes."

"What…was it like? Going there."

There was something in his voice that made her look at him, something that years of living with Maddie and listening for nuance made her able to hear. He was still whittling.

"It was…hot," she said, deliberately misunderstanding. "A hot summer day."

He looked at her then and she suddenly remembered the photograph hanging on the wall of his cabin.

"I…went on my lunch hour," she said after a moment.

"Just for something to do. There were a lot of other people going to see it, too. Families. Kids. All kinds of tour groups. Maybe some veterans, I don't know." She stopped, trying to remember the details. "On the walk to get to it, everybody was talking and laughing. The kids were running around. But…"

"But what?"

"It was…strange. The closer we got, the quieter everyone became. By the time we reached the wall, nobody was saying anything. Not a word. The kids weren't rowdy anymore. Everything was hushed and quiet. It was…" She stopped, at a loss for words suddenly. "Anyway, it's a…hallowed place—or it was that day."

He nodded and went back to whittling, the conversation clearly over.

She stood to go back into the cabin.

"If you need to go to Poppy's to buy anything—I'll hang around here while you're gone. In case…"

He didn't say in case what.

"We don't need anything," she said. She hadn't expected the offer and she simply didn't know what to do with the myriad of emotions he caused in her. He made her want to lash out at him and he made her want to weep. She had every right to feel embittered—for Maddie's sake, if not for her own—and yet he apparently refused to embrace that reality. He expected her to accept his favors, to *chitchat*, if it suited him. He didn't— wouldn't—behave like a man who had done anything wrong. She wanted to hate him, and yet here she stood, more grateful for his recent help than she would ever dare admit. Part of her wanted to know what kind of man would behave the way he did—back then, when he and Maddie were young, and now. The rest of her wanted to run him off the porch with a broom.

"We don't need anything," she repeated. "Except the blocks," she added in spite of her resolve not to give him a reason to come around.

He nodded again and she went back inside. Maddie was sleeping quietly in her newly placed bed, and when Loran looked out the window, Tommy Garth had gone.

CHAPTER 15

"Here's someone you can ask," Mrs. Jenkins said as Meyer walked into the B and B foyer. "He's trying to reach Loran Kimball," she whispered, handing him the phone. "He says it's important."

Meyer frowned and took the receiver. "Have you tried her cell?" he asked without prelude.

"Who is this?" the male voice asked, the tone suggesting a certain surprise that an unknown man would even know Loran had a cell phone and that the chest-pounding was about to begin.

"Meyer Conley. Who is this?"

"You...know Loran?" he asked instead of answering.

"Yeah," Meyer said bluntly. "I know her."

"Oh. Well, I'm trying to get in touch with her—she called me a little while ago, but we got cut off. If she's there, I really need to speak to her."

"She's not here."

"Will you...be seeing her?"

"Probably."

"Then you can tell her—"

"I'd try the cell phone again," Meyer interrupted. He handed the phone back to Mrs. Jenkins, thus ending his good deed for the day.

He took the piece of paper Mrs. Jenkins offered him

in exchange for the telephone and went back outside, reading the latest Lilac Hill chore list before he stuffed it into his pocket. The list was long, and all the jobs Mrs. Jenkins wanted done were outside. He was glad to have a reason to stay busy and not think about…anything.

He had come much too close to forgetting who he was and, more importantly, who Loran Kimball was. If seeing her wheeling and dealing investment capital hadn't been enough to remind him, then talking to the jasper she'd apparently just called did. The man on the phone hadn't sounded like a client. Or a co-worker. He'd sounded like a man who could make her cry in a B and B gazebo.

Meyer took a quiet breath and looked up at the sky. It was going to snow soon. He could feel it in the cold, damp air—Nelda would say she could smell it. He went to get a hammer out of the truck. He had gone into this situation with Maddie Kimball's daughter with his eyes wide open, and he wasn't going to think about last night. He was going to do what she'd told him to do on more than one occasion. He was going to mind his own damn business.

Oh, man, he thought as his mind filled with images of a naked Loran Kimball lying in his bed. He could still feel her, taste her. She was beautiful and loving. It had been good with her. More than good.

But she was just passing through and he was nothing but a snack at the rest stop, and he had better not forget it.

He began working on clearing the debris from a clogged downspout until he heard a noise behind him.

"I think we better have us a little talk, son," Tommy Garth said.

"About what?" Meyer asked, still trying to find the obstruction.

"About you taking advantage of my girl?"

"What are you doing?" Maddie said from the couch.

"Nothing," Loran said, still looking out the window. She had expected to see Meyer all day yesterday and all day today. She was still waiting.

"Is it snowing?"

"Yes."

"Big flakes or little flakes?"

"Little. Why?"

"If they're little, we're in for it. I think we'd better go now."

Loran looked at her. "Go where?"

"To see the doctor. I'm…running a fever."

"Mother, why didn't you say something?" Loran said in alarm.

"I am saying something. We don't have to call for an appointment first. I told him we were relying on cell phones, so, lucky us, we get to walk right in."

Loran looked at her for a moment, realizing that there had indeed been a change in Maddie's condition. Her eyes were too bright and she was trying too hard.

"I'll go warm up the SUV," Loran said, getting her coat. She waited until she was outside to take the necessary moment to gather her courage. Bad things were coming. She knew that, and the knowing didn't help.

It was snowing harder now and beginning to lie on the steps and the bare ground. She glanced in the direction of the path that led to Nelda's house, wondering again why she hadn't seen Meyer.

But she had no time to worry about that now. She ran through the snow to the SUV and started the engine.

The doctor visit went smoothly enough, but, by the time Loran had gotten Maddie's prescriptions filled, it was late afternoon and the ground was white. The wind had picked up, making the return to the cabin precarious at best, but they eventually made it. Maddie was clearly exhausted. She took one of her new pills, ate a little tomato soup, and went to bed and almost immediately to sleep.

Loran stood in the middle of the cabin, wondering what to do with herself. She had managed to speak to the doctor briefly—out of Maddie's hearing. The conversation had been less than comforting. He hadn't had the opportunity to elaborate, but Loran realized that he would treat the infection as a token gesture only because he hadn't completely ruled out a miracle.

The falling snow and the wind made her restless and edgy. She moved around the room, not really seeing any of it. She kept checking on Maddie, eventually finding her awake and staring out the window.

"Need anything?" Loran asked, which was probably only marginally better than asking her how she felt.

"I need my daughter to relax her vigil," Maddie said. "Come sit down so we can talk."

"About what?"

"Whatever you want. I want you to be…satisfied. I want your questions answered."

"I don't have any questions."

"Then who are you and what have you done with my daughter?"

Loran smiled in spite of her determination to avoid

Maddie's sudden penchant for disclosure. If Maddie wanted to answer questions, then the situation was far worse than she'd thought.

"Go ahead," Maddie said.

"Okay. What's Estelle really like?" Loran asked, picking a topic she thought would likely end the Q and A session as abruptly as it had begun. Unfortunately, the plan didn't work.

"All those years ago, she was…a force of nature," Maddie said. "Superior, opinionated—she actually tried to convert Foy."

"To what?"

"Religion and giving up his rowdy ways."

"I guess it didn't work."

"Foy was Foy. He let her think he'd turned over a new leaf for a while, until she grew confident enough to brag about it. He even stood up and confessed his sins in church one Sunday. Then he moved his latest girlfriend into the house to live with us."

"He *what?*"

"Her name was Doll—that wasn't her nickname. That was her name. My mother had been ill, and Doll was supposed to be there to help out. I don't think anything ever shocked the people here more than that did."

"Where's Doll now? Is she still here?"

"She's in the cemetery with Foy. Estelle never forgave him for making such a fool of her. I think she might have been a little in love with him."

"So what did Estelle do the rest of the time—when she wasn't saving souls?"

"She ran the church, the school, her husband—everything—except Nelda, maybe."

"Did she run Tommy?"

Maddie was quiet for a time before she answered. "I used to think she didn't. But she must have."

"Want some music?" Loran abruptly asked because of the expression on Maddie's face. "I'll turn on the radio."

"Did I teach you how to do that? I must have. You said I do it."

"What?"

"Tap dance. With an exit stage left."

"Yes," Loran said. "You did."

"We don't have time for dancing now, you know."

"Mother, I—" Loran stopped because her voice had grown husky and her eyes were burning. Maddie reached out and took her hand.

"I don't want to know anything else about this," Loran said.

"Maybe not now. But you will later."

"I…just. I don't know what to do."

"Not much to do at this point—except enjoy each other's company. I am so glad you're my daughter."

Loran bowed her head as the tears spilled over and rolled down her cheeks. "Sorry. The last thing you need is me—"

"Listen, I think I hear someone coming," Maddie said. "I'm up for company, if that's what it is."

"No, you're not," Loran said.

"Yes, I am. Go see who's come all the way up here."

"If it's Estelle, I'm not letting her in."

Someone knocked. Loran took a deep breath and wiped her eyes.

She peeped out the window. Meyer stood on the porch, holding a large cardboard box with a snowy towel over it. Even so, he had on what she took to be his military face. Tommy Garth stood next to him—he was holding a gunnysack. And, wonder of wonders, there stood Kent, too—a very unhappy-looking Kent—standing slightly behind them, clinging to a briefcase as if he thought one of them might steal it.

"Now what?" she said out loud.

"Who is it?" Maddie called from the bedroom.

"You wouldn't believe it if I told you."

She opened the door a small crack, trying to keep the snow from blowing in. She looked from one to the other, perfectly aware that her no-good father, at least, was enjoying this.

"You going to bring us in out of the snow or not, sis?" he asked.

She stood back and opened the door wider. "Come in. Please. So what brings you three here?" she asked—as if she were an on-the-spot reporter interviewing a trio of tourists she'd found sightseeing on the Parkway—in spite of the fact that two of them happened to be her lovers.

"Is your mama awake?" Tommy asked instead of answering.

"I'll see," she said to annoy him, walking toward the bedroom, not realizing until she was about to open Maddie's door that he had come with her.

"Here I was all worried about you being an old maid and you got more sweethearts than you know what to do with."

"This is *not* funny," she whispered.

"The hell it ain't," he answered in a normal voice. "Those two don't like each other one bit. You partial to one of them?"

"None of your business!"

"I'm just asking. Might be handy to know—in case I need to shoot one. Maddie, I got your blocks," he said, pushing the door open.

"I am quite old enough to do my own shooting, thank you."

He went inside, obviously still amused by the situation, plopping the gunnysack on the foot of the bed and pulling up a straight chair and making himself at home. Loran stood for a moment, then turned around. Meyer had set the box on the counter—it wasn't Nelda's favorite one. Kent was still guarding his briefcase.

"So what have you been doing?" Loran said.

"It's been hell," Kent said. "Last-minute tax shelters—"

"Not you," she said, turning to look at Meyer. "You."

"I've been…trying not to crowd you," Meyer said, in spite of Kent's presence.

The answer worked for her. "What's in the box?"

"Nelda had one of her 'feelings.' She thought you might be needing a little help in the food department. She's been baking all day—chicken pies. She says to eat one and put the rest in the freezer. And there's some gravy in here to go with it—you can freeze that, too—and an apple pie for dessert."

"I can't believe you walked all the way up here in this weather."

"I can't believe it turned into a parade," he said, glancing at Kent.

"We need to talk, Loran," Kent said. "Privately."

"Why?" she asked, ignoring what amounted to a command. If she weren't so worried about Maddie, she might have agreed with Tommy. This situation was at least a little bit funny.

"I've got some pending portfolios for you. I said I'd bring them when I came—so you could look them over and call in your recommendations."

"You've got a fire in the woodstove," Meyer said from his corner.

"Yes. With the drafts barely open for a long slow burn."

"How's the wood supply?"

"It's— I don't know."

"I'll go look," he said. "So you and Kent can talk betas and ADRs."

She looked at him, surprised because he was so obviously disgruntled, and jealous-rival disgruntled at that. She found the fact that he couldn't quite hide it fascinating. He went outside, leaving her and Kent somewhat alone. She could hear Tommy and Maddie talking in the other room—and, after a moment, Meyer chopping wood.

"Who is that guy, anyway?"

"Meyer Conley—"

"What's he to you?"

She gave him a look. "What are you doing here, Kent?"

"I want to talk to you—I told you that on the phone."

"So you did. I hope you reserved a room somewhere. You'll never make it back today in this weather."

"I'm at that…Lilac place. Loran, you can't just end everything because of what you *think* is going on between me and Celia—"

"Kent, I don't care about Celia. I care about me. I've got enough to worry about at the moment, and I don't need the extra aggravation. So I'm…cleaning house."

"What about the account we've been working on?"

"We? Oh, I see. The nostalgic widower turned you down."

"He…wants to think it over."

"Well, that's his prerogative."

"His prerogative? Since when do you care about an investor's prerogative? You need to talk to him—if anybody can get around whatever objections he thinks he has, you can."

"Well, hardly, Kent. He thinks I'm purely decorative, like his dead wife, thanks to you."

He gave a sharp sigh. "Just come back long enough to have dinner with him. You can do that."

You owe me that is what he meant.

Loran looked at him. She had forgotten how handsome he was and how he totally focused on himself. "No. I can't."

"We're talking about a huge commission here. It's for *us*, Loran. What happened to that assertive nature—that persuasiveness everyone raves about?"

Loran didn't say anything. Nothing.

"You've changed," he said after a moment. "This isn't like you *at all*."

"You don't know the half of it, Kent. Did you bring my key?"

"I can't believe you really want me to move out!" he said as both Tommy and Meyer walked in.

"I'm needing a little help setting these blocks,"

Tommy said in the doorway of the bedroom. "You, too, city boy," he said when only Meyer moved to oblige.

Kent hesitated, then put the briefcase down. Loran stayed in the kitchen area and emptied out the cardboard box—so as not to fuel Tommy Garth's amusement any more than she already had. The pies were still warm in spite of their snowy journey and smelled wonderful.

From the sound of it, Meyer and Kent lifted the bed, Maddie and all, one end at a time, while Tommy placed the blocks. Only Meyer and Kent came out of the bedroom.

"Did the blocks work?" Loran asked.

"So far, so good," Meyer said. "Maddie's happy."

"I'm ready to go back to the B and B, Connor," Kent interrupted.

"Conley," Meyer said, and Loran suddenly had some idea of how the "parade" had come about. Kent had come looking for her at Lilac Hill, and Meyer must have been called upon to accommodate a guest—snow or no snow. She didn't know how Tommy had managed to join the procession but, all in all, it must have been interesting.

Kent picked up the briefcase and headed for the door. He was not happy and he wanted to make sure she knew it.

"Kent," she said as he walked out on the porch. "Kent!"

He went down the steps before he stopped and, when he turned around, he clearly expected a capitulation.

"The portfolios?" she said.

He came back up the steps and thrust the briefcase at her.

"If you can wait, I'll give you your briefcase back."

"Keep it." He went down the steps again and hiked off into the snow without looking back. She stared after him. Her expectations regarding Kent's support in times of personal crisis had been minimal at best, but it was official now. She was going to go through the rest of Maddie's illness in a strange place, with people she hadn't even known existed, the last tie to her real life stomping off through the snow.

"He can't get far, if you want to talk to him," Meyer said. "I've got the keys to the truck."

She looked at him. "I don't want to talk to him." It was true. She didn't. Kent wasn't the solution to any of her problems.

Meyer came closer. "You all right?"

She smiled—or tried to. "Oh, just dandy."

"You've still got Nelda's number, right?" he asked, looking into her eyes.

"Yes."

"Use it," he said. He rested his hand briefly on her shoulder before he went outside.

She waited for a moment and watched him walk into the deep snow after Kent, then closed the door.

Tommy was standing by the kitchen counter.

"Your mama's wanting to sleep. I think the blocks are going to work all right. If they don't—"

"Why don't you get along with Estelle?"

The question took him by surprise—to such a degree that she almost wished she hadn't asked it. Almost.

"That's between her and me. And I'd stay away from Estelle if I was you."

"Meyer says she's not dangerous," she said as he stepped around her to get to the door.

"Meyer's wrong."

CHAPTER 16

Maddie seemed almost immediately better—but it didn't last. The fever left in a few days, and so did her stamina. To Loran's distress, she refused to give in to it, forcing herself to get up and get dressed, only to have to lie back down again. Everything her doctors had predicted seemed to be happening at once—the fatigue, the loss of appetite, the pain.

The snow melted, the wind died down, and a social worker and a nurse from the hospice agency came, neither of them daunted by the effort it took to get up to Meyer's cabin. Loran stood by helplessly as Maddie solidified her plans to stay. There was nothing she could do except review the probably token portfolios Kent had brought and stay out of the way while Maddie micromanaged the hospice recommendations. In spite of her progressive weakness, she still seemed to be on top of things. She signed all the paperwork from the agency and had Loran deliver it. She called her neighbor about her house and her plants. She wrote letters she didn't want mailed. She slept a lot, ate a little, and she visited with Tommy Garth.

Tommy came every day. *Every* day. He never stayed long, and what he and Maddie talked about, Loran had no idea. He didn't speak to her at all. She had apparently crossed some line by asking him about his relationship with Estelle. Part of her was happy for the respite and part of her wanted to annoy him with even more probing questions, for no other reason than that he didn't like it.

For Maddie's sake, she didn't. She pointedly stayed out of the way, letting them keep each other company in front of the bedroom window with the view of the "hills." Loran had no doubt that Maddie wanted him there. It was obvious that she anticipated his arrival every afternoon, grew restless if he didn't show when she expected him.

Loran looked at Maddie now, as she pretended to read, pretended that it wasn't past time for Tommy Garth's daily visit.

"Want me to go look for him?" Loran asked because she saw no point in tiptoeing around the five-hundred-pound gorilla that *wasn't* in the room.

"No, but you could take a walk. Get a little fresh air. Leave me to pine on my own."

"Are you pining?" Loran asked with some alarm. That was the last thing either of them needed.

Maddie smiled. "No. I've got cabin fever on your behalf, that's all. Go walk down to the gazebo and back. It'll do us both good."

Loran hesitated, then put on her coat. "Don't do anything crazy while I'm gone."

"Like what?"

"Like defrosting the fridge."

"You have my solemn word," Maddie said.

Loran went outside, standing on the porch for a moment before she headed for the path that led to the gazebo. It was cold and crisp, and she was halfway down the hill when she saw Tommy and Meyer standing on the path. They both looked startled to see her, so startled that she forgot her initial pleasure at finding Meyer when she didn't expect to.

Tommy recovered first, deigning to actually speak to her for a change. "How's Maddie doing today?"

"She's not defrosting the refrigerator," Loran said.

"I reckon she'll need some help then," he said, ignoring the true sentiment behind the nonsensical remark. "You remember what I said, Meyer."

"What did he mean by that?" Loran asked when Tommy walked in the direction of the cabin.

"I wonder why that minding-your-own-business thing only applies to me," he said instead of answering the question.

"Because in this case I think I'm the 'business.'"

"He's…just looking out for you."

"I look out for myself. I don't need any help from Tommy Garth—especially at this late date."

"Right," he said. "You want to go get something to eat—I'm buying."

"Why?" she asked suspiciously, still not satisfied that her not-so-illustrious father wasn't up to something she wouldn't like.

"Because I think he wants to talk to Maddie and he doesn't want you underfoot."

"Is that what he said?"

"No, that's what I think."

"Is that the only reason you want me to go? To accommodate Tommy Garth?"

"You know it isn't. Come on," he said. "You can order anything on the menu you want."

"What…menu would that be?"

"The restaurant close to the Parkway."

"The one with the apple pies that taste like Nelda's?"

"That's the one, and they are Nelda's. You want to tell Maddie we're going?"

She still hesitated.

"Did you hear the part about me buying?" he asked, and she smiled in spite of herself.

"Yes."

"That doesn't happen every day, I can tell you."

She looked off into the distance before she answered. "All right. Let's go—but I can't stay long."

They began walking up the steep path.

"Heard anything from Kent?" she asked him.

"Who, me?" he said, clearly taken aback. "Hell no."

She couldn't keep from grinning. "Gosh. And I thought you two hit it off."

"You're pretty cute, you know that?" he said.

"I do, yes."

"Now behave," he said as they stepped up on the porch. "Don't go picking a fight with Tommy while you're in there."

"Why ever not?"

"Because he grew up butting heads with Estelle. He can probably whip us both."

She managed to say goodbye to Maddie without incident, but it was all she could do not to couch her departure in admonishments designed to guarantee Maddie's safety in her absence. In lieu of that, she offered to bring Maddie something—anything—from the restaurant. Maddie firmly declined and there was nothing left to do but go.

The restaurant wasn't that far away, but it was surprisingly hard to leave Maddie alone—except that she wasn't alone. Tommy Garth was with her. For as long as it suited him, anyway.

"Quit worrying!" Meyer said when they were halfway to the restaurant.

"Okay!"

"All right then."

By the time they got there, Loran was glad she'd accepted Meyer's invitation. There was no awkwardness between them, and she needed to be in the company of a man who could make her laugh. There were people at the restaurant who knew him—and her—thanks to the welcome-home party Tommy had given. And all of them came by the booth to speak to her and to ask about Maddie.

"Thank you," she said to Meyer when they were in the truck and on their way back to the cabin.

"For what? You wouldn't let me pay for your meal."

"For…" She looked out the side window toward the mountains and gave a quiet sigh.

"You're welcome," he said after a moment.

They didn't talk anymore until he had parked in the yard near the cabin. Loran unbuckled her seat belt, but she made no attempt to get out. The sun was no longer shining, and the mountainside looked bleak and cold. The wind shook the truck from time to time and she dreaded having to step into it.

"I think about you," Meyer said. He turned his head to look at her. "All the time. I just wanted you to know that. I don't want you to think it didn't mean anything to me—the other night—"

She moved toward him then, leaning over the console between them to cling to him for a moment—hard—before she abruptly let go and got out, then all but ran to the cabin, looking back at him once before she went inside.

Trouble and heartache.

She stood with her back against the door, her eyes closed until she heard him leave. She thought about him all the time, too, but she couldn't say it.

The cabin was so quiet. She didn't hear anything but the refrigerator running. She turned on a lamp because the room was too dark, then walked to the bedroom to check on Maddie.

Maddie was awake, sitting up in bed and looking out the window.

"How was your lunch with Meyer?" she asked, but she didn't turn her head in Loran's direction.

"It was fine. I saw some people I knew there. They all asked about you."

"That's nice," Maddie said, still not looking at her.

"I thought Tommy was going to stay until I got back."

"He didn't."

"So I see. Mother—"

"You know, I'm really tired. I think I'll take a nap." She made a great show of rearranging her pillow and settling in to do just that.

"Mother, are you—"

"Not now, Loran. Close the door, will you?"

Loran stood for a moment, then went out of the room and shut the door quietly behind herself.

Maddie slept, but not for long. She awoke pale and tired-looking and determined to get up and try to putter around the cabin. She had a light supper of onion soup and lime sherbet, after which she decided to take one of her pills, the first of the high-powered pain pills, as far as Loran knew.

"Come sit with me until this takes effect," Maddie said matter-of-factly, as if taking the pill weren't an indicator of things to come. She went back to her raised bed and Loran tried not to hover, tried not to bombard her with questions about how she was feeling or what had become of Tommy Garth.

Maddie wanted the light off. The room was illuminated only by the lamp in the other room. They both looked out the window, but there was nothing to see but an occasional pinpoint of light coming from other cabins and houses on the hillsides.

The pill seemed to work quickly.

"A good place to hide," Maddie said drowsily at one point.

"What?"

"The mountains. That's why our Scotch-Irish ancestors came here—to hide."

"From what?"

"Persecution. Religious and political. They came with nothing…but their…pride and their suspicion of authority. They wanted—needed—the isolation to feel…safe. I think that must be why…we're the…way we are now."

Loran looked at her, the feeble remnants of what little hope she had left of getting Maddie to leave dissipating. *We*, Maddie had said. Not *they*.

Maddie gave a quiet sigh and reached for Loran's

hand. "It's…home. I never thought so when I was living here, but I can feel it now. Nobody understands us, not…really."

She grew quiet, and Loran thought she had fallen asleep.

"It's so…strange," Maddie said when Loran was about to leave.

"What is?"

"My accent."

"Your accent?"

"I'm having to work…really hard to keep it…from coming back."

"What did Tommy do?" Loran asked suddenly, without even realizing she was going to, and Maddie let go of her hand.

"Something happened while I was gone, Mother, and since you won't tell me anything, I have to guess. I'm guessing he did something you didn't much like. Hence the question—what did he do?"

"Nothing."

"Oh, good. That certainly puts my mind at ease."

"I don't want to talk about Tommy—"

"I'll go hunt him down if you want."

"No." Maddie said. She took a another deep breath before she continued. "I don't want to see him. I don't want to talk to him. And I don't want to talk about him. I mean it."

"Works for me," Loran said, but it wasn't true. And there was nothing she could do about it.

"How is she?"

"Well. Long time, no see. Again."

Loran looked Tommy Garth in the eye and she could feel the sudden attention of the rest of the people in Poppy's store—Bobby Ray, and the old men playing checkers by the stove and the two women looking for something in the canned goods.

"I asked you a question, sis."

"What do you care how she is?" Loran said, lowering her voice—for Maddie's sake, not his.

"She's scared. You need to stay by her."

"*I* need to stay by her? And where are you going to be, you jerk? You did it again, didn't you? You made her think she mattered to you, then you walked away."

"Is that what she said?"

Loran ignored the question. "So was it fun for you—fooling her again? Make you feel like a big man?"

He didn't say anything, but he didn't back down, either.

"You don't know what the truth is—"

"And I don't care. Get out of my way."

Finally, he stepped aside. Loran carried the groceries she had in her arms up to the counter where Poppy stood waiting, his face worried and anxious.

"What?" she said faintly because she didn't understand what he'd said to her.

"Ten dollars and seventy cents, honey," Poppy said again.

She paid him the money, letting him see her hands shake because she couldn't do otherwise. She grabbed up the groceries before he had them all in a bag and walked out of the store, sitting for a moment in the SUV before she calmed down enough to leave. She still had errands to run and, after a moment, she was grateful she only had half of them done. It would give her a chance to settle down before she went back to the cabin.

She's scared.

"You think I don't know that!" Loran said out loud. She abruptly started the SUV and drove away.

But she was hardly calm again when she returned to the cabin. A trip to the post office to pick up more pending portfolios, and to the discount department store to buy some sheets and blankets and extra pillows—and nightgowns, because Maddie wasn't all that interested in getting up and getting dressed anymore—hadn't really helped. Loran desperately needed the portfolios to keep from thinking about Maddie's dwindling strength and resolve.

The hospice nurse was coming more often now, every third day unless Maddie needed something beforehand. And Nelda was helping—Loran was so grateful for Nelda. Her appearance on the doorstep every day was like a gift from heaven. Nothing seemed as bad when she was there. She mothered Loran and Maddie both, making one rest and the other eat, doling out her cheerfulness and her serenity until they both felt renewed. Meyer had told her she would like Nelda, and she did.

She hadn't seen Meyer in several days, but he'd sent her a small gift via his beloved great-aunt—a *Wall Street Journal* he'd picked up for her when he'd had to drive a B and B guest to the airport in Asheville. She smiled whenever she thought about it. Who else but Meyer would give her a financial newspaper? Or a can of snuff.

Nelda was unusually subdued when Loran returned, but she waited for Loran to put the groceries away before she said anything.

"Your mama's wanting to talk to you, honey."

"About what?"

"She'll tell you."

Loran stood for a moment, then went into the bed-room.

"There you are," Maddie said, smiling slightly. It was getting harder for her to smile, and seeing her having to work at it broke Loran's heart.

"Do you need something, Mother?"

"I...need you to promise."

"Promise what?"

"I need you to promise me you'll do what Nelda asks you to do."

"I don't understand."

"Nelda..." Maddie stopped and took a quiet breath. "Nelda knows what I want. She'll tell you when it's time," she said when Loran was about to interrupt. "What she asks you to do, it's for me, from me. I want you to promise me you'll do it."

"No. I can't promise when I don't know—"

"Promise me!"

"Mother—"

"Promise me, Loran. I'm asking you."

"I...all right. Whatever it is, I promise."

"Good. You're a good daughter, a good person...."

Maddie closed her eyes and didn't say anything else. Loran stood for a moment, then left the room.

Nelda was waiting for her.

"I don't understand," Loran said.

"She's just a-trying to take the burden off you, that's all. She's made her plans."

"What plans?"

"For when she goes home, honey."

Loran looked into Nelda's kindly face and knew that she didn't mean *home* in the literal sense.

I can't do this, she thought. She didn't know where this kind of calm acceptance came from. And Kent had been right. She had always been a person who never paid attention to someone else's prerogative.

"Your mama's set down what she wants and she don't want you worrying about it. Come on over here now and sit a spell. You're looking all weak-eyed and peaked. Tell me, did you see anybody whilst you was out?"

"I saw Tommy when I was at Poppy's," Loran said, sitting down on the sofa with Nelda next to her. "I…called him a jerk."

"Well, I reckon he is one, by most folks' account," Nelda said.

They sat for a time in silence, neither of them feeling the need to manufacture any conversation. Loran was tired, more tired than she realized, and it was easier to rest when Nelda was around.

She leaned back and put her feet up. "What was the other secret? For a good marriage. You said there were two."

Nelda thought for a moment before she answered. "Well. I reckon the second one is the hardest—us women being like we are. It's a good thing to love your husband a lot—I reckon everybody knows that. But you don't never want to love any man so much you think you can't live without him. It ain't good for you, and it ain't good for your children. That was one thing what was so wrong with Foy and Adeline. Foy Kimball, he was as handsome as he was wicked. Weren't many women around he couldn't have if he'd a-wanted them. All Adeline could think was how lucky she was to get him to the altar. She didn't see how he was after her daddy's timberland. She thought she'd done something no other girl could, and she thought she couldn't live without him. She was plum mindless about it, so she put up with all kinds of things. Bad things what caused her a heap of misery. And it weren't just her that suffered. She was so scared of losing him, she let your mama suffer right along with her, poor little young-un. You know about Doll, I reckon."

"Maddie told me."

"Well, I always thought a body ought not be judging other people and casting stones like the Bible says. But when that happened, I just couldn't help it. I asked Adeline why she was putting up with him bringing Doll right into her house like that. And the question surprised her. It did. It *surprised* her. She looked at me like I'd lost my brain somewhere on the way over to see her, and she said, 'Nelda, you don't want a man nobody else wants, don't you know that?'

"I knowed right then there weren't no help for her, or for your mama. It ain't right to put up with that kind of thing when you got little ones. No, sir, it ain't. Who's going to look out for the wee babes of this world if they own mama won't do it? Like to have broke my heart."

"Maddie lived all right without Tommy, though."

"Yes, she did. She done a good job with her life and with you. I can't say if she would have been happy with him, and I don't know how happy she was without him. She ain't nothing like Adeline, but I don't know that she and Tommy could have ever made it together—not with Estelle getting in between them."

"I was thinking maybe I ought to go see Estelle."

"Oh, Lordy, no, honey. You don't want to do that."

"Why not? Everybody's talking about Maddie coming back home, and Estelle is my grandmother. I don't want her to think I'm ashamed of Maddie or that I'm scared of her."

"If she looks at you, she ain't going to see nobody but Foy. And she pure hated Foy Kimball, just like she hates—" Nelda broke off and gave a quiet sigh.

"Who? Maddie?"

"Well. It just ain't a good idea, that's all. Estelle can't see she makes her own misery. I don't reckon she ever will."

"Do you know what happened, why Tommy didn't marry Maddie?"

"I reckon you need to ask him about that."

"He's not very good at answering my questions. I asked him about Estelle—why they didn't get along. He didn't speak to me again for days."

"You asked him about Estelle? Lordy, child. You're just like a whirlwind. But don't go whirling around Estelle. I'm thinking it would be more trouble than it'd be worth, and you wouldn't learn nothing, not from her. Ask Tommy again. It might go better now that he's had some time to get used to the question."

"Maddie—she's not getting better," Loran suddenly said, trying not to cry. "I know she can't, but I—"

Nelda reached out and wrapped her in her arms, the same way she must have done with Maddie all those years ago. She smelled of baby powder and freshly ironed clothes.

"She ain't ready to give in yet. She's been fighting, honey, and fighting *hard*. It's not easy to just stand by while she does it, wanting to help and you can't."

"I don't think I can stand this."

"Yes, you can. You're stronger than you think, but sometimes you need to bend a little, so's you don't break."

"I don't know what that means."

"It means I'm a-wanting you to do something for me," Nelda said. "I'm wanting you to go down to my house."

"Is this what Maddie made me promise?" Loran asked.

"No, honey. Right now it's just me asking you. Meyer's going to be there. He'll tell you about it."

Loran hesitated, not because she didn't want to go, but because she was so tired. Maddie had her days and nights turned around, something Nelda had predicted would happen at some point.

"Sick people is afraid of the night," she said, and Maddie was no exception. She couldn't, or wouldn't, sleep during the night hours anymore. Neither did Loran. Sometimes they talked all night. Sometimes Loran read to her—poetry usually. Emily Dickinson or Edna St. Vincent Millay. And all the while, the sand in the hourglass ran.

Loran stood up and put on her coat. She went in to tell Maddie she was leaving for a little while, but Maddie was sleeping.

"Are you sure Meyer knows what you want?" she asked Nelda.

"I'm sure. Take your time walking down. It's cold, but it's a pretty day, what's left of it."

Loran stepped out on the porch, standing for a moment to look at the sky and the bare trees before she began the walk to Nelda's house. She realized suddenly that she didn't even know what day of the week it was and she most certainly didn't know the date. Time had come down to the sequence of events required to manage Maddie's illness—when to give her her pills, when to help her take a bath, when to try to entice her to eat and sleep. There was nothing else.

Loran's head and back ached. She hadn't realized how hard this would be physically. Sometimes—like now—the fatigue was nearly overwhelming. She forced herself to go down the steps and take the path to Nelda's. She had all but forgotten what it was like to be outside, to breathe fresh air and, for once, she actually savored the cold. She took her time. The late mountain fall would have passed for a full-blown winter anywhere else, but the land was still beautiful. There had been one ice storm since she and Maddie had taken over Meyer's cabin, but she had yet to see an event Maddie had once described, a full moon rising above the mountainside and making all the icy trees look as if they had been decorated with diamonds—something the little girl Maddie, so deprived of beautiful things, had once witnessed and still cherished.

She saw as she came out of the trees that Pearl's pasture was empty. There was no sign of the mule as she passed by the fence. Meyer's truck was parked in the yard near the porch. It had been a while since she'd even spoken to him. She'd managed to miss him every time he'd come to the cabin because she had been dozing, try-ing to catch up on her lost sleep, and he hadn't awak-ened her.

She walked across the yard, the ground ice crunching under her shoes as she went, and she ran up the steps onto the porch. Meyer opened the door before she could knock. She was so glad to see him. He, on the other hand, frowned.

He started to say something, then didn't, then didn't again.

"I bet you say that to all the girls," she quipped, but it occurred to her suddenly that she must look exactly the way she felt.

"In," he said. He stepped back to let her inside, then followed her into Nelda's warm kitchen. He'd been washing dishes at the sink. Something was simmering on the stove.

"Take off your coat. Sit down," he said, pulling out a chair from the table. "Before you fall down."

"I'm not that—" she started to say, then let it go. She was every bit as in need of a chair as he clearly thought she was. She took off her coat and sat.

"Nelda sent me," she said as he rummaged in a cup-board and took out a glass canning jar of something he poured into a light blue teacup. "She said you'd know why."

"Here," he said, handing her the teacup. "Take a sip, but not a big one."

She looked into the cup. It definitely wasn't water.

"Go on," he insisted.

She sighed and took a sip. It went down like liquid fire.

"What—is—this?" she asked, trying not to cough.

"Ninety proof," he said. He came close and rubbed her back until the urge to cough subsided. "One more."

"What, Nelda told you to get me drunk?"

"No," he said, taking the cup out of her hand. "She told me to give you a bath."

CHAPTER 17

"I have to go," she said in the dark. Meyer's arms tightened around her and he pressed his lips against the side of her neck.

"Nelda's expecting to stay at the cabin all night," he said, pulling the quilts closer around them. The room was cold now that the heat of passion had subsided.

She buried herself deeper into the quilts. They smelled of cedar and lavender.

"Isn't this kind of...scandalous?" she asked sleepily. "Nelda sending me down here to be with you?"

"Maybe she didn't know I'd ply you with untaxed liquor and drag you off to the bathtub."

She smiled in the dark. "I knew she didn't tell you to give me a bath."

"Nelda is a worldly woman."

"Not that worldly. I need to go," she said again. "Maddie might need something."

"Poppy's wife is going to be there to help. The two of them can manage. And Bobby Ray is staying. He'll come down and get you if anything changes."

"Bobby Ray is afraid of the dark."

"No, that one's negotiable. He likes to coon hunt too much to put it very high on his list. Mostly, he's afraid of haints and thunder, and he's not going to run into either one between here and there. Besides that, he's got my big flashlight. He can't wait to go tripping through the night with it."

"All of you got together and planned this?"

"Well, not *this*," he said. "But we thought you needed a little R & R."

"I—it's—"

"Hush," he said against her ear. "Let me take care of you. Let me keep you warm and let Nelda and the rest of them watch over Maddie."

"I'm so…tired, Meyer."

"I know. You need to stand down. It's all right. You can let go for a little while."

"How are *you*, Meyer?" she asked, suddenly remembering that he had demons of his own.

"I think you had too much corn liquor."

"No, tell me."

"I'm…good, Loran."

She reached up to caress his face, then closed her eyes and relaxed against him, savoring the feel of his arms around her, knowing that however brief it might be, he was giving her something Foy Kimball would never have given Adeline, and Tommy had never given Maddie.

Someone to cling to in the dark.

"She seemed stronger the last couple of days," Loran said to the hospice nurse when she came out of the bed-room—a different one who had come because Maddie needed an unscheduled visit.

"It's like that sometimes," the nurse answered, looking at Loran with such compassion that she wanted to weep.

Loran didn't say anything. She walked over to the kitchen table and sat down.

"I know you wanted that to be a good sign, but—"

"I understand," Loran said. She looked out the window and gave a quiet sigh.

"It's good you have people to help you and Maddie. It makes all the difference in the world."

Loran nodded her agreement, wondering what it would have been like if she'd managed to convince Maddie to go back to Arlington. Not like it was here, with the church women bringing food and coming to sit with Maddie night and day, quietly doing whatever was needed just to give Loran a little respite.

Some church women, Loran thought. Estelle was never among them, even though, by all accounts, she supervised the church's business. No one mentioned her. No one mentioned Tommy.

Tommy Garth.

Surely he must know what was happening with Maddie now. Loran kept expecting to see him, regardless of their last encounter.

No. *Expecting* wasn't the right word. *Hoping* was the word, and this time she couldn't say it was for Maddie's sake. It was for herself that she wanted him to come, and how could she possibly miss the presence of a father she'd never known?

Sometimes she would go outside for a little while and sit in a patch of sunlight on the porch, trying to do what Maddie had once said, trying to outlast the misery. Once, she was almost certain that someone had stood out of sight among the trees watching. It had to be Tommy— or Estelle. She still wondered about Estelle, and how much delight the woman must be taking in the prospect of having Maddie Kimball forever out of her precious son's life.

"What?" Loran said, when she realized the nurse had spoken.

"I'm going to be staying for a while."

"Oh. Good," Loran said absently, trying to distance herself from the reality the woman was trying to impose on her. After a moment, she forced herself to look at her. "I'm sorry. I've forgotten your name."

"Deanie," she said, but she wasn't diverted by pleasantries. "I want to talk to you about something, about the promise you made Maddie."

"I can't talk about it," Loran said. "I don't know what it is."

"Sometimes…when a person is very ill, they want their loved ones with them at the end," Deanie said anyway. "Sometimes, they don't."

Loran looked away. Deanie waited until she looked back again.

"The very idea of it is too…distressful for them," she said. "Especially when they and the ones they leave behind have been really close. Dying feels like a…terrible failure to them. They know you need them. They know how much you want them to stay, but they can't, and it may be the only time they've ever let you down—"

Loran abruptly got up from the table.

"Maddie doesn't want you with her, Loran," she said quietly. "That's what you promised her, that you won't be there, you won't see her die."

"No, I—"

"It's what she wants. And it's what she asked Nelda to

tell you. Nelda didn't have the heart, in case you're wondering why I'm doing it. Nelda says there's been a big change in Maddie's level of alertness. Based on what I see now, I don't think Maddie will be awake again. I think the last couple of days was like a candle flaring up just before it goes out. I also think, in a little while, she won't know if you keep your promise or not. But if you mean to, if it's important to you to do what she asked, you need to tell her goodbye and go down to Nelda's house."

"No, I can't," Loran said, tears spilling down her cheeks. "I can't!"

The nurse didn't say anything. She waited.

Loran looked up at her. "You mean right now, don't you?"

"Yes."

"How can I? How can I do this!"

"It's your decision, Loran. You know your mother best. And you know what's best for you. I know this is one of the hardest things you've ever had to do, but I can tell you, either way, there are people who care about you here, and you won't be alone."

Loran was sobbing now.

"I'm so sorry," the nurse said, putting her arm around her.

"We talked—a—lot—yesterday. All day—"

"That's good. That helped you both."

"But I still have—things I want—to say—"

"Say them now."

Loran took a deep wavering breath. Nelda came out of the bedroom. She embraced Loran for a moment, then stood back to wipe away her own tears with the pink-flowered handkerchief she had in her hand.

"I'm going to stay out here," she said. "So you can talk to your mama."

Loran stood for a moment, then nodded. She got a paper towel and wet it at the sink, wiping her face with it in an effort to gain control. Then, she took a deep breath and walked into the room where her mother lay.

Was Maddie so much different from earlier? Loran sat down on the chair by the bed and took her hand.

Yes, she thought. Maddie's hand was so cold. She cupped it in both of hers, watching Maddie's chest rise and fall. There were gaps in the rhythm of her breathing.

"Maddie to the end," she whispered. "Still picking and choosing what I get share with you. I'm glad you came home to the mountains, though. I know I gave you grief about it, but I can see it was a good thing. Parts of it, anyway. I don't know about Tommy. I'm not sure if he was a good thing for you or not. He's—I don't know what he is, Mother."

She gave a heavy sigh.

"When did I start calling you that—*Mother?* I can't remember. It was so…pretentious, wasn't it? Why didn't you make me stop, switch my legs or something? I wish we'd talked more. You tried to tell me I needed my questions answered—"

She abruptly looked out the window toward the mountains, wanting the sight of them to comfort her as Maddie had been comforted.

Home.

She stared at them for a long time. She had never felt that about any place she'd ever lived—that it was home, not the way it apparently was for Maddie. And Tommy Garth. And Meyer.

"Meyer is a good thing," she whispered to Maddie now. "Did you guess about Meyer? If you didn't, I bet Nelda did, didn't she? She knew about you and Tommy. She said you and he were married…."

She suddenly put her face down on the bed. "Oh, Mom…"

Nelda and Deanie were sitting at the kitchen table when Loran finally came out. She had no idea how long she'd been with Maddie. She stood looking at them, not quite knowing what to do. She felt dazed and disoriented and all cried out.

Nelda got up from the table. "Are you ready to go now, honey?" she asked gently.

Loran nodded, not trusting her voice.

"All right. Come on now. Keep your heart on doing what your mama wanted, and it'll be all right."

Loran picked up her coat and Nelda helped her put it on, then opened the outside door.

"These ones have been a-waiting for you. They want to walk with you."

Four little boys stood on the porch, their faces so grave—nothing like when she'd driven them around in the SUV at Tommy's party. She gave Nelda a final hug before she went outside. All four boys fell into step with her; one took her by the hand as they walked, as if he'd been the one chosen to do it.

"You can cry if you want to," he said as they went down the path. "It'll be all right."

She nodded, the tears already running silently down her face.

She hadn't thought that there would be people at Nelda's house, but there were. Mary Ann and several other women from Lilac Hill met her at the door. Mrs. Jenkins herself was in the kitchen, unwrapping a platter of sandwiches. And Poppy was there, and his wife.

"I reckon you're not wanting anybody hanging over you right now," she said. "Come on in here in the parlor. Poppy's built a fire in the stove so it'll be warm for you."

"Thank you for walking with me," Loran said to the boys. "Maybe Mrs. Jenkins can find you some sandwiches."

Mrs. Jenkins looked startled, but took the suggestion to heart. "How about some cake, too," she said. "You boys like chocolate cake?"

"Thank you," Loran said to Poppy. "Which way?"

"That way, honey," Poppy said, but he took her hand in both of his. "Now we want you to do whatever feels right to you. Stay in there where you can be by yourself as long as you want to, or come out to the kitchen and set with us. We'll be here, and we ain't wanting to trouble you, just help if we can."

"Thank you," Loran said again. She walked to the parlor, past the door to the room where she'd spent the night with Meyer. He wasn't here. She had thought he would be.

The parlor was warm and smelled of red furniture oil. She looked at the stove for a moment, thinking that she could have built a fire in it herself now. Lace curtains hung at the window, and green shades had been pulled

halfway down. There was a horsehair couch and two up-
holstered rocking chairs, and a piano. A large pendulum
clock in an intricately carved case sat on the mantel. It
had been wound, and the pendulum ticked back and
forth. There were photographs next to it—a very young
Nelda and the man Loran thought must be her beloved
Delman, and a portrait photo of a stern-looking Meyer
in his army uniform. There was also a framed snapshot
of him and a young woman, both of them in desert-cam-
ouflage uniforms and clearly in an exotic place. They
were both smiling, their fingers discreetly entwined, as
if they had to be careful not to flaunt the joy they clearly
took in each other.

Jolie.

Loran turned away to look at a spinning wheel in the
corner, and a curio cabinet full of figurines—some clearly
Asian, some Swiss-German-looking, some she couldn't
identify. She wondered if Meyer had sent them, if they
were a kind of testimony to his deployments. A huge
family Bible had been placed on the coffee table in front
of the couch. Loran sat down and opened it.

Births. Deaths. A lock of strawberry-blond hair tied
in a blue ribbon.

She took her time reading the names that had been
written in various shades of sepia and black ink, sometimes with great flourish, sometimes painfully executed
and barely legible.

She found Meyer's name and thought suddenly of the
lost woman on Lady Ridge, the one whose name had
been removed from the family record. That woman
might have been one of her Garth relatives, someone
who'd felt forced to leave the valley as Maddie had.

Maddie.

She was going to cry again. There was nothing in her mind and her heart but sorrow.

She got up and walked to one of the rocking chairs, removing the crocheted afghan from the back of it and sitting down. She put the afghan over her knees. The clock ticked quietly, and she began to rock back and forth in front of the fire.

People came and went—heard but not seen, except for Mrs. Jenkins and Poppy. Loran ate a little of the cake and drank the tea Mrs. Jenkins brought her, and she bowed her head when Poppy came in for a moment to pray. She might have even dozed from time to time. Mostly, she waited, the struggle not to break her promise growing harder and harder as the mantel clock marked the passing seconds, minutes, hours.

Maddie wanted this.

She got up from the rocking chair. She didn't want to be alone any longer. She could hear the quiet murmur of voices in the kitchen as she stepped into the hallway, and she walked in that direction. Except for the boys, the same people who had been in the house when she'd arrived were now sitting around the big harvest table. Everyone had apparently just eaten. One of the women was about to wash the dirty dishes.

They all looked around at the sound of a truck pulling into the yard.

"It's Meyer," Poppy said. "I reckon he—"

He abruptly stopped talking, apparently because his wife kicked him under the table. Loran didn't wait to try to decipher what that meant. She got her coat and walked outside, intercepting Meyer before he reached the porch.

"Is Maddie—"

"I haven't heard anything, Loran," he said. He looked tired, but she still asked.

"Can we take a walk?"

"Yeah. Let's go feed Pearl."

They walked together to the barn. She stood just inside, thinking she would watch while he pitched the hay, but he put the pitchfork into her hands and set her to doing it. She was grateful for the activity—who would know better than he did how to manage sorrow? She was grateful, too, that he didn't ask her if she was all right or offer her any platitudes.

"I've been looking for Tommy," he said when she'd made Pearl happy.

"Did you find him?"

"Yeah."

She waited for him to continue, but he didn't.

"I thought he'd come back to see Maddie—before it was too late," she said.

"I think he wanted to."

"All evidence to the contrary."

He didn't say anything else and neither did she. They began walking up the hillside, hand in hand, following the same route they'd taken before. She stared at the stand of trees and underbrush where the old school had been.

Nothing lasts, she thought. Not people. Not the things they build.

When they reached the crest, she stood for a moment, facing into the sharp wind, barely registering the cold.

Nothing lasts.

"Bobby Ray's coming," Meyer said quietly.

She looked around and, the moment she saw him making his way up the hill, she knew. She must have made a sound because Meyer reached out to steady her. She didn't walk forward. She couldn't make herself go out to meet the news that Maddie was gone. She stood and waited, the tears streaming down her face.

Bobby Ray stopped a few feet from her.

"Nelda says for you to come now," he said, his mouth trembling.

Loran didn't say anything, and Bobby Ray suddenly began to cry, noisily and without restraint like a child. She reached out and put her hand on his arm. "It's all right, Bobby Ray."

"Can't—help it," she thought he said.

She began walking down the hill with Meyer on one side and Bobby Ray on the other. Halfway down, she noticed a large plume of smoke rising in the sky in the direction of Lilac Hill and Poppy's store. The church bell began to toll in the distance, and Bobby Ray's sobbing grew louder.

She looked at Meyer. "What is it? What's happening?"

"It's Tommy," he said. "He's thawing the ground. He's going to dig Maddie's grave and he's calling the men to come and help him."

CHAPTER 18

Loran hadn't realized that the quaint parlor in Nelda Conley's house was so multipurpose, that Maddie's body would lie in state there and that people would come to pay their respects and some, by choice, would keep an all-night vigil until it was time to go to the church.

Flowers began to arrive almost immediately—from the Kesslers and, more surprisingly, from Kent. Nelda had been delegated to call Maddie's neighbor—yet another of Maddie's finely tuned plans for handling her demise—but Kent was a puzzle. Loran kept staring at the card with his name on it.

"Meyer told him, honey," Nelda said quietly. "He got the phone number from Mrs. Jenkins. He reckoned he ought to know about your mama."

Loran nodded and put the card away. In spite of herself, she kept expecting to see Tommy somewhere in the rush to get Maddie into the ground. Maddie had taken care of almost everything. She had wanted the funeral over and done quickly, so quickly that Loran was having to go to the funeral service in a black sheath dress she'd borrowed from Mary Ann. There was no time to buy anything. The only thing Maddie hadn't designated was who would dig her grave, and Tommy had usurped that.

"It's time to go to the church now," Nelda said, and

everything became a blur the people and their well-meaning words of comfort got lost in the haze of sorrow and sleeplessness. Meyer came briefly and went away again. He and Bobby Ray and the regulars at the store were acting as pallbearers—but there was still no Tommy Garth. There was no Estelle, either. Loran imagined her in her house on the hillside with her face pressed to the window, taking down the names of the people who'd flouted her judgment and had come to bury Maddie Kimball.

Loran sat between Nelda and Poppy on the pew and listened to the songs Maddie had wanted—joyfully morbid songs sung a cappella and in tight harmony. She listened to the pastor Maddie had apparently sought out for spiritual comfort at some point during her stay. He was kind and earnest and just nervous enough to make Loran want to believe that Maddie was in a better place.

She walked with the procession across the road to the cemetery, barely noting that a cold rain had begun to fall. Someone put an umbrella into her hands. Someone else told her where to stand. The chairs were too wet to sit on in spite of the canopy. She cried, when she thought she couldn't possibly cry any more. Meyer came to stand behind her, taking the umbrella and holding it over her.

And suddenly it was over. She stood there as the mourners quietly took their leave, until there was no one left but Meyer and the pastor.

"I'm going to stay here for a little while," she said, glancing in the pastor's direction.

Meyer made no effort to try to talk her out of it. He didn't point out how tired she looked or that she hadn't eaten or how hard the rain was coming down.

"You want me to wait for you?"

She shook her head. "No."

He gave her the umbrella and the keys to the SUV. "Come to Nelda's when you're ready," he said, and when he left, he took the pastor with him.

Loran watched them walk back across the road, watched them both get into the pastor's car and leave. She stood by the grave a long time, staring at the raw earth and the rain falling on the flowers, trying to find Maddie somewhere in all of it.

But Maddie wasn't there. Loran had more of a sense of Tommy Garth in this place than she did of Maddie. Tommy, digging and digging, finally accepting help from Meyer and the rest of the men who had answered the tolling bell.

She walked slowly back to the church, regardless of the rain, but she didn't get into the SUV when she reached it. Instead, she went inside the church. The lights were still on, and she realized almost immediately that she wasn't alone. Estelle Garth was already hard at work, putting things back the way she wanted them.

Humming as she worked.

Loran waited—until Estelle realized that the job of cleaning up after Maddie Kimball's funeral might be more complicated than she'd anticipated. The floor creaked under Loran's tread, and Estelle suddenly whirled around. They stared at each other across the pews. Estelle started to say something, but didn't. There was no sound but the rain on the roof.

"Are you going to throw me out of the church again?" Loran asked.

"No," Tommy said from the back of the sanctuary. "She ain't. Are you, Estelle?"

He walked down the aisle and sat down on one of the pews. He was as drenched with rain, and she could almost see Estelle flinch as he dripped water and tracked mud everywhere he stepped.

"This is her, Estelle. Mine and Maddie's girl."

Loran looked at him, forgetting her grandmother for the moment.

"Why?" she asked him. "Why did you leave her like that?" She hated that her voice broke, but there was nothing she could do about it.

"If you're talking about now, I done what she wanted. If you're talking about before, ask *her*."

Loran looked in Estelle's direction. At first she thought the woman was afraid, but that wasn't it. It wasn't fear that Loran saw on her face. It was indignation. And...self-righteousness.

And that alone made her ask.

"What did you do to them...Mrs. Garth?"

Estelle didn't answer her. She gripped the hymnal she had pressed hard against her breasts, her eyes darting around like a trapped animal looking for the chance to escape.

"Tell her, Estelle," Tommy said. "Or I will. She's got a right to know why she had to grow up without a daddy."

"Liars," Loran thought Estelle said.

"I couldn't get out, could I, Estelle?" Tommy went on. "See, the Garth house has got this old stone cellar. One of the first Garths cut it out by hand to keep his winter crops from spoiling. I reckon it took him a long time to do it. Estelle, she kept her canning down there in the cool, didn't you, Estelle? What was it you wanted that day? Oh, yeah. I remember. Peaches. She was making peach cobblers for the dinner on the ground at the church, but her hip was paining her. Said she couldn't make it down those narrow steps. So I went. I was a good son. *I* went.

"She locked the goddamned door behind me. And she left it locked. She didn't care how much I begged her. She weren't worried about me. I had all that canning she'd done to eat—Estelle takes great pride in her canning, don't you, Estelle? And I had a couple of jugs of water. There was even an old latrine down there. I could stay locked up a *long* time. I couldn't see much, though, once the matches run out. Couldn't dig through the stone. Couldn't claw open that heavy door. Couldn't tear through it with pieces of glass. When Estelle found out I was AWOL enough that the army was looking for me, she called the sheriff to come and get me. Said I'd been hiding out and she caught me in the cellar to keep me from running off to Canada. Nobody was surprised she'd do that—our Estelle believed in right and wrong. She'd turn her own *son* in if she had to.

"Addison, the sheriff, he wouldn't let me see Maddie before they hauled me off to jail. I should have told him right then and there what Estelle done, but I was too ashamed, so I didn't do it. You got the best of me there, Estelle—me a trained soldier, too.

"The army was pretty forgiving. I got sent to Vietnam anyway. They needed me over there more than they needed me in a stockade. I never heard from Maddie again. Not one word. Nobody here knew where she got to. When I come back from the army, I still couldn't find her no place. I even went down to Atlanta looking. Her and me, we used to talk about Atlanta, living there in the big city. I looked for her a long time, didn't I, Estelle? Tell my girl here how long I looked for her mama—you're not saying anything, Estelle! And you *always* got something to say—"

"You weren't looking for her when you made that other bastard out yonder!"

Tommy gave a bitter laugh. "That's what you think, Estelle. I'm sitting here now, in this church you think so much of, right where God can see me and hear me—so maybe you'll believe me when I tell you. I loved Maddie Kimball more than I loved my own life. I loved her! She's dead in the ground, you hateful woman, and I still love her!"

Tommy took a long wavering breath and looked at Loran. "I…wanted to tell your mama what happened, how come I didn't show up that night. I was going to swallow my pride and do it, but she wouldn't let me. And I wanted to know why she never come back, why *she* never gave me not one chance to tell her how it was. She wouldn't talk about none of it. She wouldn't listen. She said it didn't matter anymore."

He turned his face away so Loran wouldn't see the tears rolling down his face. "It mattered to me! I still wanted to marry her but she…"

He had only known the young Maddie, not Maddie the woman, who'd decided that her child would have a good life no matter what. He didn't know that that obsession was what had kept her from tainting Loran's life with her sadness and her anger, and what had made it possible for her to see him again. See him—and nothing more.

Loran glanced in Estelle's direction. She was still clinging to her hymnal, but she looked smaller somehow, as if all that relentless self-righteousness was being stripped away, layer by layer.

Loran moved closer to her father. "Maddie was afraid."

"Of her?" Tommy asked. "She was right to be afraid of *her*."

"Not her. You."

"Me!"

"She was afraid you were like Foy—and she had me to think about. She would never let her daughter go through what she had."

He didn't say anything. The silence lengthened. The rain still beat on the roof. The sanctuary had grown colder.

"Nelda says you *were* married," Loran said, hearing a gasp of protest from Estelle. "She said you and Maddie were as married as anybody who ever had a license and a ceremony. She said people could look at the two of you and know it." She glanced at her grandmother. "Estelle saw it. *I* saw it."

Tommy finally looked at her.

"It ain't enough," he said.

Loran was so tired suddenly, tired and filled with regrets that didn't even belong to her. And she couldn't bear anyone else's sadness. She had enough of her own.

"I'm sorry," she said, not certain if he even heard her. "I'm sorry for us both." She turned and walked out of the church.

CHAPTER 19

Everything was back the way it was. The blocks were gone. The bunk beds were stacked again. Loran made one last check of the cabin, looking for anything she might have missed or forgotten. There wasn't much to forget. Just her few changes of clothes and the toiletries. Maddie's things had already been boxed up. Nelda had helped her do that two days after the funeral, and it hadn't been nearly as painful as she might have thought. Nelda talked the whole time, about the little girl Maddie, about life in the valley, about the people Loran now knew by name.

"Will you come back again?" Nelda asked now as they stepped out onto the porch.

Loran pulled the door closed behind herself. The sun was shining. It was going to be a beautiful day. "I don't know, Nelda."

"You got ties here, honey, you know that—"

"I've got a grandmother who hates the sight of me."

"Your daddy don't hate you. These mountains called your mama back. I'm thinking they'll be calling you, too."

Loran gave a heavy sigh. "I think—I don't know what I think. It's all too complicated. Tommy is at war with Estelle. And I make it worse."

"Meyer's here," Nelda said, looking into her eyes.

Meyer.

Trouble and heartache.

"He don't know what to think, either," Nelda said.

"About what?"

"About you, honey. He knows you got to go back yonder to Washington. You got a lot of things you need to study on and not just your mama dying. I reckon you don't even know who you are anymore, much less where you're going."

"Nelda—" Loran said. "I just—"

"I know, honey. I know. Here. Take this with you." Nelda picked up a box covered with a towel she'd left sitting on the porch. "A little something to help you on your journey—I'm lending you the box."

Loran smiled. It was *the* box. The one so suitable for pie-carrying—Nelda's subtle hint that she was to come back again, if for no other reason than to return it to her.

Nelda walked with her to the SUV. Loran put the box inside on the front seat, and she couldn't keep from looking toward the sound of a vehicle on the highway below.

"He ain't coming, honey," Nelda said, so gently it made Loran want to weep. She had already guessed as much. Meyer knew she was leaving this morning. She'd told him yesterday in Nelda's long hallway. She'd told him; he'd nodded. She hadn't expected to see Tommy before she left. But Meyer…

She gave a quiet sigh, exhausted from trying to keep up with the whereabouts of the men in her life—Kent, Tommy, Meyer. At least one of them seemed to be per-petually unaccounted for.

"It's hard to tell somebody goodbye when you care

about them, especially if you're thinking maybe that's all there is between you—a goodbye. I reckon Meyer is like Joseph."

"Joseph?"

"Mary's husband. In the Bible, honey. Joseph, he never said much—he just *did*. It ain't never what a man says. It's what he does."

Loran smiled again because it sounded like another secret for a happy marriage. But her smile faded.

"I want you to remember something," Nelda said. "This—now—it's your blackberry winter."

"I don't know what that means, Nelda."

"It means you got to have hope. See, every year, just when you think spring is here to stay, it turns all cold and stormy. That's when the blackberries bloom, and we call it the 'blackberry winter.' But it don't last. Pretty soon it goes, and then it's spring again, and before you know it, you got blackberries. Your coldness and storms is going to go, too, and there's something good on the other side of it.

"Now, I'm going to say goodbye to you, and I'm just going to walk back to the house—I need to be a-thinking about some things, and walking is a good way to do it. You take good care of yourself, sweet girl. I loved your mama, and I love you, too."

Nelda embraced her one last time, kissed her on the cheek and walked away.

Loran wiped her eyes and stood for a moment. She'd had no sense of Maddie's presence in the cemetery, but she did here. All around her. Everywhere she looked.

She got into the SUV and drove down to the highway. She slowed down as she passed Lilac Hill. Meyer's truck wasn't there.

So what does not saying goodbye really mean? she wondered. That whatever he felt where she was concerned was too painful or too meaningless?

When she reached the church, she pulled into the circle drive and got out. She crossed the road and began to walk among the headstones to the black marble one that marked her little half brother's grave, then beyond to Foy's and Adeline's, wondering how far away the notorious "Doll" might be. She even went to the Garth plot, knowing she was trespassing.

My family, she thought. *The good and the…not so good*.

When she was young, she had wanted to belong to some place with a name, wanted to have roots and a host of relatives, but she'd grown out of it. She had learned to rely on herself—and Maddie.

She continued to walk through the cemetery until she reached Maddie's grave. The flowers had faded. The headstone hadn't yet been set into place. She could still see traces of scorched earth where Tommy had built the fire.

She stood in the bright sunshine, staring at the mound of dirt as a shadow fell across it.

She looked up. Estelle stood a few steps away.

"Yes, Mrs. Garth," Loran said. "Here I am again."

"What do want anyway?" Estelle asked—demanded.

"What do I want? I want my mother, Mrs. Garth. Maybe I want my father, too. What do you think of that?"

Not much, from the look on her face. Clearly, Loran had just confirmed her worst fear.

"Are you going to tell it?"

Loran knew exactly what "it" was.

"Don't worry, Mrs. Garth. I'm not going to tell people what you did—but I'm not keeping quiet for your sake. I'm keeping quiet for my father's. I see what a proud man he is, how ashamed he is of you. So you're safe, Mrs. Garth. Nobody is ever going to know how much Tommy Garth loved Maddie Kimball."

She turned and walked back to the SUV, then drove to Poppy's store to get gas, taking the time to say goodbye to him and Bobby Ray and the rest of the men who more or less lived there.

"You seen Meyer today?" Poppy asked, clearly fishing.

"No, not today."

"Well, I reckon he's pretty busy. Meyer, he works hard—got a lot of jobs. Always working."

"Yes," Loran said. "Would…you tell him goodbye for me when he comes in?"

"Yeah, honey, I'll do that. If I was to see Tommy, you want me to tell him you said goodbye, too?"

"If you see him," she said.

"I reckon they'll both turn up sooner or later. You could wait around and do it yourself. I reckon Bobby Ray could find them for you."

"No. That's all right. I've got a long drive. I want to get home before dark." She had to force herself to look at him.

"Well. You take care on them big highways—them people always drive too fast. And you come back, you hear?" Poppy said.

She wanted to say she would, but she couldn't. She stood for a moment, then paid for the gas and left, looking over her shoulder as she got into the SUV. They were all standing in the window—Poppy and Bobby Ray and the others.

She gave them a little wave and drove away, her eyes burning, her throat aching.

When she was about to turn left on the highway that would eventually take her into Virginia, she saw Meyer's truck at the restaurant near the Parkway.

"You wanting more coffee, Meyer? Meyer!"

He looked away from the window.

"More coffee or not?" the waitress asked, clearly unhappy about his inattention when she had better things to do than chase after customers with the coffeepot.

"Yeah, Lou," he said, pushing his mug in her direction. He looked out the big plate-glass window again while she poured it.

"What's the matter with you today?"

"Same thing that's the matter with me every day," he said. "Too handsome and too broke for my own good."

"Was that one of your army buddies you was talking to a while ago?"

"Yeah," Meyer said, his attention back on the occasional traffic at the intersection fifty yards away.

"He coming back or going?"

"Coming back."

"Thought so," she said. "He's got the look."

Like you do hung in the air unsaid.

"It's good you all can run into each other now and again—I reckon it helps to talk to somebody what's been through the same thing. You heard anything from Clay?"

"No."

"His mama and daddy ain't, either. His mama's about worried to death."

"Tell her no news is good news. If something bad happens, the army gets in touch with you pretty quick."

"Too many high-country boys over there, if you ask me."

He nodded, but he wasn't really listening. He was watching the intersection. When Loran left, she'd have to come this way, and he was—

He didn't know what he was—except miserable. He hadn't felt this…empty since Jolie had died, and it was his own damned fault. He'd walked into it with his eyes wide open, knowing that Loran Kimball wouldn't be around long. And even if he hadn't, he'd gotten enough insight about the situation from Tommy Garth and from Maddie. Tommy had threatened to kick his ass from here to Knoxville if he took advantage of his little girl when she already had too much to deal with, and Maddie—

He had the letter she'd asked Nelda to give him in his coat pocket. Maddie had wanted him to understand that Loran's whole life had been turned upside down and that he would need to give her the time and the room to set it right again—if he cared about her as much as she suspected he did. Maddie was like Nelda. Not much got by her.

Loran.

He loved her name. He loved to aggravate her and make her laugh. He loved the way her mind worked, learning, always learning—about the valley and the people in it, about herself and Maddie and Tommy Garth, and about him. He loved to look at her, to touch her.

He didn't know what he'd do if he never saw her

again, and yet he was going out of his way to make sure that happened. The only thing he knew for certain was that he couldn't tell her goodbye face-to-face without making a fool of himself, so here he sat, hiding.

It wasn't that he was surprised by the depth of his feelings for her. He was stunned. He had loved Jolie, been devastated by her death, and he'd never expected anything good to happen in his life again.

But it had—for a little while.

He looked out the window as a big SUV stopped at the intersection and stayed there for a time. He couldn't see inside the vehicle, but he knew who it was.

Don't go, he thought—but must have said.

"I ain't got time to stand around here jawing with you," Lou said. "You sit here much longer, and I'm going to make you buy something," she added as she walked away. "*Spend* some of that money you say you ain't got. All you Conleys is tighter than Dick's hat band."

He suddenly got up from the table and walked out the door and into the parking lot. He expected the SUV to make the turn away from where he stood, and it did. Almost. At the last minute, it swerved and came in his direction, stopping at the edge of the dirt parking lot just off the road. Loran immediately got out and walked in his direction.

"What are the rules?" she asked bluntly.

"Rules…?"

"Those army rules of…something."

"Engagement?"

"Yes. What are they? My guess is they've changed again. The 'no kissing' thing pretty much went out the window, so now what are they? Are we just going to forget about—everything?"

"I'm not going to forget," he said. "Ever."

She looked at him. She was so beautiful, and she was trying so hard to be tough. He didn't want to take advantage of her. And he didn't want to give her time *or* room. He wanted to grab her up and run with her—anywhere, he didn't care. He wanted to work for her, the way old Delman had worked for Nelda. He wanted to live with her until the day he died.

"I should have chained you to a porch," she said, her mouth trembling now. "And not—"

He reached for her then, grabbing the front of her coat and pulling her into his embrace. They stood there in the parking lot with their arms around each other, her face pressed into his shoulder.

"Is that all you have to say?" she asked, holding on to the back of his jacket.

He tightened his embrace. "Don't marry Kent," he whispered against her ear.

Everything was back the way it was.

There was no trace of Kent in the house or the bedroom, except for one empty closet. Loran stood staring at it, surprised and not surprised that he'd done as she'd asked and had actually moved out. She closed the closet door. She hadn't heard anything from him since the flowers he'd sent to Maddie's funeral.

She had made good time on the way back to Washington, taking three interstates instead of the Parkway. She was tired from the drive, and restless. So restless. It was all she could do not to pace around the room.

She stripped the bed and put on clean sheets, removing whatever trace of Kent's presence might remain. Then she went into the kitchen to make herself some tea. Everything seemed so…loud around her. The relentless traffic noise she'd craved, lying in her bed that night at Lilac Hill, now made her want to cower and cover her ears. There were Christmas decorations out everywhere, and how could that be? How far away was Thanksgiving, anyway? Not far, apparently.

She gave a heavy sigh. She would get used to urban living again. A few weeks and it would be as if she'd never left.

The phone suddenly rang, making her jump. She let it ring again before she answered it.

"Is Kent there?" a woman asked.

"He doesn't live here," Loran said.

"I know that," the woman said. "I asked if he was there."

"No, Celia, he isn't. I don't know where he is. I haven't seen him in…oh, two or three weeks."

"You saw him two or three weeks ago?"

"Celia, I'm sorry you've misplaced him, but he's not here. Happy…Thanksgiving."

She hung up the phone and stared at nothing, wondering if Celia realized she might be better off if she never found him.

Nelda's holy box sat on the kitchen island where Loran had left it. She began to empty it out. Apple pies—two of them. And three jars of homemade apple jelly. She carefully set the jars on the windowsill, leaving them out in the open because she found them comforting somehow.

She looked out the window, but she couldn't see anything but the paved driveway between her house and the house next door. No trees. No mountain ridges.

She found a small envelope standing on its edge in the box. Her name was written on the front of it and she recognized the handwriting immediately.

Meyer.

There was a photograph inside the envelope and a folded piece of paper. The photo was of Maddie—a laughing Maddie dancing with Bobby Ray. It was wonderful. Just looking at it made Loran smile. She hadn't even realized that someone had been taking pictures.

She unfolded the piece of paper and read what he'd written:

Poppy's nephew was running around with a digital camera, and he took this picture. I thought you'd like it.

I'm glad I got the chance to meet Maddie. I've tried to remember her from when I was a boy, but I never could place her. I wouldn't have missed getting to know her for the world. As Nelda would say, she was a rare jewel. Take good care of yourself. Don't forget us.

He had written something else before the word *us*, but he'd marked it out. She held it up to the light to see.

Me.

He'd written *Don't forget me*.

She sat there, staring at the photograph, remembering. The night of the party—the night she and Meyer had first made love.

She still didn't regret it. Even as sad and lonely as she felt now, she didn't regret it.

She put the photo and the note aside. There was still something left in the box. It was solid and rectangular and wrapped in several thicknesses of newspaper—a piece of wood with beveled edges.

She turned it over. It was a plaque with an intricately carved border of flowers and raised embellished lettering in the center. She recognized the style immediately. She sat there, tears running down her face, remembering the first one she'd seen like it and the conversation on the porch that must have inspired this one. Her fingers gently caressed the words:

Tommy's Daughter's House

CHAPTER 20

"How are you?"

"Fine, John," Loran said, waiting until her immediate superior had taken a seat on the other side of her desk before she sat down. She was surprised that he'd come to her office instead of the other way around, and she watched him notice the can of snuff sitting next to the only photograph she'd ever put on her desk.

"You did a fine job for us. We'd all but given up on the Barrett account."

She didn't say anything. Kimball women didn't give up. They might give out, but they didn't give in. Even Adeline. In her own sad way, she had been the most tenacious of them all.

"I wore them down," she said finally, and he smiled a surprisingly fatherly smile. She wondered idly if he could play a fiddle and carve wood.

"The bonus will be…notable," he said.

She smiled. "Notable" was good. She liked "notable."

"I know it was hard for you after you lost your mother."

"Yes," Loran said. She looked out the window behind him, at the first budding of green leaves, wondering what the valley would look like now.

"It doesn't have to be…permanent," John was saying.

"John, I can't do this anymore," she said bluntly.

He seemed to be waiting for an explanation, but she had none. All she knew was what she'd just said. She couldn't work at this job. She couldn't be in this city. She had to go…someplace else. She had to find "home"— like Maddie.

Home.

She had only recently come to realize that home could be a person *and* a place.

"If you change your mind…" John said.

"Thank you, John. For everything."

"Well—" He stood, and so did she. They shook hands across the desk, but when she walked with him to the door, he stopped and hugged her, startling the onlookers in the outer office. John the Terrible did *not* hug.

"Yikes," Carole, her personal assistant, said, coming in on the heels of his departure. "And you didn't turn to stone or anything."

Loran laughed, remembering when she herself thought that that could be a distinct possibility.

"Loran? They—the girls—want me to ask you something."

"What?"

"Now that you're leaving, we thought it would be all right."

"What is it?"

"What's with the snuff?"

"A man gave it to me," Loran said, smiling. "To cheer me up when I was going through a tough time."

"Snuff cheers you up?"

"The thought behind it does."

"Oh. He's…not the banker type, I guess."

"No."

"Is it—is he—" She stopped when Loran raised her eyebrows.

"Sorry. It's just—we all want you to be happy."

"Thank you. I want all of you to be happy, too," Loran said.

They stood looking at each other, both of them suddenly getting teary.

"You won't just disappear, will you? You'll come back and take us all out to lunch? Maybe bring the snuff guy?"

"I'll take you out to lunch—I'm still working on the snuff guy."

"Is he cute?"

"Very cute."

"What else, what else?"

"He's…ex-army," Loran said, suddenly wanting to talk about him. "Wears flannel shirts. Teaches at a community college sometimes. Plays the banjo. A country boy."

"Oooooo. I *love* banjo-picking country boys. I bet he says 'yes, ma'am' and stuff like that. He does, doesn't he—?"

"Go make your report to the troops," Loran said, laughing.

"Need any help packing up?"

"No. Just a couple of things left."

"I hope it works out—for you and the country boy."

"Thanks. Maybe it will."

When Carole had left to tell the others the latest intelligence, Loran opened the desk drawer and got her purse.

Maybe, she thought, remembering Clay and Mary Ann that first day at Lilac Hill, in love and carrying a big green garbage can.

Maybe forty wasn't too old to find what they had. Maybe she wasn't too afraid.

Maybe.

She picked up the can of snuff and the picture of Maddie and Bobby Ray dancing and walked to the door.

She looked back once.

Everything was back the way it was.

Flowers everywhere.

Even her father stood holding an armful.

She walked in his direction—over the carefully trimmed grass, past the scrubbed headstones, and more flowers.

He didn't see her as he bent down to place his bouquet just so among the ones already on Maddie's grave. She didn't say anything. She waited until he'd finished.

"What was that song?" she said and he looked sharply around.

"What song?" he asked, recovering quickly. She hadn't seen him since that terrible scene with Estelle in the church after Maddie's funeral and, clearly, he hadn't expected to find her here in the cemetery today—Decoration Sunday. If he was glad she'd come—or not glad—she couldn't tell.

"Maddie's song," she said. "The one you played for her at her welcome-home party."

"How do you know it was for her?"

"Everybody there knew it was for her. What was it?"

He looked up at the bright blue sky instead of answering. He'd grown thinner since she'd been gone, but he was still very much Tommy Garth.

"It doesn't have a name?" she persisted.

"It's got one," he said, but he still didn't look at her. "'Yesterday's Waltz.'"

"What's it about?"

She could see him trying to decide whether or not he was going to put up with her pestering him about something he didn't want to discuss.

"It's about regret, sis," he said abruptly. "The only one the man had—losing the woman he loved."

He looked at her finally. "She wrote me a letter, did you know that?"

"No," Loran said. "I knew she wrote some, but I didn't know who they were for."

"Gave it to Nelda to give to me. After…" He took a deep breath. "You knew your mama, I'll say that. She wrote down why she never come back—it was what you said—her thinking I was like Foy and not wanting you to be hurt like she was. She changed her mind in the end, though. She turned you over to me after she was gone— for safekeeping."

"I stayed mad at her for a while."

"I stayed mad at her for forty years."

"You and I…missed a lot, not knowing each other."

"Maybe. I don't know. If Maddie was wrong to keep you away from here like she did, she made up for it the best she could. I don't reckon neither one of us needs to waste time worrying about it now."

Loran didn't say anything.

"What did you do with that wood carving I made you?" he asked after a moment. "You hang it up or did you burn it?"

"I didn't burn it," she said. "It's packed away. I'm…moving."

"Where you going, sis? Heading for Wall Street after all?"

"No," she said, barely able to get the word out. "I'm…"

She trailed off without answering.

He pursed his lips to ask a question, then didn't. He smiled suddenly. "I reckon you better go see about him," he said, nodding in the direction where Meyer stood waiting. "He's worried about you again."

Loran put her own flowers on Maddie's grave and turned to go.

"You going to marry him?" Tommy asked.

"Depends," she said.

"On what?"

"On whether I can get him to the altar."

"I reckon I can help you with that."

"What, with a shotgun or giving me away?"

"I don't reckon I'd want to ever do that—give you away."

They stood looking at each other. Maddie slept quietly between them.

"Don't wait too long, sis. He's a good man."

"So are you," she said. "I'm…glad Maddie turned me over to you."

"Might be more of a job than I'm up to," he said, and she didn't miss it this time—that subtle teasing he and Meyer did so well.

"It just might," she assured him, making him smile.

She watched him walk away. Later, she would go up on the ridge to see him. She would learn from him— about life, and the mountains she was coming to love, and Maddie. Together, they might even try to do something about taming Estelle.

But not now. Now, she was home at last, and Meyer was waiting to welcome her.

A bear ate my ex, and that's okay.

Stacy Kavanaugh is convinced
that her ex's recent disappearance
in the mountains is the worst
thing that can happen to her.
In the next two weeks, she'll
discover how wrong she really is!

Grin and Bear It
Leslie LaFoy

Kate Austin makes
a captivating debut
in this luminous tale
of an unconventional
road trip…and one
woman's metamorphosis.

dragonflies AND dinosaurs
KATE AUSTIN

REQUEST YOUR
FREE BOOKS!

2 FREE NOVELS
TO INTRODUCE
YOU TO OUR
BRAND-NEW LINE!

There's the life you planned. And there's what comes next.

Three friends, two exes and a plan to get payback.

The Payback Club
by Rexanne Becnel
USA TODAY BESTSELLING AUTHOR

HN25TALL

Available January 2006
TheNextNovel.com

HARLEQUIN®
Next™